THE REGENCY
HIGH-SOCIETY AFFAIRS
COLLECTION

**Passion, Scandal and Romance
from your favourite historical authors.**

THE REGENCY
HIGH-SOCIETY AFFAIRS
COLLECTION

Available from the Regency High-Society Affairs
Large Print Collection

THE RELUCTANT ESCORT

Mary Nichols

First published in Great Britain 2000
Large Print edition 2010
Harlequin Mills & Boon Limited,
Eton House, 18-24 Paradise Road, Richmond, Surrey TW9 1SR

© Mary Nichols 2000

ISBN: 978 0 263 21607 3

Harlequin Mills & Boon policy is to use papers that are natural,
renewable and recyclable products and made from wood grown in
sustainable forests. The logging and manufacturing process conform
to the legal environmental regulations of the country of origin.

Printed and bound in Great Britain
by CPI Antony Rowe, Chippenham, Wiltshire

Chapter One

1816

When Duncan first saw Molly, it was an early summer day, with the sun shining and the skylarks hovering above the heath. She was walking on the grass alongside the track with her shoes and stockings in her hand and the hem of her striped dimity skirt wet and muddy. Her cottager hat had fallen down her back on its ribbons and her soft blonde hair lay tangled on her shoulders. He took her for a child, a very pretty child.

She looked up when she heard the slow clop of the horse's hooves behind her and brushed her wayward hair from her eyes to watch him approach. Strangers were a rarity at Stacey Manor, it being on a promontory of land which was not *en route* to anywhere, and she concluded he was probably lost.

His black stallion, seen with the eyes of someone who adored horses, was a beauty, strong and muscular and somehow out of keeping with the look of the man.

He was a rough sort of fellow, with a half-grown beard and clothes which were crumpled and dusty as if he had slept in them. But he held himself upright and his hands, holding the reins with a light touch, were brown and strong. There were lines about his dark eyes which could have been caused by frequent laughter or continually squinting in strong sunlight. A soldier home from the Peninsular War, she deduced, and immediately imbued him with the character of a hero.

In her mind's eye she imagined the heat and smoke of battle, heard the gunfire, saw the enemy hordes and the man, slashing this way and that with his sword and emerging triumphant. The only thing wrong with that vision was that the man's coat was not scarlet but a drab brown and he was not carrying a sword but a rifle in a holster on his saddle.

She waited, expecting him to stop to ask the way, but though his lips twitched into a smile as he passed he did not speak nor even acknowledge her, which piqued her. She hardly ever spoke to anyone but Lady Connaught or the servants and the chance of a little conversation with someone new, however brief, was something to be savoured.

She watched as he continued unhurriedly on his way and then sat on the side of the road to put on her stockings and shoes. Her feet were still wet from paddling in the brook and the footwear was tight and uncomfortable.

She had seen the green and blue flash of a kingfisher swooping along the bank and had waded into the shallow water to see it better. She ought to have known she would startle it and it would abandon its prey to sit in a tree overhanging the water until she had left its domain. And then she had spotted a trout under the bank and tried to catch it as she had seen Jeremy Bland, the poacher, do, but it, like the kingfisher, was gone in the blinking of an eye.

She had turned for home, knowing she would be in for another scolding from her godmother if she saw the state she was in. 'Molly Madcap', Lady Connaught called her. And though she grumbled and threatened, Molly knew her bark was far worse than her bite and she would escape punishment. Besides, what could her ladyship do, except lock her in her room? And that was easy to escape from. There was enough ivy clinging to the walls of the old house to make a secure ladder from her window to the ground.

There was no other punishment available, no social occasions she could ban her from attending, no friends she could be forbidden to see, no shops she could be barred from visiting, unless you went to Norwich or King's Lynn, which the old lady did twice a year. Molly hadn't been staying with her long enough to have enjoyed that experience yet, but she didn't hold out much hope that it would be the adventure she craved. She was bored. Even the stranger had ignored her. She might as well be invisible.

Once in sight of the big house, standing on its promontory, four-square to the North Sea, she hurried her pace, darting between the scattered shrubs which were euphemistically called a garden, and in at the kitchen door.

'Lord a'mercy, Miss Molly!' Cook exclaimed. 'What have you been up to now?'

'Trying to poach a trout for dinner.' Molly's smile lit her face; it was the kind of smile that made everyone around her feel more cheerful, however ill their humour had been beforehand. It started in rosy lips and even white teeth and ended in blue eyes, bright as cornflowers. Cook could not resist it, and even the Dowager Lady Connaught found it difficult to maintain her severity. 'But I'm not sad it escaped. It was too beautiful to be cooked and eaten.'

'Seventeen years old, you are,' Cook reminded her. 'Seventeen. Some young ladies are married at your age. Will you never grow up?' It was a rhetorical question. Cook knew perfectly well why Molly was still so childlike. It was her mother's fault. Harriet could never stand competition and Molly showed promise of being even more beautiful than her parent. So the poor girl had been kept a child for as long as possible, but when that would no longer serve she had been brought here to stay with the old lady while Harriet herself had set off for London to find husband number four.

'Has Aunt Margaret asked for me?' Lady Connaught was not really her aunt, but a cousin twice removed, but that was how Molly's mother addressed her and Molly, who had been named after her, had been told to do the same.

'No, but she will do so soon. We have a visitor…'

'A visitor?' Molly brightened, thinking of the stranger who had passed her on the road, and then wondered why her ladyship should entertain such a one. He had come to bring her some stupendous news: a long-lost love found. No, her godmother was too old for such fancies. Then news of some distant battle in which a relative had distinguished himself? But as far as Molly knew, her ladyship had no relatives except the Earl of Connaught who was her grandson, and he lived at Foxtrees on the borders of Hertfordshire and Essex.

Perhaps the stranger had been wounded and had come to be nursed back to health. Oh, that would be best, then he would stay a little, instead of disappearing as all visitors to Stacey Manor were wont to do. 'Who is it?'

'You'll see. I suggest you go and change and do your hair and be quick about it.'

Molly crept up the servants' stairs to her own room and stripped off her soiled clothes. She washed and dressed again in a pale blue sarcenet gown with a shawl collar of white lace, white stockings and blue kid shoes, then set about brushing out the tangles in her hair. When it was once again lying smooth and shining on her shoulders, she sat down and surveyed herself in the looking-glass, wishing she didn't look so young; Lady Connaught's guest would hardly converse with her unless she could make herself look interesting and intelligent. Perhaps it would help if she put her hair up.

She scooped it up in her hand and looked this way and that, then scrabbled in her drawer for combs and pins. Oh, if only she had a lady's maid to help her! But Mama had said it was not at all necessary at Stacey Manor where the simplest of clothes would be perfectly adequate. She had been right, of course. There was nothing to do, except walk and ride and read, and make occasional visits of a charitable nature to the local villagers.

Pinning up her thick hair was not easy but she achieved it in the end, though one strand refused to be confined and curled lovingly into her neck. She left it there and went down to the withdrawing room.

Lady Connaught, dressed as always in unrelieved black on account of being widowed thirty years before, sat in a high-backed chair by the hearth. Her visitor stood facing her, with his hand on the mantel. He turned when he heard Molly come into the room. She wasn't sure whether his smile was one of amusement or pleasure, but was gratified that he smiled at all.

He had changed out of the grubby clothes he had been wearing and was now in biscuit-coloured pantaloons and a blue superfine coat, beneath which was a canary-yellow waistcoat with brass buttons and a cravat of white muslin, cleverly tied. He had shaved and his hair had been washed and brushed until it shone. He was now Molly's idea of a man about town and the war-like fantasies she had been weaving about him faded to be replaced by others.

He was part of the Prince Regent's court and had been sent to rescue her, to take her to London to be courted by all the eligibles and marry the most handsome and attentive of them all. She might be presented to the Queen at one of her drawing rooms and everyone would say how well she looked.

She knew she should not indulge in these day-dreams; it was foolish and childish, as her mother had told her often enough, but they lightened a dull afternoon when there was nothing else to do. Dreams were no substitute for reality and it was the reality she craved.

'Molly, come and meet…' Her ladyship paused and looked at him for a moment as if unsure of his identity, then went on, 'Captain Duncan Stacey. Duncan, this is Mrs Benbright's daughter, Margaret. You remember Harriet Benbright, do you not?'

Molly did not see the look which passed between them, nor did she hear his murmured comment as she dropped a very deep curtsey before moving forward, wondering if he recognised her as the girl he had seen on the road. She hoped he would not mention it, because it would spark off a jobation from Aunt Margaret and that would be too mortifying. Besides, she didn't want him to think of her as Miss Molly Madcap, but as a woman with whom he could enjoy social intercourse.

She looked up into his eyes and realised that he was trying to convey a message in them. It was a kind of reassurance and she gave him a conspiratorial smile which startled and then charmed him.

'Your servant, Miss…' In the middle of taking her hand and bowing over it, he paused. 'Forgive me, I do not know which one you belong to.'

He was referring to her mother's three husbands, she realised. 'I should have thought it was obvious,' she said. 'The first one, Monsieur Martineau, of course. Mama was only seventeen when she married him and I was born less than a year later. It is why we are more like sisters than mother and daughter, so Mama says. If I had been the child of Mr Winters or Colonel Benbright, I would still be a child, would I not?'

'Of course,' he said, stifling an inclination to laugh. 'How stupid of me not to have worked that out for myself. Miss Martineau, I am pleased to make your acquaintance.'

'Sit down, both of you,' her ladyship said. 'Dinner will be served at three. We don't keep London hours here.'

'No, I did not think you would,' he said. He turned to Molly. 'Miss Martineau, are you enjoying your stay in Norfolk?'

'Yes, thank you,' she said.

'But it is somewhat dull, I think.'

'Sometimes.'

'How do you amuse yourself?'

She looked up at him sharply, wondering if his

query was leading up to some comment about wandering about the countryside in bare feet. 'I walk and ride and read, and visit the cottages. The people are very poor, you know, and we must do what we can for them.'

'Indeed, I do know. It is commendable that you are concerned about them; isn't that so, my lady?'

'Yes,' her ladyship said. 'Though there is little we can do about the weather and it is the heavy rain that ruined last year's harvest.'

'And the end of the war,' Molly put in. 'All those soldiers coming home and needing work. No wonder they riot.'

'Do they?' he queried. 'Hereabouts?'

'Everywhere. You must have been out of the country not to have known about it. But perhaps you are one of those soldiers yourself. I collect you are a captain.'

'I am, yes.'

'Were you in any big battles?'

'Indeed I was.'

'Which ones?. Tell me all about them. Have you ever seen Napoleon Bonaparte? Or spoken to the Duke of Wellington? How much do you think the different styles of leadership of Napoleon and the Duke contributed to the final outcome?'

'Styles of leadership?' he echoed, taken aback. It

was not a subject he would have expected someone of her years to show an interest in.

'Why, yes. Napoleon likes to march to battle with a great deal of noise and show and banners flying, while the Duke hides his men away and does not reveal himself until the last minute. He also dresses in a very nondescript way and Napoleon struts like a turkey-cock. Is that not so? Do you think Wellington learned his tactics from Agincourt? Henry V hid his bowmen behind palisades until the enemy was almost upon them, didn't he?'

'Goodness, so many questions all at once,' he said. 'I hardly know where to begin.'

'I shouldn't answer any of them,' Lady Connaught put in drily. 'It will only lead to more. Molly's curiosity is insatiable.'

'But that is how we learn, is it not?' Molly said. Ever since she had been taught to read by her father, she had devoured everything she could lay her hands on, whether suitable or not. Simple moralising tales given to her by her nursemaid were soon replaced by novels, both good and bad, and the contents of her succeeding stepfathers' libraries.

Geography and horticulture and ancient history were digested along with the rudiments of wine-making. And from Colonel Benbright's vast collection of military books she had read about war and military campaigns and those who directed them. 'I have read about such things,' she told the Captain. 'But it is not the same as talking to someone who was there.'

'Some things it is better not to know,' the Captain said. 'I shall certainly not enlighten you or I shall be blamed for giving you nightmares.'

'You think I am so lily-livered I have to be protected from anything disagreeable? I assure you, Captain, I am not so lacking in imagination that I do not realise that some things in life are very unpleasant. One must learn about the bad as well as the good.'

'But better not dwelt upon,' Lady Connaught said. 'Duncan, you may escort us in to dinner and I do not want to hear another word about the war. You may tell us what is going on in London instead.'

They moved into the dining room and over a frugal meal of turbot, game pie, vegetables and a fruit flummery Duncan regaled them with the latest gossip from the capital, including the Prince Regent's long dispute with his wife Caroline, and Princess Charlotte's love match with Prince Leopold, a story that delighted Molly, who had a very romantic streak in spite of her hoydenish ways. But he had been to no social gatherings and could tell them nothing of the latest fashions.

Duncan stayed behind to smoke a cigar and drink

a glass of port after the meal but soon joined them in the withdrawing room where they played three-handed whist until it was time for Molly to retire.

'You will be staying?' she enquired, when she bade him goodnight. 'I shall see you tomorrow? You can tell me all about your experiences then.'

'Alas, no, I must be gone by daybreak,' he said. 'But I shall look forward to meeting you again in the future.'

'Oh, must you go? We so seldom see anyone interesting at Stacey Manor. It is the most boring of places. Nothing ever happens here. Begging you pardon, Aunt Margaret, but there is so little to do and no one to converse with at all.'

Duncan's smile was a little crooked. 'I am afraid if it is social discourse you are looking for I am a poor one to provide it.' He stood up and bowed to her. 'Goodnight, Miss Martineau. May your dreams be pleasant ones.'

When she had gone, Duncan settled down again with his grandmother. 'The poor child must find it very boring here. Why in heaven's name did Harriet not take her with her to London?'

Lady Connaught smiled. 'And have everyone wondering how she can be old enough to have a daughter of seventeen? It would certainly be a stumbling block to her own prospects. Harriet has promised Molly a Season when she has landed a wealthy husband for herself. She is still a beautiful woman, not in the first flush of youth but not too old to want a husband.'

'She has had three already! I should think anyone contemplating marriage with her might well consider how long he might live after the ceremony.'

'Oh, that is unfair, Duncan. Her first husband, the French diplomat and Molly's father, was a widower and an old man when she married him. Unfortunately her expectations on his death were not realised; he left his fortune to his first family in France and only a small portion came Harriet's way.'

'And her second?'

'George Winters. He was a wine importer and plump in the pocket when they married, but the blockade of French ports ruined his business and he went to America to look for new sources of supply. He died out there of a fever in 1812 or 1813—I am not sure which it was. That marriage lasted eleven years, but it left Harriet no better off than before. Her third husband was Colonel Benbright...'

'He was killed at Waterloo. I met him once. An old stick-in-the-mud, who believed it was dishonourable to retreat whatever the circumstances. He had been ordered by Wellington to withdraw from his position, but he chose to ignore the order and took a great many good and brave men with him to their deaths.' He stopped, hearing again the sound of the unremitting guns and the cries and groans of the wounded men in that terrible conflict.

He had thought himself battle-hardened, but even he had been appalled and sickened by the carnage. And some of it was so unnecessary. Colonel Benbright's men, not knowing his orders, had obeyed his commands and died at his side. Duncan had been glad not to be one of them, even though, at the time, he had been feeling sick at heart and would have welcomed a good clean death.

'So now Harriet must find another husband.' His grandmother broke in on his reverie and brought him sharply back to more mundane matters. 'Her daughter is an encumbrance, if not a serious rival, so she sent her here to stay with me.'

'Fustian! She is no more than an attractive child; how can she possibly be in competition with her own mother?'

'She is not a child, Duncan. She is seventeen, nearly eighteen.'

'She looks more like fifteen. A mere schoolgirl.'

'That is Harriet's fault for trying to keep her young. Poor Molly has not been allowed to grow up, but underneath that childish exterior there is the heart and mind of a young woman who could blossom into a real beauty.'

'I do not doubt it. It makes me feel like horse-whipping that selfish mother of hers.'

'That would not serve either. What Molly wants is someone to help her grow up. I can't do that; I am too old and set in my ways. And Stacey Manor is too isolated.'

'So?' he asked, wondering where this conversation was leading.

'You need to settle down, Duncan. It is about time you abandoned your scapegrace ways and made something of your life.'

'With Molly Martineau?' he asked in astonishment.

'Why not?'

'Grandmama, have you any idea what sort of life I lead?'

'Yes, and it is not to your credit. You did not have to abandon your inheritance and take to the road. It was done in a fit of pique…'

'No, Grandmama, it was not. When I came home and discovered I had been reported killed in action at Vittoria…'

'The report of that action was detailed enough for no one to doubt it,' his grandmother put in. 'You were seen to fall and a French officer dismounted and finished you off with his sword…'

'He meant to, but charitably changed his mind when he saw I was wounded and took me prisoner instead.'

'It is a pity you could not have managed to let anyone know you were alive…'

'I tried, but because I would not give my parole not to attempt to escape I was denied all privileges and no one would take a letter. When I did escape, I brought important intelligence and the Chief sent me back to discover more. I was not free to come home until after Boney surrendered. Too late. My father had died, my title had been usurped, the lady I was to have married had wed my brother and produced an heir.' He paused, remembering the consternation his return had caused.

If it had not been for that spell as a French prisoner of war and Old Hooknose sending him back behind the lines as an agent, he would have come home long before and claimed his birthright. He would have arrived before his father's death and there would have been no question of who was the heir. He would be head of the family, running his estates, married to Beth… Married to Beth.

He mused on that for several seconds. It was a prospect which had kept him going all the time he had been in the Peninsula. He had dreamed of it, sure that she was waiting for him. He had spent hours wondering what she might be doing, how she looked, whether she missed him and longed for his return as much as he missed her and looked forward to being reunited with her.

The reality had been very different. Coming home and finding her married to his brother had shaken him to the core. He had been angry and miserable and then anxious only to get away, to leave them to their happiness with each other. He had told them he did not care for the settled life, had not really wanted to be the Earl, that he was a soldier and would remain one. He would not bother them again; they might continue to believe him dead.

He had given a harsh laugh. 'You may even continue to mourn me,' he had said.

Hugh, though clearly discomfited, had not tried to dissuade him, but had offered him an income from the estate, saying it was the least he could do. He had refused it, being more concerned with salvaging his pride. He had wished them happy and reported to the War Office for further service. Napoleon's escape from Elba and the second phase of the war was fortuitous in that respect.

'What else was Hugh to do?' she demanded. 'He truly believed he had become the new heir and was entitled to inherit. We all did. And Beth had expected to marry the Stacey heir ever since she was a child; it was what both families wanted. You can hardly blame her for turning to your brother.'

Logic told him that Hugh and Beth were not at fault, but his heart was still sore. Beth had been so quick to change her allegiance that he began to wonder if, after all, it was Hugh she had wanted all the time and his reported demise had been a blessing. 'Oh, I can quite see how it happened. My return was an acute embarrassment to everyone. It were better I had stayed dead. I returned to my regiment to give Napoleon another chance to finish me off at Waterloo. 'Tis a pity he did not.'

'Don't be bitter about it, my boy,' she said softly. 'You chose to renounce your inheritance for the sake of Beth and their son, so now you must put it behind you and make a fresh start. Careering about the countryside getting into scrapes will not do. It just will not do.'

'How do you know I have been getting into scrapes?'

'Why else would you come here? And in the state you were in. I am not a fool, Duncan, even if you take me for one.'

'Oh, Grandmama, I know you are no fool, but it is better you do not know…'

'Running from the law, I shouldn't wonder, or your creditors. Using Stacey Manor as a bolt-hole…'

'Grandmama…'

'Enough. You are right—I do not want to know.

But what about settling down? What about Molly?'
She laughed lightly. 'Scapegrace and madcap, it
might be the making of you both.'

'You are surely not in earnest?'

'Why not?'

'It's out of the question. You said yourself, I am
a rakeshame, always on the move, getting into one
scrape after another...'

'Precisely.'

'I cannot change into a fan-carrier overnight. We
should both be miserable. And what do you suppose
Miss Martineau would think of the matter?'

'She will be guided by her elders.'

'Her mother! I hardly think she would provide
wise guidance with three husbands already dead
and buried.'

'No, but as Harriet has left Molly in my care and
Molly is an obedient girl she will listen to me...'

'Then she would be lacking in spirit and that would
not commend her to me. Besides, it would mean
taking Harriet Benbright as a mother-in-law and I do
not think I could stomach that. Such pretensions I
never did see in a woman of no consequence.'

'Harriet's father was a baronet and I hardly think you
are in a position to talk of consequence now, my boy.'

'No, which is why Harriet would not entertain an
offer from me for her daughter. I have nothing to

commend me. And any children we had would have no prospects of inheriting the title. I could not go back on my word to Hugh. That alone would exclude me in Harriet's eyes.' He smiled disarmingly. 'Grandmama, I thank you for your concern, but I must continue to live my life in the way that suits me. I have a small pension from a grateful country and Hugh has been kind enough to make me an allowance from the income of the estate.' He did not want her to think ill of his brother, nor intervene on his behalf, and so he told the lie.

'So he should! It is yours, after all. Where are you off to tomorrow?'

He smiled, concluding she had not been serious or she would not have capitulated so easily. 'Wherever the fancy takes me.'

'But I collect it must be done under cover of darkness.'

'I am afraid so. I shall be gone long before you wake, so I will say my farewell now and retire.'

She sighed. 'Very well. But you know you are always welcome here, no matter what.'

'Yes, I know, but I would be grateful if no one knew of my presence here tonight. In fact, I should deem it a favour if you were to say, if asked, that you were unaware that I had survived the second war and returned to England.'

'That I will do, but I shall also pray that you come to your senses before you find yourself preaching at Tyburn Cross.'

'Oh, I do not think it will come to that,' he said lightly. 'Hanging is certainly not part of my plan for the future.'

'Then what is?'

'I do not know. Not yet. But undoubtedly something will occur to me. Now, if you will excuse me.' He bowed over her hand, putting it to his lips. 'Goodnight and God bless you, Grandmother. Tell Molly… No, tell her nothing, for there is nothing good you could say of me.'

He strode from the room and made his way upstairs to bed, though he did not intend to sleep for more than an hour or two. Long before dawn, he was up and creeping down to the back door, from where he crossed the cobbled yard to saddle his horse.

Molly's room overlooked the stables, and as she had stayed up reading *Don Quixote* by the light of a candle she heard him leave the house. Going to the window, she watched him enter the stables. He was escaping, getting away on that beautiful black horse of his, and she was sure he would have many fine adventures and his life would not be at all boring, as hers was.

There was something a little mysterious about

him; he had talked all through dinner without giving away a single thing about himself, not even why he had chosen to come to Stacey Manor in the first place, nor how he knew her mother. Until a few months ago, she had not heard of her mother's Stacey connections. And she was curious as to why it was necessary to creep away in the dead of night.

Without stopping to think of the consequences, she scrambled into her riding habit and hurried downstairs. She was in the kitchen, pulling on her boots, when she heard the quiet clop of a horse walking across the cobbles of the yard. By the time she had let herself out of the house, the sound of the horse was fading in the distance. She ran out to the stables to saddle her mare, Jenny. Lady Connaught had long since given up riding and there were only a couple of men's saddles belonging to the groom, who rode pillion when her ladyship went out in the carriage. Molly had used the smaller of these on many occasions and had become proficient at riding astride.

Two minutes later she was galloping after the enigmatic captain, without any idea of what she would say to him when she caught up with him. It was simply that she was wide awake and longing for something to give her life a little piquancy. She would follow him and solve the mystery of who he was and what he was about.

It was a quiet night and she could hear the hooves of his horse ahead of her, cantering easily along the dry road. She would stay a little behind him until he stopped to rest his mount; she could catch up with him. Then he must either escort her back himself or share his adventure with her. Either way she would learn more about him.

She suddenly became aware that the hoofbeats had stopped and she pulled up to listen and look about her. She had left the familiar heath behind and was on a road with open fields on one side and a copse of trees on the other. There was a village not too far way, for she heard a dog bark. Close by an owl hooted, startling her for a moment, but there was no sound of man or horse.

Surely he could not have outrun her so completely? She began to walk her mare forward more slowly, straining to hear the slightest sound. Had he turned off? But she could see no other road or bridleway. Had he gone into one of the houses in the village? Could he have an assignation there? She ought to go back, but it would be so disappointing not to have her curiosity satisfied.

A mile or two further on, she became aware of the sound of a horse behind her. She stopped and pulled her mount into the edge of the wood, concealing herself behind a bush, refusing to admit she was more than a little afraid. The other rider approached at a walk, singing quietly under his breath. He stopped when he came level with her hiding place.

'Are we going to play hide-and-seek all night?' he asked mildly.

Recognising his voice, she gave a sigh of relief and emerged from her hiding place, ducking under the low branches of a tree. 'How did you get behind me?'

'I heard someone riding after me a long time ago, but when no one caught up with me I deduced I was being followed and that is something I do not like, so I hid in the trees to see who it might be. You are very lucky I didn't take a pot shot at you.'

He was annoyed; she could tell by the set of his jaw and the steely gleam of his eye in the darkness, and she supposed he had every right to be, but she was not one to back down from a confrontation. 'And when you realised it was me, why did you not show yourself?'

He chuckled, in spite of his annoyance. 'The follower became the followed. I wanted to see how determined you were. If you thought you had lost me, you might have turned back.'

'And now you know the answer to that, what are you going to do about it?'

'Send you home, of course. I cannot for the life of me think why you set out after me.' He paused as a new thought crossed his mind. 'Lady Connaught did not send you, did she?'

'Lady Connaught?' she queried in surprise. 'Why should she do that?'

He ignored her question. 'Then why?'

'I wanted to see where you were going. You are undoubtedly going to have an adventure and...'

He threw back his head and laughed. 'I am sorry to disappoint you, Miss Madcap, but I am simply going to join a friend...'

'In the middle of the night?'

'It will be dawn before I reach the rendezvous.'

'Is it a lady friend? You have a tryst?'

'Certainly not!'

'Why so adamant? Have you an aversion to ladies?'

'Not at all. I have known some very accommodating ones. Now, if you have finished interrogating me, it is time you turned back to Stacey Manor.'

'You are surely not sending me back alone? I might lose my way or be set upon and robbed. Or raped.'

He felt sure she did not know the real meaning of the word but, looking at her youthful figure and bright eyes, he conceded she might very well be right. But they had met no one on the road and in a quiet country district like this, so far from the evils of civilisation, she was safe enough. Besides, he had his reputation of being a hard man to consider and Frank waiting at the Red Lion in Aylsham for him. He did not have the time to go back. 'You came alone.'

'Ah, but I knew you were not far away and would have come if I had called for help.'

'You scheming little madam! Well, it will not serve. Back you go.'

He was angry again. His moods changed with lightning speed; one minute he was scowling, the next laughing, and it was difficult to know which it was likely to be, but that was half the fun of the adventure. She opened her mouth to answer him, but before she could do so he had reached down to take her reins. Turning her horse the way they had come, he slapped its rump. It set off at a canter.

She could easily have brought it under control, but decided to let it have its head and pretend it was bolting with her. She turned it off the road and they crashed through the trees, startling an owl which swooped down and skimmed so close to her head, she let out a genuine scream of terror. The horse panicked and reared and the next minute she hit the ground with a bump.

'Molly, where are you?' In a daze, she heard Duncan coming after her. She lay still, her eyes closed. She heard him pull up and dismount, felt his warm breath on her face as he bent over to see if she were breathing and then let out a shuddering sigh.

'Thank God! Molly, open your eyes, there's a good girl. Let me see you are not injured.'

She allowed her eyelids to flutter. 'Where am I?'

'Safe now. Are you hurt?'

'I don't know. My head aches.'

'Can you sit up?' He was surprisingly gentle as he helped her to sit. 'That's better.' He felt round the back of her head with gentle fingers. 'Nothing broken that I can see. Now stay there while I catch your mount.'

He disappeared through the trees, but he was only gone a minute because Jenny was cropping the undergrowth close by, calm as you please.

He walked both horses out to the road and tethered them, then came back to pick her up in his arms and carry her through the trees to sit her on the mare's back. She was still a little dizzy and not at all sure she could ride. Afraid he would set her off alone again, she moaned softly and fell forward on the horse's neck.

'Oh, damnation!' she heard him mutter. She was glad Jenny was being good because she had allowed her hands to fall from the reins.

He lifted her down again and put her on his own horse, then, leading Jenny by her reins, got up behind her in order to support her as they rode. She leaned back on his rough coat, wondering what he would do next.

'Can you hear me?' he asked. 'Molly, stay awake for God's sake.'

'Am awake,' she murmured. 'Bad head.'

'Very well, Aylsham is nearer than Stacey Manor and there'll be a doctor in the town, so we will go there, but as soon as you have sufficiently recovered I shall put you on the stagecoach to take you back.'

She did not argue. His arms were strong around her and the clop of the horse's hooves soporific; she was almost asleep.

'How did you come to be such a madcap?' he murmured, more to himself than to her. 'It was that silly woman, your mother, I have no doubt. You have to grow up some time, kitten, and I have a notion it will be very soon and very sudden. I wish I could protect you, but I cannot. I need protecting from myself, as Grandmama was quick to point out…'

'Grandmama?' she murmured.

'Oh, you are not as sleepy as you pretend, are you? Grandmama is Lady Connaught.'

She lifted her head from his shoulder and turned towards him. In the moonlight, his face seemed sombre beneath a large black hat. 'You are surely not the Earl of Connaught?'

He laughed under his breath, a harsh, rather bitter sound which troubled her a little. 'No, I am not the Earl of Connaught. I belong to a different branch of the family.'

'The poor side. Every great family has a poor side, does it not?'

'And its black sheep.' This time his laugh was one of genuine amusement.

'Oh, I see. But I should guess you are her ladyship's favourite, all the same.'

'Perhaps.'

'Oh, how romantic! I expect you have had hundreds of adventures.'

'So, your headache has magically vanished.'

'No, it is still there.' She hurried to assure him. 'It will be better tomorrow, perhaps.'

'It is already tomorrow. See, the sun is on the horizon and soon it will be daylight.'

'So it is.' She could see the road winding downhill to a group of buildings and a church. 'Is that Aylsham ahead of us?'

'Yes. The Red Lion is a respectable hostelry. We will stay there for a few hours until you are feeling better. Then I will see you safely on the coach to Cromer. If your horse is tied on behind, you will be able to ride from there to Stacey Manor.'

'Where are you going?'

'Wherever the fancy takes me.'

'That's sounds very indecisive to me and you do not seem to me to be an indecisive man. A secretive one, perhaps. Do you not want me to know where you are going?'

'There is no need for you to know. Your little adventure is at an end.'

She was silent for a moment. 'When you have seen your friend are you going on to London?'

'I might. On the other hand I might not. It depends.'

'On what?'

'On what transpires,' he said enigmatically.

'I should very much like to go there…'

'Perhaps one day you will. I collect my grandmother saying you had been promised a Season.'

'Oh, that will only happen if Mama finds herself a rich husband.' She sighed. 'I am afraid she is not very good at judging how wealthy a man is and may very well mistake the matter again. I hold out no great hope.'

'So young and so cynical!'

'Realistic, Captain. So, will you take me to London?'

He chuckled, unable to take her seriously. 'Minx! You have been play-acting the whole time. It will not serve, you know. What would my grandmother say if I were to carry you off?'

'We could ride back and tell her. She will be quite content to let me go with you.'

She squirmed to turn and look at him again when he roared with laughter. He laughed so long and so loud, the tears ran down his face.

'I amuse you?' she asked stiffly.

'Oh, I was not laughing at you but at myself. How anyone could be such a gowk, I do not know.'

'Gowk?'

'Fool, Molly. I am a fool. I have fallen for a ploy as old as time.'

'Then will you take me to London? To Mama?'

'I doubt your sudden arrival would please your mama.'

'Oh, she might ring a peal over me to start with but I shall turn her up sweet, then she will take me out and about with her.'

The idea amused him even more than knowing Molly had inadvertently played into Lady Connaught's hands. Harriet would be furious. It was almost worth considering just to discomfit her. But that would not be fair on Molly. And between the Red Lion and London were a great many miles and every one of them fraught with danger. Miss Molly Martineau must be returned to Stacey Manor.

He turned into the inn yard and dismounted before lifting her down and setting her on her feet. He ordered the ostler to look after the horses and escorted her inside. Not until he had bespoken a room and tipped a chambermaid to help her to bed did he feel free to go in search of Frank.

Frank Upjohn, once a sergeant in the Norfolk Regiment and now his servant, had taken two rooms along the corridor. Duncan tiptoed along and quietly let himself in, but Frank had been watching for him and was wide awake, sitting by the window.

'You're late, Captain,' he said. 'I had all but given you up for lost.'

'I was delayed.'

'Yes, I saw her. A pretty little filly, no doubt, but a distraction we could well do without.'

'You mistake the matter,' Duncan said. 'She is a distant cousin. I shall put her on the Cromer stage when she has rested.'

'No, Captain, you cannot do that, unless you want to upset all our plans. 'Tis the stage our target will be on.'

'How so?'

'He travels a day early. It were meant to confound anyone with an eye to waylaying him. He will be coming through here in two hours' time.'

Duncan swore roundly. Now what was he to do? He could not involve Molly in what he was about to do and he needed to get away quickly after the deed was done. 'She will have to stay where she is for another day and go on tomorrow,' he said, hoping Molly would be docile and do as she was told without further argument about sharing his adventures.

'We had no plans to come back here,' Frank reminded him.

'Then we shall have to change our plans.'

'I don't like it,' Frank muttered. 'Don't like it at all. Petticoats are the very devil…'

Duncan laughed. 'You never said a truer word, old friend, but what would we do without them, eh? But enough of that. Tell me all you have discovered and let's get down to business.'

Chapter Two

Molly woke with a start when a coach rattled into the yard outside her window. For a moment she lay staring at the ceiling, wondering where she was. And then it all came back to her—the ride in the night, the fall from her horse, the comfortable feeling of Captain Stacey's strong arms around her, and his determination to send her back to Lady Connaught. She sighed heavily. It had been a kind of adventure, she supposed, but only a little one and nothing of any importance had happened. She still did not know his secret.

She rose and went to open the window. The yard outside was busy with horses being changed on a coach and the passengers were coming into the inn for refreshment. She guessed it was late in the morning, for the smell of roasting beef wafted up to her and reminded her she was hungry. Without a nightgown, she had slept in her underwear and it did not take her long to wash, using cold water from the jug on the wash-stand, and put on her riding habit again. It was crumpled and dirty, but that could not be helped. Having secured her hair as best she could, she went downstairs in search of Captain Stacey.

'He and his friend left two hours since,' the landlord told her. 'He left a message that you were to wait here for him.'

She was puzzled. 'He did not say to take the stage to Cromer?'

'It left soon after the gentlemen, miss. If that was where you were bound, then you must needs wait until tomorrow.'

'Oh, I see.' She did not see at all. Unless the Captain had decided to take her to London, after all. But even she could see that was impractical; she had not thought of a long journey when she'd left Stacey Manor; it had been a spur-of-the-moment thing, coming to her as they rode together. She had no change of clothes, no baggage at all. No money either. In the unlikely event of him agreeing, they would have to return to Stacey Manor to make the proper arrangements for a journey.

Supposing the Captain had abandoned her? He was not at all a chivalrous man; he was the black sheep of the family; he had said so himself. He would have no conscience about leaving her to find her own way, especially if he had met up with a friend. 'Did he say where they were going?'

'No, miss.'

'But he did say he would be back?'

'Oh, yes, miss. Most particular he was as to that. And I was to see that you did not stir from the premises.'

'In that case, please bring me something to eat. I am starving. I am sure…' She paused. Was the Captain here under his real name? What was his real name? Would she upset some deep-laid plan by revealing the one she knew him by? 'My friend will pay.'

The landlord's smile did not reveal what he thought about young ladies arriving at his inn in the arms of gentlemen in the early hours; it was not his business, but if she had been a daughter of his he would have spanked her soundly. 'Do you wish to have it sent to your room?'

'No, I will eat in the dining room. And bring me paper and ink to write a letter, if you please.'

He conducted her to the dining room and offered her a table by the window where she could see everyone who came and went. Given the writing things she asked for, she sat down and scribbled a note to her godmother—telling her she was safe and well and under Captain Stacey's protection—

which she gave to the innkeeper to put on the next mailcoach, before beginning her meal.

She had hardly begun to eat when a rider galloped into the yard and dismounted. He was obviously in a great hurry and very agitated. Molly watched as a crowd gathered round him. From their shocked expressions, she gathered he was bringing news of some importance. He left the crowd outside and came into the dining room, where he announced to all and sundry that the Cromer stage had been waylaid by highwaymen on a quiet stretch of the road a dozen miles to the north.

'Was anyone hurt?' enquired the innkeeper while Molly reflected that if she had not overslept and if Captain Stacey had not decided to disappear she would have been on that coach. That really would have been an adventure and she was rather cross that she had missed it.

'No. But they made everyone get out and they searched the coach very thorough,' the man said. 'They took Sir John Partridge's gold and his watch and papers, but they let the ladies keep their jewellery.'

'Where was the guard? Did he not try to stop them?'

'The stage carried no guard. Sir John's man had a pistol but he was so slow fetching it out, he was useless. The high toby took it from him as easy as you please.'

'Then what happened?'

'They made everyone return to their seats and told the coachman to drive on. Sir John demanded to know their names, as if they would be foolish enough to give them to him. One of them laughed and said he was called the Dark Knight.'

'Where were you when all this was happening?' demanded mine host.

'I came upon the scene quite by chance, but there was nothing I could do. They had pistols and I was unarmed…'

'How many of them?'

'Two. Very big men, they were, and masked. I hid in the trees until it was safe to proceed.'

'Which direction did the robbers takc?'

'To the coast, I think.'

The landlord sent a boy off to fetch a constable and there was talk of sending for the runners from London, but it was decided that by the time they arrived the highwaymen would be long gone. Doubtless Sir John would report the incident when the coach arrived in Cromer and constables sent from there to help search for the robbers.

In the middle of this discussion, Duncan strolled into the inn and sat down opposite Molly. He was dressed in soft buckskin breeches, a brown coat and a yellow and brown checked waistcoat. His boots and white neckcloth were pristine. She surmised that he could not have ridden very far, for the roads were dusty and there wasn't a speck of it on him.

'You have missed all the excitement,' she told him. 'The Cromer coach has been held up. They are even now sending for the watch.'

'Is that so?' He affected little interest. 'I'm devilish hungry. Have you finished with that?' He pointed to a tureen of vegetables and a platter containing pork chops.

'Yes. Please help yourself. You will be paying for it, after all. I have no money.'

'Dear me! Not even for the coach fare?'

'No. I did not think I would need money. I was on horseback.'

'And what would you have done if I had not returned?' he asked, piling a plate with food. 'I could simply have ridden off and left you. The landlord would not have been pleased when he discovered you could not pay for what you had eaten.'

'He assured me you had said you would be back. I had no reason to doubt you.'

'No reason not to doubt me either. You are too trusting, my dear.'

'But you did come back, so I was right.'

'Tell me,' he said, tucking into the chops. 'What did you intend when you followed me last night?

Not a journey to London, I'll wager, or you would have come better prepared.'

'No, I saw you leave and was curious as to why you travelled by night, that was all. I wanted to see where you were going. And riding in the dark is something I never tried before and I like doing new things. I did not think of Mama, until we started to talk about her. And then it seemed the very thing to join her in London.' She sighed. 'And you left me asleep, so I missed my adventure.'

'Adventure?'

'Yes, being held up by highwaymen. Do you suppose they stole a kiss from the ladies? But I collect the man said they took nothing from the ladies, only from Sir John Partridge.'

'What man?' Duncan tried not to let his real interest show.

'The man who saw it all. I think he must be a little nervous and not at all heroic, for he said he hid and only rode on when it was all over.'

'What else did he say?'

'There were two of them, heavily armed, and afterwards they rode towards the coast. Everyone seems to think they had a boat waiting for them and are long gone.'

'Very likely,' he said, allowing himself to relax. 'Now, what are we to do about you?'

'The landlord says the next Cromer coach is not until tomorrow. We shall have to ride back.'

'We, Miss Martineau? I cannot spare the time escorting a chit about the countryside; I should have been on my way long ago…'

Before he could go on, they were interrupted by the arrival of the local constable, who had come to take charge of the investigation into the robbery. He began by questioning the witness whose tale lost nothing in repetition. In fact, it gained a detail or two. The chief of the highwaymen was of a dark countenance, dressed all in black, and he rode a big black horse with a white flash on its nose. His accomplice was older and smaller by six inches and had a scar near his left eye, though it could not all be seen on account of the mask he wore.

Molly had pricked up her ears when she'd heard the description of the horse. She had ridden on the back of such a one not five hours since but, she told herself severely, there must be many black horses with white noses and many men with dark looks. She glanced across at the Captain who was placidly eating and told herself she was imagining things. To have arrived back in the inn so soon after the hold-up, he would, like the man who had witnessed it, have had to ride hard, but he was completely unruffled and showed every evidence of a leisurely toilette.

She noticed Duncan lift his head as another man came in. Did she imagine he nodded towards Duncan before passing through the room and out of the door towards the stairs? What was unmistakable was the scar on his face.

'Captain,' she whispered, reaching across and touching his hand to attract his attention. 'That man who just went out. He had a scar…'

'So have a great many men, I should think,' he said, without even bothering to look up from his meal.

'But one of the robbers…'

'Miss Martineau, you must learn to curb your imagination, you know, or you will land yourself in more trouble than a little.'

'You know him, don't you?'

'Miss Mar…' He stopped short when the bulk of the constable loomed over them.

'Sir, may I ask what you know of this matter?' he asked. 'I am told you have recently arrived and from a northerly direction.'

'If by recent you mean five hours or thereabouts,' Duncan said laconically, 'then I suppose you could say I have.'

'Hours, you say? I was told you entered the room but fifteen minutes ago.'

'So I did. From my bedroom. My man will vouch for me. He is even now packing for our departure.'

'It is quite true,' Molly said, turning her ingenuous smile upon the constable. 'I, too, can vouch for the Captain's whereabouts, though I own he did leave me for twenty minutes or so. He had to arrange transport for us.'

'Twenty minutes? No more?'

'Oh, no more, I do assure you.'

'And who are you, miss, if I might ask?'

'Why, I am Captain Stacey's wife,' she said, favouring the man with a dazzling smile and ignoring the sound of Duncan choking on his food. 'Who else would I be?'

The constable inclined his head towards Molly. 'I beg your pardon, ma'am, but I must leave no stone unturned.'

'And while you waste time turning over stones the thieves will have gone to ground.' Duncan, who had quickly regained his scattered wits, decided he could not embarrass her by contradicting her, but it put him in a devil of a coil. He could hardly put her on a coach to Cromer and ride off in the opposite direction if they were supposed to be husband and wife travelling together. 'Get out to the scene of the crime,' he said in his most commanding voice. 'Surely that is where you should begin?'

The man bowed again and left them and Duncan

called the waiter to bring a pudding; he was still hungry, he said.

'Don't you think we should go?' Molly asked. 'If the constable sees your horse—or the man with the scar…'

'I see you have added two and two and made five,' he said, making inroads into the plum duff which had just been set before him. 'Have some of this; it is delicious.'

'No, thank you. I am no longer hungry. And I don't know how you can sit there and eat so calmly when you know…'

He smiled at her. Her blue eyes were looking troubled; surely she was not worried on his account? He felt an unaccountable frisson of pleasure at the thought. 'What do I know?'

'More than you are saying. If you were not on the road this morning, you know very well who was.'

'But you gave me an alibi. Surely you do not condone highway robbery?'

'I know nothing of it. If you were to tell me…'

'There is nothing to tell. And I wish you would not refine upon it. What I do is none of your business.'

'I think it is,' she said promptly. 'If you had not panicked my horse, I would not have been thrown and you would not have had to bring me here. That was your fault. And now, because there is no coach going to Cromer until tomorrow, we must stay here like sitting ducks. Besides, you have already said your man—and I doubt not he is the robber with the scar—is packing to leave and I have confirmed you have been out to arrange transport, so leave we must.'

'Of course we must; you made sure of that,' he said. 'We shall have to find another way of returning you to Stacey Manor.' He stood up unhurriedly and beckoned the landlord for the reckoning. 'Wait for me in the yard. I will be out directly.'

She went outside and, while waiting for him, wandered round to the stables. There was no sign of his horse, nor Jenny either; they had been spirited away. By the man with the scar? She turned as Duncan joined her. 'Where are the horses?'

'I did not like the stabling here; I have had them moved elsewhere where the fodder is better and the accommodation more to their liking.'

There was definitely something have-cavey going on and she was more intrigued than ever. 'Then how do we go on?'

'I have hired a curricle.' He stood looking down at her; she was completely unafraid, but that was because she had never in her life come across anything to be afraid of. He hoped she never would, but she was more astute than he had given her credit for and now he must protect her. He had commanded men in battle, been responsible for their lives, but never before had he had such an obligation as this and it was making him uncomfortable.

His experience with women was with women of the world, who asked nothing for their favours but money or costly presents. There were female relatives, of course, and Beth, whom he had expected to marry. But Beth would never put herself into the position that Molly had done; Beth was too aware of what Society expected from her and what it was and was not permissible for a lady to do. Chasing after a man in the middle of the night would not have occurred to her.

'Where are we going?' she asked, as he escorted her back to the front of the inn, where a spanking curricle and a small brown horse were ready and waiting for them.

'Norwich.'

'South! Why, that is halfway to London!'

'Not quite,' he said laconically, helping her onto the vehicle and climbing up beside her. 'But you have made it necessary for us to leave together and going north is not sensible, so Norwich it will have to be. Besides, the place is big enough for shopping and you need a change of clothes.' He turned to look at her as he spoke.

Her riding habit was of some dull silk material

and the matching skirt was quite plain, not distinc-
tive, except that it was unusual for a young lady to
wear such a garment for riding in a carriage and the
skirt was too long and cumbersome for her to walk
comfortably in town. It would be noted and if, in
her innocence, she let slip whatever it was she
thought she knew, suspicions would be aroused.
Once she was suitably attired, he could put her on
the coach to Cromer, under the chaperonage of
another lady passenger.

'We are going shopping! Oh, Captain, how very
thoughtful you are! But I have no money.'

'So you have said before. My pocket is at your
disposal.' He flicked the reins and they turned out
of the yard at a smart trot.

'And is it a very deep pocket?'

'Not at all. We must be frugal.'

'But I heard Sir John had a great deal of gold...'

'You think I robbed that coach for gain?' The annoyance was plain on his face as he turned to answer
her. 'Rakeshame I may be, but I do not stoop so low
as to profit from another's loss, unless it be at the
card table.'

He had not exactly denied his involvement, she
noted, only that he had not gained by it; she was
more curious than ever and determined not to be
sent back to Stacey Manor until she discovered the

truth. 'There are gentlemen highwaymen. I have heard of many instances where…'

'And I collect you are a great reader. Romantic fiction, I'll wager. The real world is not like that.'

'No, perhaps it is not. But fiction hurts no one, does it? And if it provides a little light relief and entertainment, where's the harm? I have my feet firmly on the ground.'

He laughed suddenly. 'And your head in the clouds.'

She was silent for a moment, but only a moment. 'What shall I be allowed to buy?'

'Whatever you need for a coach ride and an overnight stay. By the time we arrive, it will be too late to go on.' He knew perfectly well he was endangering her reputation, had in fact already compromised it, but it was her own fault; he had not asked her to provide him with an alibi. That was not to say he need not put his mind to finding ways and means of preserving her good name and he thought he might have the answer.

'Mama said she would buy me a wardrobe when I went to London,' she said rather wistfully. 'You know you need a great many clothes for a Season. You should have seen what Mama bought. Trunks full. She showed them to me. Gowns for mornings, afternoons and evenings, for riding in carriages and walking and habits for riding, and hats and bonnets and ballgowns. She said it was absolutely essential to be well kitted out.'

'Yes, ladies change their clothes a great many times a day, I believe,' he said, watching her upturned face and sparkling eyes.

'Mama's ballgowns are all very beautiful. Of course, she is taller than I am, so they would not fit me. And she said they were unsuitable. I am not…' She paused and treated him to her infectious laugh, which made the corners of his mouth twitch. 'I am not as well rounded as Mama.'

'No, indeed not,' he said, thinking of the voluptuous Harriet. 'But I think your figure is very pleasing as it is.'

'Do you? Oh, that is very civil of you. I think you are the most handsome of men, even if you are lacking in chivalry.'

'Am I so?'

'I have been reading *Don Quixote*. You know he was always rescuing damsels in distress. You are not at all like him. He would never have slapped Jenny's rump while I was unprepared for it.'

'He was also more than a little touched in the attic, I collect. He thought windmills were giants.'

'But it didn't stop him wanting to fight them, big as they were. He was very brave.'

'There are times, my dear, when bravery is foolhardy in the extreme. Have you never heard the saying "discretion is the better part of valour"?'

'Yes, but that is a very dull maxim.'

'Then I must be the dullest of men.'

'Oh, I do not believe that. Why, you said yourself you are a rakeshame and you cannot be that if you are too cautious. And I am sure you are not cautious at all. I believe you thrive on risk. Look how you came back to the Red Lion and sat and ate your dinner as calm as you please. And the way you answered the constable.'

He smiled. 'You didn't do so badly yourself, though I cannot think why you did it.'

'I was afraid they would go up to your room and find the man with the scar. Not to mention the gold.'

'Gold?' he repeated furiously. 'I have already told you I have no gold.'

'So you have,' she mused aloud. 'I wonder what you can have done with it?'

'Molly, you will make me very angry if you mention that again.'

'Very well, have your little secret, if you must, but how am I to help you, if I do not know the truth?'

He turned to her in astonishment. 'Help me?'

'Of course,' she said placidly. 'A man travelling to London with his wife is not the same as two masked men on horseback, now is it?'

'London?' he repeated. 'Wife?'

'Oh, I do not mean you to marry me, but we could pretend. Just until we reached the capital.'

'I do not have to make an honest woman of you, then?' he teased. 'I thought in the best tradition of the lady novelists you would insist upon it.' Talking to her made a refreshing change from the horrors which often invaded his thoughts; she was like a breath of spring air, light and joyful, the foretaste of the warmth of summer. And he had been too long in the cold.

'I am not such a ninny as to want to shackle myself to a man who has no great love for me. That would spell disaster. And besides, I mean to enjoy my Season if I am so fortunate as to have one, and how can I do that if I am already married?'

'How very sensible of you,' he murmured, smiling a little.

'You are laughing at me,' she said.

'No, I was thinking of your mama and what she might say when she found you on her doorstep.'

'She will be very pleased to see me.'

'Oh, I am sure she would.' And this time he did not hide his smile as he added, 'When she recovered from the shock. How are we to explain your arrival in my company? I am, after all, a rakeshame and you have no chaperon.'

She had no idea what she was talking about, he realised. The romantic reading which had been so large a part of her education might talk of ruined reputations, but he doubted if she had any conception of what it meant in practice. 'Have you any idea what would happen when we arrived in London and it became known you had openly admitted to spending a whole night in my company?' he asked.

'Two nights,' she corrected him.

'You would be vilified. Everyone would cut you dead. There would be no Season. Your mother would disown you. And every ne'er-do-well in the capital would take it into his head...' He paused. 'No, I will not go into that.'

'Then you must become a reformed character, concerned only for my welfare and good name. Lady Connaught charged you with bringing me safely to my mother and you discharged that duty faithfully.'

'She would never do that unless you were travelling with a female companion, a maid, who slept in your room.'

She laughed. 'Don't be a goosecap, Captain; even I know maids do not sleep in the same room as a married couple.'

'Not married,' he said. 'Being escorted, very properly escorted.'

'Oh, I see. But I have no maid. Mama said it was not in the least necessary for me to have one. Her maid always helped me when I was at home, but since she sold the house…'

'Sold the house?' he queried in surprise.

'Yes. The Colonel did not leave a great deal and all Mama had was a small pension. She was in debt and being dunned by everyone. She needed to realise all her assets to pay for her Season in London. It was an investment. She explained it all to me. She has rented a house in Holles Street and bought a carriage and horses. But when she has found her next husband we shall have a new home and everything we need.'

'I can hardly credit it,' he said, his fury with Harriet almost boiling over. He had always known Harriet was selfish and a gambler, but he had never thought she would treat her own daughter in such a ramshackle manner. 'Do you mean to say you are homeless?'

'I have—had—a home with Lady Connaught until Mama came about. And I suppose I could say I have a home in Holles Street. And if you are going to London…'

'Who said I was?'

'No one, but you are, aren't you?'

'No,' Duncan said firmly. 'The idea is out of the question.'

'Oh, please, Captain. I will not be a trouble to you, I promise. I will be as quiet as a mouse and do as you bid…'

'Impossible,' he said. 'I am ready to wager you could not keep quiet however hard you tried; I never heard such a chatterbox. And as for doing as you are told, give me leave to doubt that too.'

'Then I shall not promise it, only that I will try my best.' She turned a smile on him that made his heart turn over and almost took his breath away. 'I cannot say fairer than that, can I?'

'No,' he admitted.

'Then you will take me?'

'I cannot.' The further they went from Stacey Manor, the more difficult it would be for him to return Molly to his grandmother, but the young chit had been right when she said a husband and wife would attract less attention. They were still too near the scene of the action. But it was impossible. Out of the question. He had not yet stooped so low as to ruin a young lady's reputation.

She was silent for a moment, but only a moment. 'Have you been in London during the Season, Captain?'

'Many years ago, before I became a soldier.'

'And did you not find the lady of your dreams there?'

'I thought so at the time, but nothing came of it.'

'Oh, you were crossed in love. How sad for you. Is that why you have become a gentleman of the road?'

He laughed again but this time she detected a little bitterness in it. 'I have admitted to being no such thing. Now do you think we might change the subject?'

'Certainly, if you find it painful. Tell me, what do young ladies do during the Season? I have read some of Miss Austen's books and others on etiquette and it seems to me there are a great many pitfalls. How do they know who is eligible and who is not? So much of it seems to rely on hearsay. Surely one needs more than that? After all, everyone must have a different idea about what makes a perfect partner. And how can mere acquaintanceship turn to love if you are never allowed to be alone with a man even for a minute? After all, he might seem very charming and unexceptional when in company, but turn out to be the very opposite when it is too late.'

'That happens.'

'And once she is committed she must make the best of it, I believe.'

'That is another of your mama's truisms, is it?'

'Is it wrong?'

'No. But courtship works two ways. The lady might not turn out to be all the young man had hoped for. A pretty face and a fetching figure are not the only attributes for a good wife.'

'So, tell me what you think they are.'

He turned to smile at her. 'What do you think?'

'Love and compassion,' she said promptly. 'Gentleness, but not so much as to make her dull.'

'Oh, you are so right,' he said, only half teasing. 'I should abhor dullness in a wife.'

'I should not like a dull husband either. Not top-lofty or arrogant. I would expect him to be sensitive and kind.' She paused to look at him, a smile playing about her lips. 'And chivalrous.'

'Oh, dear,' he said mournfully. 'I should fail on all counts.'

'Oh, I wasn't thinking of you, Captain. You are far too old.'

'And that has put me firmly in my place,' he said, smiling a little ruefully as he flicked the reins to make the horse go a little faster. 'There is an inn ahead of us which I should like to reach as soon as maybe. And for your information I have seen but thirty summers.'

'Old,' she affirmed. 'But perhaps that is no bad thing. One would expect a man of thirty summers to have sowed all his wild oats and be ready to settle down.'

'The problem with that theory is that some men never want to settle down. Sowing wild oats is a deal more fun.'

'As ye sow, so shall ye reap,' she said.

'And what is that supposed to mean?'

'You will have a poor harvest.'

'Quite the philosopher, aren't you?'

'No, but I am interested in people and why they do the things they do. You, for instance…'

'I am a dull subject for your studies.'

'Not at all. You may be from the poor side of the Connaught family, but I believe you have been educated as a gentleman, you have served as an officer and you have a grandmother who is very fond of you, so you cannot be all bad. With a little instruction and application, you could become a real gentleman and find some more fitting occupation.'

'Heaven preserve me from reforming women! I am as I am and that is an end of it.'

'Very well,' she said meekly. 'I am, after all, in your hands to do with as you please. I have no wish to fall out with you.'

He smiled to himself as they bowled along. She was an amazing mixture of innocence and wisdom, child and woman, and one day, when she had learned the ways of the world, she would be a charmer, even a heartbreaker. And he did not want his heart broken again.

Unaware of his introspection, or perhaps deliberately ignoring it, she continued to chat happily to him until they turned into the yard of the Crosskeys at St Faith's just short of Norwich, and drew to a stop.

'Well,' she said, turning towards him. 'Are we to test my theory?'

'Theory?' he queried. 'It seems to me you have a great many theories. Which one are we to test?'

'Why, that it is Captain Stacey and his wife who will stay here overnight.'

'Good God, child, have you any idea what that means?'

'I believe it means we must share a bedchamber.'

'And what happens in that bedchamber?'

'How am I to know that?' she asked. 'I never did it before. But it doesn't signify, does it, because we are not really married but only pretending?'

'And if there is only one bed?'

'Oh, Captain, I am quite sure you can contrive something.'

Before he could find a suitable reply an ostler came out from the stables to see to the equipage. Duncan jumped down and reached up to help her alight. 'Come inside and we will decide what's to be done with you,' he said.

The inn was small and very old. Duncan had to duck his head to enter the doorway. He stood looking round the company, which consisted of a farmer and his wife who were quarrelling loudly, and four men, intent on playing cards. They were evidently playing very deep for there was a pile of coins on the table between them and their conversation consisted of grunts, unintelligible except to each other. The only other customer was the man with the scar. Duncan led Molly over to join him.

"Bout time too,' the man said. 'Did you stop to admire the wayside flowers?'

'No, but I had to answer questions from a bumbling town constable and I could not appear too eager to depart.'

'And you still have the trailing petticoats, I see.'

Duncan turned to Molly and took her hand to draw her forward. 'Miss Martineau, may I present my good friend, Sergeant Frank Upjohn? Frank, this is Miss Molly Martineau. We have spoken of her.'

'Miss Martineau, your obedient.' He did not seem particularly pleased to see her, she noted as he rose to acknowledge her.

The innkeeper came forward, wiping his hands on his apron, to ask their requirements.

'Food,' Duncan said. 'And plenty of it.'

The man went away to give the order to his wife and Duncan and Molly joined Frank at the table.

'You do not approve of me, Mr Upjohn,' she said, arranging her long skirt about her as she sat down; it was now more crumpled than ever. 'No doubt you think I am an encumbrance, but I assure you, I intend to help you both.'

'Whether we will it or not,' Duncan murmured, leaning back in his chair, a faint smile playing about his mouth.

'You said I did not do so badly,' she protested. 'And if you were escorting me from Stacey Manor to London you would not have had time to hold up a coach, would you?'

'Hold up a coach?' Frank repeated, looking sharply at Duncan. 'Who said anything about holding up a coach?'

'I certainly did not,' Duncan answered. 'Madam, here, has added two and two and made five, as I pointed out to her.'

'There is nothing wrong with my arithmetic,' she said. 'Two men, one bigger than the other, one riding a fine black horse with a white nose-flash, and the other with a scar beneath his eye. I cannot think of a better description of you both. You were absent from the inn at the relevant time and the horses were removed from the stable on a pretext I find unbelievable, not to mention the fact that you did not deny it when I said you had been with me all night.'

'I could hardly contradict a lady,' Duncan said, smiling at the look of astonishment on Frank's face at this statement. 'And if you were so sure, why did you not denounce me, instead of dreaming up another cock-and-bull story?'

'I was curious as to why you did it, if not for gain.'

'I thought you were going to send her back where she came from,' Frank muttered as the innkeeper's wife brought plates and tureens to the table.

'How?' Duncan demanded. 'There was no public coach, her mare had been hidden and I had no time…'

'It was necessary to put the constable off the scent,' Molly added. 'Besides, I want to go to London and I thought of a great ruse…'

He turned to Frank. 'She wanted us to pretend to be married; she even told the constable at the Red Lion that we were. I have persuaded her it will not do. We can't look after her. Quite apart from the practical difficulties, just think what it would do to her reputation.'

'And yours,' Frank said with a wry smile. 'The hard man who has no time for females, making a cake of himself over a chit. And we have work to do, or had you forgot?'

'No, I hadn't forgotten,' Duncan said, watching Molly pile her plate with roast chicken and vegetables. He disliked women who picked at their food in the pretence of daintiness. The longer they were together, the deeper became the coil he was in, and the inn, though perfectly adequate for him and Frank, was certainly not suitable for a lady. He wished he had thought of that before suggesting the rendezvous. It just showed how long he had been out of genteel society and how unmannerly he had become. 'But I must admit it would be easier to take her with us than try and return her to Stacey Manor.'

He could not tell Frank the other reason why he was even considering taking her with them because it had nothing to do with his own plight. He wanted to make her happy and if taking her to her mother made her happy, then why should he not do it? But not as his wife. Never that. 'We must make ourselves into a proper escort and that means another female and a coach and horses.'

'Oh, yes, please,' Molly said, brightening. 'That would be the very thing. I could enter London in style and no one would think any the worse of me.' She stopped and gave him a meaningful look. 'Nor you either. Everyone would admire you for it and your reputation would be quite restored.'

'What do you say, Frank?' Duncan asked him. 'Would Martha act the maid?'

'Martha?'

'Yes, why not?'

'Who is Martha?' Molly demanded.

'She is my wife,' Frank said. 'But she has never been a lady's maid. She would have no idea how to go on.'

'Oh, I could soon tell her,' Molly said. 'There is really nothing to it and I should so like a female companion. Do say you agree.'

'What is the alternative?' Duncan demanded of his friend. 'Turn and ride back to Stacey Manor and take our chances with the local constabulary, who will by now have been reinforced by those from Cromer and Norwich, or leave the young lady here to manage by herself?'

'No, I am not so lacking in conduct as to do that. I'll fetch Martha.'

'Good. Where are our horses?'

'Fed and watered and grazing in a field nearby.'

'Then Molly and I will ride into Norwich in the morning with your mount. You take the curricle and bring Martha to us at The Bell.'

Molly, who did not fancy an evening spent in the company of the card players and the nagging farmer's wife, said she wanted to retire as soon as they had finished supper. Duncan cast a glance at the men, who seemed intent on their cards, but he knew they would hear any orders he gave; he could not let it be known she was a single lady and was left with no alternative but to ask for a room to be prepared for his wife.

Once this was done, she bade him goodnight with a great show of wifely affection. She was in a cheerful mood because he had fallen in with her scheme to pretend to be husband and wife, if only for one night. This was a grand adventure and so long as he remained with her she had nothing to fear.

As soon as Molly had been conducted from the room, Frank turned on him. 'Captain, you must be mad. Do you know how much this escapade is likely to cost? And we have nothing left, unless you have been holding out on me. Every farthing of what we took has been passed on as you instructed.'

'Good. I knew I could rely on you.' He was beginning to realise how poor people felt when their whole lives must be lived in search of money to buy food and shelter. There was never any time for anything else. No wonder some of the soldiers returning from the war with no way of earning a living and a family to care for turned to crime.

'But now we have pockets to let again,' Frank went on, speaking more bluntly than would have been considered fitting between master and servant in any other circumstances. 'It is always the same with you, Captain. It seems money is an embarrassment to you.'

'It is when so many of my fellows have nothing. They fought as hard as I did, and under more difficult conditions; they deserve all I can do for them. Especially for their widows.'

'So, how will you convey the lady to London?'

'With good luck, by post chaise, with a little less by stagecoach.'

Frank sighed heavily. 'I suppose it is useless for me to point out that petticoats are a bad omen…'

'Not this one. I have a feeling she will bring me the best luck in the world. Nor can you say Martha has brought you anything else.'

Frank owned himself defeated. 'Do you want me to leave now?'

'Yes, otherwise Molly will be unchaperoned yet another night.'

Still grumbling, Frank got up and left the inn. Duncan watched him go, then put the rest of the evening to good use by joining the card players when one of their number lost everything and was forced to stop. By dawn, he was richer by several guineas. It was enough to pay for their lodging and for Molly's shopping expedition, though he would have to warn her against extravagance.

Pretending to be too drunk to go to bed, he dozed for an hour or two on a settle. He could not join Molly and asking for a separate room would have looked decidedly odd. Besides, he risked over-sleeping and he wanted to be on hand if Molly took it into her head to do something foolish or talk to strangers; she could not know how risky that might be.

Chapter Three

As soon as Molly woke, she rose, washed in cold water from the jug on the wash-stand and, once more attired in the now bedraggled riding habit, went downstairs. In the corridor, she met the innkeeper's wife busy sweeping the floor. Molly bade her good morning and asked if the Captain was up and about.

'Yes, ma'am. Did you sleep so sound you didn't know he hadn't come to bed?'

She was momentarily disconcerted, but, remembering her role, smiled. 'I must have.'

'He's pacing the floor, chafing at the bit, waiting for you.'

Molly hurried to join him, but, far from pacing the floor, he was sitting at the breakfast table, apparently at ease. There was no one else in the room. He rose as she came towards him and pulled out a chair for her.

'Good morning, my dear. Did you sleep well?'

'Yes, thank you. But you did not, I believe. The innkeeper's wife told me you did not go to bed. Where were you?'

'In the next room, enjoying the company of friends.'

'Friends? I did not know you were acquainted with anyone here.'

'I used the term loosely.'

'Is that the usual behaviour of a man towards his wife when travelling?'

'It is certainly not so out of the ordinary as to excite comment and it was better than invading your privacy, my dear. Besides, I put the time to good use.' He jingled a pocketful of coins.

'Gaming.'

'Yes.'

'And did you win?'

'Naturally, I did.'

'Is that how you make a living?'

'It is one of the ways. Now, please have some breakfast. We must be on our way as soon as you are ready.' He indicated the platters of ham and eggs as he poured her a cup of coffee from the pot at his elbow.

She sat down and helped herself. 'And another way is holding up coaches. I cannot believe that someone as educated as you are should stoop to crime. I do believe there is more to it than meets the eye.'

'Is that so?' he asked laconically, wondering if she

could possibly have stumbled on the truth. But no; clever she might be, but not that clever. 'And are you going to tell me your theory?'

'I don't have one, not yet. Of course, you could tell me and then I would not worry about you.'

'You worry about me?' he queried. 'Why?'

'Naturally I worry about you. You are family, even if it is I don't know how many times removed. And I am very fond of Aunt Margaret…'

'So, it is not for my own sake?' he asked, and wondered why he asked. Did it really matter what a chit of a girl thought of him?

'That, too, of course.' She smiled at him and popped a forkful of food into her mouth. 'Tell me, Captain, just what are you about?'

He smiled suddenly. 'I believe I am escorting a young lady to London to be with her mama.'

'Oh, so you do think I am a lady?' she said.

'I do not know what else you might be. Hoyden or schoolmiss might be to the point, but I give you the benefit of the doubt. Now, if you have finished, we must be on our way.'

'I should write another letter to Aunt Margaret before we go,' she said. 'I sent her one yesterday, but as I did not know our destination I could not be very precise. I shall tell her you are going to take me to Mama and that will set her mind to rest.'

He wondered whether it would, considering the jobation his grandmother had given him about his way of life, and decided to add his postscript to the letter assuring her he would take good care of the young lady. He could imagine the old lady's smile when she read it; he was playing right into her hands and if Molly had not assured him otherwise he would have had no trouble believing she had concocted the whole escapade to bring him to heel.

The letter was soon written and given to the landlord to put on the mail and they went outside where three horses stood patiently waiting for their riders. He helped her to mount Jenny, then picked up the reins of Frank's horse, which she learned was called Good Boy, and sprang nimbly into his own saddle.

They turned and rode towards Norwich, sometimes cantering and, now and again, when it was safe to do so, putting the horses to a gallop. She rode well, he noticed. He noted other things too: her softly rounded breasts and trim waist, her bright eyes, always so full of life, her pink lips and the way a strand of her hair curled so lovingly into her neck. And he asked himself what in heaven's name he was doing with her. Frank was right—he had run mad.

When they crossed the river and entered the city, she was so diverted by the size of it, the busy streets, full of carts and carriages, the pedestrians and hawkers crying their wares and the shops and taverns, she could do nothing but gape.

'I did not know it would be such a big place,' she said. 'Is it as large as London?'

'Not quite. But it is an important centre of commerce. You will find all you need here.'

He smiled indulgently as the road took them past the castle. She pulled up her horse to stare up at its looming grey wall. 'Is it occupied?'

'Oh, yes, by several hundred criminals.'

'It's a prison?' She shuddered, imagining the Captain being confined there, and it occurred to her that the life he led was dangerous in the extreme. If he were arrested and taken from her, what would she do? Might she be arrested too for aiding him? Adventure for adventure's sake was suddenly not so appealing. 'Then the sooner we leave it behind the better,' she said.

'We must wait for Frank and Martha. In the meantime we shall go shopping.'

'Good,' she said, looking down at her habit, which was so dusty and crumpled it looked as though she had slept in it. 'I tried to get the creases out but it proved impossible.'

'We need to refresh ourselves first and the horses need stabling,' he said, deciding that taking her as she was into a genteel establishment to buy the things a lady needed to travel to London would invite strange looks and he could not afford to arouse curiosity.

He took her to The Bell where the rooms were superior to any they had had so far: a well-furnished bedroom and a sitting room with a table and chairs and an upholstered sofa.

While she shut herself in the bedroom to strip off her clothes and wash, he changed into pantaloons and a clean shirt, tied a fresh cravat about his neck, donned waistcoat and frockcoat and left the building.

He returned just as Molly came out of the bedchamber into the sitting room. She had asked the chambermaid to press her habit and it was a little more respectable than it had been but still bore evidence of a long ride. She had cleaned her face and now it was pink and glowing and her blue eyes sparkled. She had evidently borrowed a brush and spent some time on her hair, because it gleamed with health and she had put it up into a Grecian style, which suited her piquant face.

His grandmother had been right, he decided; Molly Martineau would one day turn heads with her beauty. She was inexperienced and that was part of her charm, but he felt his loins stirring at the sight of her and realised he was not so impervious as he'd thought he was.

'Here,' he said, almost embarrassed, handing her the parcel he carried. 'Put this on. It is, I think, more suitable for a shopping expedition than a riding habit.'

She opened the package eagerly to reveal a simple round gown in turquoise muslin, with little puff sleeves and a round neck filled with lace. There was a little matching cape, white stockings, blue kid shoes and a reticule. 'Oh!' she exclaimed. 'It is very pretty. I could not have chosen anything I liked more. But will it fit?'

'There is only one way to find out,' he said, smiling at her enthusiasm. 'Put it on and we will go out and buy more.'

She needed no second bidding and disappeared into the bedchamber. Twenty minutes later she emerged once again, looking very fetching and smiling happily. 'You guessed my size exactly, Captain. How very clever of you. Except the shoes are a little tight.'

'I am sorry about that. Perhaps you could wear your riding boots…'

'Oh, no, that will spoil the effect. I shall manage.'

'Madam.' He smiled at her, offering her his arm. 'Shall we go?'

Laughing, she laid her hand upon his sleeve and

together they went out into the street and strolled towards the centre of the city to the emporium where he had bought the gown and where he knew there were other establishments offering ladies' apparel, as well as things like fans and reticules, parasols and footwear, underwear and toiletries.

'Kit her out with everything she needs for a stay in London,' he told one proprietress, whose name, according to the legend above the door of her establishment, was Mrs Hannah Solomon.

'I am to have a Season,' Molly told her. 'Is that not exciting?'

'Yes, indeed,' the woman agreed. 'So very sensible of your uncle to buy your requirements in Norwich. The prices in London are much higher.'

Molly looked at Duncan when she mentioned her uncle and stifled a little giggle. He simply smiled and said nothing to put right the mistake.

The morning flew by as he sat and watched her parade before him in day gowns, carriage gowns, riding habits, gloves, shoes, half-boots, hats, bonnets, capes, spencers and pelisses. His resolve to limit her spending was abandoned in the face of her pleasure.

'Which shall it be?' she asked, looking from a carriage dress and matching pelisse in soft green velvet to an afternoon gown of blue sarcenet. 'I cannot make up my mind, so you choose.'

'Then have them both.'

'Oh, you are the most generous of men!' she exclaimed as Mrs Solomon began folding the gowns to pack into boxes before he should change his mind. 'I am beginning to revise my opinion that you are not chivalrous.'

He bowed towards her. 'And I am gratified to hear you say so.'

'Madam will need underthings?' Mrs Solomon queried, determined not to let this customer go until she had wrung every last drop out of the transaction.

'Naturally she will,' he said.

'And she must have at least one ballgown,' she went on. 'I have just the thing.' She disappeared through a curtain at the back of the premises and came back carrying a large dress box. 'This was made for a young lady who changed her mind about buying it. You are of a size, I think.' She opened the box and held the gown up against Molly.

The overskirt was made of the palest blue-green crepe with an open front which floated round her like shimmering water. It had puffed sleeves and a deep round neckline filled with rouched lace and the bodice was caught under the bosom with a cluster of silk flowers in pale colours of pink, blue and lilac; more of the flowers trimmed the hem. The underskirt was of white satin. Molly ran her hands lovingly over it. 'Oh, it is beautiful, but I do not know…'

'Try it on,' Duncan said.

He watched as she disappeared into an adjoining room to put it on, a procedure which had been going on all morning. He had thought he would be bored by it, but he was captivated. She was so easy to please and he guessed she had had few such pleasures in her young life. He was prepared to wager that Harriet had all the gowns she needed, while her daughter had nothing but what would suit a schoolgirl.

He looked up as Molly came back to stand before him. The gown fitted perfectly and her simple beauty took his breath away so that, for a moment, he could not speak.

'What do you think?' she demanded. 'Is it not beautiful?'

He swallowed hard. 'Indeed, yes.'

'It could have been made for the young lady,' Mrs Solomon said.

'But it was not,' Duncan put in. 'It has been left on your hands…'

Molly held her breath; she wanted to have the gown so very much and if the Captain haggled the woman might not let him have it.

'I am sure we can come to an arrangement,' she said with a simpering smile. 'For such a good customer.'

'Wrap everything up, put it into a trunk and send it to The Bell Hotel,' he instructed, pulling a purse out of his frockcoat. 'And I want a discount for cash.'

'Certainly, sir.' The sight of Duncan's hoard of hard-won coins was too much to resist.

Molly could hardly contain her excitement. Somehow or other, she was going to make an opportunity to wear that gown when they arrived in London. Already, she could imagine the occasion— the ballroom, the lights and music and the elegant young men clamouring to dance with her. Her mama would be very proud of her and not ashamed of her as she always seemed to be.

She chose to ignore the fact that they still had a long way to go before reaching the capital and she was almost sure the Captain was a wanted man. A more crucial problem was that she did not know how to dance. 'Captain,' she said, as they left the shop and turned back towards their lodgings, 'can you dance?'

'Tolerably well,' he said. 'But if you think I am going to take you to a ball…'

'No, not that; I was hoping you might teach me the steps. Mama always said there was plenty of time for that and so I never learned. And I should like to waltz.'

'I am not sure young unmarried ladies are allowed to waltz.'

'Why not?'

'I believe it is considered improper.'

'Why?'

'Because of the way the man holds his partner. It is a little…' He paused and smiled. 'A little too intimate for unmarried ladies.'

'Oh. There is a very great deal I do not know, isn't there?'

'Yes, I am afraid there is.'

'Then you must teach me.'

'Oh, no,' he said, laughing. 'I have undertaken to take you to your mother, nothing more. It is her place to instruct you.'

'Yes, but she is always so busy and it would be so much better if I could learn it all before we arrive in London. Then if an important invitation should come my way I would be ready.'

'No.'

'Why not?'

'I have more pressing things to do.'

'Like holding up coaches and gaming. I wish you would not do such dangerous things. I cannot bear the thought of you being shut up in that castle.'

He turned to look at her, trotting along beside him, trusting him completely, and a twinge of conscience smote him. What he was doing was highly improper and what was worse he was allowing himself to use her to allay the suspicions of the custodians of law and order. The fact that he had spent almost his last sovereign paying for her clothing in no way relieved his feelings of guilt.

'I have no intention of allowing myself to be shut up inside it,' he said brusquely.

'Why are you so blue-devilled? Is it because you have laid out more money on me than you intended? Mama will reimburse you, I am sure.'

'I have not laid out more than I intended,' he said, knowing perfectly well he would never accept repayment from Harriet, even if it were offered, which he doubted. 'What use are sovereigns except for spending?'

'Especially when they are not your own,' she retorted.

'I did not notice you refusing to take advantage of them,' he snapped.

'You said your pockets were at my disposal. I think it is very unkind of you to fly into the boughs just because I said I should not like you to be shut up in the castle.'

'Then there is no more to be said on the subject.'

'What are we going to do now?'

'Go back to The Bell and eat a good dinner.'

'Do you think Mr Upjohn will have arrived?'

'I certainly hope so.'

He shut his mouth so firmly after speaking, she knew it would be unwise to pester him. She walked on beside him, hobbling a little because the tight shoes were pinching her feet, and she wished she had asked if she might wear a pair of the new ones he had bought for her. But it was not the tight shoes which had spoiled the pleasure of the outing but his tetchiness. His mood was not improved when they returned to the hotel and found no sign of Frank and Martha.

'Perhaps Mrs Upjohn was not agreeable,' she suggested.

'Like all good wives, she will do as her husband bids her.'

'I should not like her to come against her wishes, Captain, and I should hope Mr Upjohn would not insist.'

'Then you would have to go back to Stacey Manor. I am determined we shall not continue alone.'

'I know what it is,' she said, speaking in a whisper, so that others in the crowded room would not hear her. 'You are afraid you will be forced into making an honest woman of me. That is not at all flattering.'

'And you are not at all consistent,' he said, also keeping his voice low. 'Yesterday you told me I am too old and you would not consider such a match. Now you seem to be saying the opposite…'

'No, I am not. I simply said you were afraid you

might have to. Let me set your mind at rest, Captain. I have no wish to marry you, but, having come this far, it would be foolish to turn back, especially as we are like to run into more trouble going back than going forward.'

'How so?' he queried, wondering what she understood by the term marriage. She could have no conception of physical desire, the love and passion that, in his view, should exist between husband and wife. The novels she read and her mama's conversation had filled her head with nonsense. The man who married her would have a pleasurable time educating her.

'Why, Mr Upjohn may very well have been taken up; had you thought of that?'

'Yes, I had,' he said irritably. He was beginning to wish he had not drawn Frank into this escapade, though it had seemed like a good idea at the time.

They had shared so much during the Peninsular campaign, both the comradeship and the danger, but Frank had had enough of war by the time Napoleon surrendered in 1814, and decided to return home to his wife. He had not taken part in the Battle of Waterloo. Duncan had come back to England in late 1815, after recovering in a Brussels hospital from a wound in his side received at Waterloo, but he could not bear the thought of going home and so he had reported to the War Office, hoping to be given active service. Instead he had been sent to track down a traitor. His enquiries had taken him to Norfolk and it was in Norwich he had met Frank again.

He smiled, remembering the night of revelry they had enjoyed as they'd reminisced and talked about old battles and the people they had known. But it had been obvious Frank was in a bad way. He was thin as a rake and his clothes were in tatters. He had admitted he could not find work and had turned to crime. Duncan had been appalled and infuriated. There was something wrong when a good and valiant man like Frank should be so little thought of by the country for which he had given years of his life, while men like Sir John Partridge prospered. He had asked him to join him.

'There won't be regular pay,' he had warned. 'But there will be something at the end of it, if we are successful.'

And so they had joined forces. Becoming a highwayman and living the life of a ne'er-do-well had been one way of dealing with a personal situation he found difficult to come to terms with and he justified it with the argument that he was obeying orders. Taking risks was a way of finding release. Until he met Molly.

She had made him see life with a different perspective, had forced him to examine his motives. And in spite of her conviction that he was a criminal, which was only half true, she trusted him. Did he deserve that trust? Did he deserve anyone's trust? Martha's? Or Frank's?

'Do not look so cross.' Molly's voice broke into his self-analysis. 'It is not my fault you were seen holding up that coach. Indeed I have done my best to help you.'

He was about to tell her that she was more hindrance than help and that if she had not told the constable they were married he could have sent her back to Stacey Manor and forgotten all about her, but changed his mind. Not only would it hurt her feelings, it was palpably untrue. He could no more have sent her on alone than fly. Besides, he and Frank had brought their troubles upon themselves.

She smiled suddenly. 'Mr Upjohn might be here soon and I am hungry, so do you think we could have something to eat while we wait? I am starving.'

In the face of her imperturbability, he could do no more than take her into the dining room and order a meal, in the hope that Frank would arrive before they had finished it.

Molly hated long silences, and though she tried very hard not to speak she could not resist trying to bring him out of his ill humour. But he would have

none of it and she turned her attention to the conversation going on at the next table, which was
occupied by four men—tradesmen or perhaps
farmers, judging by their plain trousers and gaiters,
frieze coats and shallow hats.

'He says he gives them homes and educates them
which is more than they had where they came from.'

'Don't make no odds,' another said. 'It's trading
in human beings and I don't hold with that.'

'But they ain't exac'ly human, are they?' queried
a third. 'They're savages. Black savages.'

'That's on account of they don't know no better.'

'Well, ain't that just what I've been saying?' the
first man put in. 'He educates 'em in the scriptures
and teaches 'em to work in the house.'

'Only so's he can get more money for 'em. Why,
I heard he makes ten thousand a year.'

'You seem to know a lot about it.'

'My brother-in-law was on one of his vessels. In
the navy in the war, he was, but had to come out at
the end of it. Surplus to requirements, he was, even
though he was in ten years and didn't know nothin'
else. Grunston offered him a berth and he took it,
but when he comes back the tales he told fair made
me shiver, I can tell you. He didn't go only the once,
said he'd rather starve than serve on a slaver again.'

By the time they had finished their meal, she had

discovered that Mr Grunston owned two ships going out from Lynn to buy his human cargo, some of whom he sent on to the Indies, and the ships returned with cargoes of sugar from the plantations there—a double profit. Others he brought home and, having cleaned them up and taught them how to behave, he sold to Society ladies for whom having a black page or footman was the height of fashion. Two days hence he was off to London to purchase another decommissioned ship from the Admiralty to enlarge his fleet.

Molly leaned forward in order to whisper, 'Captain, did you hear that?'

'Hear what?'

'Those men at the next table. They are talking about a slave trader earning ten thousand a year. Don't you think that is disgraceful?'

'It is not unlawful…yet.'

'Well, I think it is reprehensible. I am persuaded the Dark Knight would have something to say on the matter.'

'The Dark Knight?' His only concession to being even slightly disconcerted was to raise one dark eyebrow quizzically. 'Is he another of your fictional heroes?'

'Oh, no, he is a real person, as you very well know.'

'Do I?'

'Oh, yes. I believe he models himself on Robin of Locksley.'

'Who is Robin of Locksley?'

'He is a mythical figure I read about. He lived a long time ago, in the time of Richard the Lionheart, and he was always holding travellers up and giving their gold to the poor.'

Duncan was diverted. 'And what would this Dark Knight do, if he were here now?'

'Hold the man up. Take his ill-gotten gains from him and set his slaves free.'

'That would be a crime,' he said drily.

'But justified, don't you think? You could distribute his wealth to deserving people and prevent another cargo of poor black men, women and children being sold into slavery.'

'Me?' he queried in astonishment.

'Why not?'

'Miss Martineau, I abhor the trade as much as anyone and I support those who advocate its abolition, but that is not the way to bring it about.'

'Oh, I did not think you were so pudding-hearted.'

'Molly, I wish you would put the Dark Knight from your mind. The Dark Knight is not Robin of Locksley, nor yet Don Quixote.'

'Indeed he is not, if he will not tilt at a few windmills.'

He laughed in spite of himself. 'Oh, you will be the death of me.'

'Oh, no, but you must admit you would like to do it.'

'Indeed I should,' he said. 'But that is not to say I will.'

'No, perhaps it would not be wise without Mr Upjohn to help you.' She liked to tease as much as he did and was gratified when he rose to the bait. 'I think we should have waited at the Crosskeys and not come here without him.'

'Do you? I recollect you wanted to go shopping.'

'That was your idea. I did not ask to go.'

'You could not go to London dressed in nothing but a filthy riding habit.'

'No, but I was not in such haste that I would want you to abandon your friend.'

'I have not abandoned him. He is well able to look after himself, which is more than can be said for you, who are young and vulnerable and whose head is filled with fantasy.'

'My head is not filled with fantasy. You do not know me very well or you would know I am a very practical kind of person.'

'Is that so?' He smiled for the first time for over an hour. 'I have seen no evidence of it so far.'

'Then I will prove it. I shall come back with you. We may well meet them on the way.'

'Not so long ago you were of the opinion we would run into greater trouble going back than going forward.'

'I am sure you are clever enough to avoid anyone searching for you if you go carefully, and I am not afraid of a little adventure.'

'No, that I had noted. And not above inciting a man to crime either.'

'Oh, that,' she said airily. 'I was bamming. But you must allow that you are troubled about Mr Upjohn.'

He sighed heavily, admitting she was right. He *was* worried and his conscience *was* troubling him. Frank must be in trouble or else Martha was proving difficult. But if that were the case Frank would have come on without her.

If it were not for Molly he would not have hesitated, but if it were not for her he would not have been in this predicament in the first place. He was not at all sure he liked being so accountable for another human being, and one who was so artless. 'Very well,' he said. 'We will go back, but only as far as the Crosskeys. He may be there.'

He rose from the table, leaving Molly to scramble under it in search of her shoes which she had kicked off.

'Now what?' he asked in exasperation.

'Nothing. I am simply looking for my shoes. They

were tight and... Oh, there they are.' She bent to retrieve them and squeezed her white-stockinged feet back into them, to his unfeigned amusement. 'It will be a relief to go back to my riding boots.'

She went up to their rooms to change while he gave orders for Molly's new trunk to be kept for them when it arrived, and then they set off on horseback, retracing the route they had covered that morning, meeting a little traffic—a coach or two, several loaded haycarts, people on horseback and on foot—but not the curricle.

'Where are we going now?' she asked him when he'd returned from questioning the innkeeper at the Crosskeys and been told his friend had not returned there.

'To his home. We'll find out if he reached it.'

'How far is that?'

'An hour's ride. Are you tired? Do you want to rest?'

'No. I can keep up, never fear.'

They had been riding for perhaps an hour and were passing through a wooded area, when they came upon the curricle. It was tipped on its side in the ditch beside the road and there was evidence of a struggle, but of Frank or Martha there was no sign. Nor could they find the horse, though they stopped and searched the area.

'What do you suppose happened?' she asked him. 'Did the watch catch up with him? Or was it robbers?'

'Robbers?' he queried. 'What could robbers want with him?'

'Why, Sir John Partridge's gold, of course. They could have overheard the man who witnessed the hold-up of the coach and recognised Mr Upjohn from his description.'

'Don't be ridiculous!' he snapped, his concern for his friend making him speak sharply to her. 'There is no gold.'

'I am not being ridiculous. You are the most uncivil man I have ever come across. I am beginning to wish I had never consented to ride with you.'

He gave a bellow of a laugh at this statement. 'Consent to ride with me! Tell me, when did I ask you to?'

'Oh, well, if you are going to split hairs, then I might as well remain silent.'

'Do that. There is nothing I would like more than your silence. How a man can be expected to think with you chattering like a magpie all the time, I do not know.'

He went back to the curricle and examined it again but it revealed no more than it had before. From the direction in which it was pointing, he deduced that Frank had been on his way to join them and not on his way home. In that case, had Martha been with him?

Molly, following behind him and peering over his shoulder as he bent to move aside the splintered wood, spied a piece of torn jaconet attached to the broken door. 'Captain, would the watch have arrested Mrs Upjohn too?'

He sighed; his companion was determined to make her presence felt and it took all his self-control to keep his temper. If it hadn't been for her riding after him, none of this would have happened. He was angry with her but more angry with himself for allowing a slip of a schoolgirl to dictate to him.

'I do not think so; why do you ask?'

She pulled the tiny scrap of material from the wreckage. 'This. It is from a lady's gown.'

He took it from her. 'Come on, mount up. There is no time to lose.'

Not a word of gratitude, she noticed, not even an admission that she had seen something he had missed, just a curt order to get on her horse. She could almost hate him for it. Except, of course, that she knew he was very worried about his friend, even though he pretended not to be, and worry often made people crotchety. She must make allowances.

He almost flung her into her saddle and mounted himself with a curt, 'For goodness' sake, keep up.' And then he was off at a swift canter with Good Boy beside him. When he realised she was right behind him and grimly determined, he increased their pace to a gallop. She was too busy hanging on to call out to him to slow down or ask him where they were going.

They eased the horses into a walk as they entered a small hamlet and he picked his way over the village green and stopped outside the gate of a cottage. 'Wait there,' he commanded as he dismounted and went up the short path to knock on the door.

Molly watched as a young woman in a plain brown dress with a white apron and cap answered the summons. She stood for a moment, staring at him, then, recognising him, gave a little cry of relief. 'Oh, Captain Stacey, it is you. I have been praying you would come. The most dreadful thing has happened and I do not know what to do. Come in, please.'

She looked up and saw Molly. Her eyes darkened and she looked annoyed, but in the face of Molly's friendly smile she softened. 'The young lady too.'

Molly slipped off Jenny and joined them as Duncan ducked his head to enter the cottage. Mrs Upjohn stood to one side to allow her to precede her. Molly dipped her knee and lowered her head. 'Mrs Upjohn.'

Martha inclined her head in acknowledgement. 'Miss Martineau, I believe?'

'Yes. I suppose Mr Upjohn told you of me?'

'He did.'

'I am truly sorry if I have been the unwitting cause

of trouble for you.' She stood and looked round the tiny cottage. There were two rooms downstairs, a small sitting room in which they stood and a scullery behind it. A ladder led up to a hole in the ceiling, presumably to a bedroom under the roof. It was very plainly furnished but was clean as a new pin.

'Never mind sorry,' Duncan put in as Mrs Upjohn indicated a sofa and bade them be seated. 'Martha, tell me what happened.'

'We were on our way to join you and the young lady,' she explained, standing by the hearth. She was very pale and trembling a little, Molly noted. 'It was a bright sunny day and we were not hurrying. Frank said we had all the time in the world. And then three men galloped up behind us. Frank drew to one side to allow them to pass, but they didn't want to pass. They surrounded us and forced us to stop.

'One said he was a constable from Cromer and he was arresting Frank for holding up Sir John Partridge's coach and stealing gold and other valuables. Of course that was nonsense and so I told them, but they took no notice of me. Another said he had been a witness and he would swear Frank was one of the robbers. I never heard anything so outlandish. Why, Frank would never do such a thing.'

'Then what happened?' Duncan asked, while Molly looked on, shocked into silence. Mr Upjohn had obviously been deceiving his wife about his activities with Captain Duncan Stacey. No doubt he had been lured into a life of crime by the Captain and that was very wicked of him.

'He struggled, but they overpowered him. They took the horse from the curricle and tied him onto it. They said they were taking him to Cromer to face charges. They said he would come up before the justices and one of them was Sir John Partridge. It afforded them a great deal of glee.'

'I'll wager it did,' Duncan said laconically. 'When did it happen?'

'This morning. About eight of the clock. Please, Captain, do something. Go after them, tell them it is all a mistake. Tell them he was with you the whole time. They will listen to you.'

'Of course we will go,' Molly said.

Duncan turned to her in astonishment. 'What are you saying, miss? There is no question of you going. If I go, I go alone.'

'But they will not believe you without me to vouchsafe your alibi; you know that.'

'I need no alibi. And if you continue to make public statements like the one you made at Aylsham it will ruin your reputation.'

Molly sighed. 'Why? I shall tell everyone we have done nothing improper and they will believe me. It is not as if we are running away to Gretna Green…'

'I should hope not!'

'You need not be so emphatic about that, Captain, it is not at all flattering.'

'Oh, Molly, Molly, what am I to do with you?'

'Take me to my mama, as you promised.' She paused and smiled at Martha. 'After we have rescued Mr Upjohn, naturally. We cannot let him languish in prison.'

Duncan had no intention of allowing Frank to languish in prison, nor of confronting magistrates, but that did not mean he would not do all in his power to free his friend and before he reached Cromer. Sir John Partridge would do anything rather than have Frank reveal their true interest in his baggage, which was certainly not the gold; he would make sure Frank never came to trial. His friend would meet with an unlucky 'accident'. Nor would Sir John rest until the damning papers Duncan carried in his saddlebag were once again in his possession.

The last thing he needed was Molly Madcap at his heels the whole time. It was time something was done about her. 'You are going back to Stacey Manor on the first available coach, which is what I should have insisted upon from the first,' he said. 'You are nothing but a liability.'

'Oh, that is not fair!' she cried. 'It was not my fault you are suspected of being a highwayman. That would have happened whether I was with you or no. You have just made a mull of everything and now you are blaming me. I begin to think I do not like you at all.'

In spite of the seriousness of the situation, he grinned. 'Only begin not to like me? Why, you have been ringing a peal over me these last two days.'

'I was bamming before, but now I am in earnest. You are not a hero, nor even a gentleman.'

'Then, miss, I wonder at your wanting to be in my company.'

'I did not know you were a rakeshame when I met you, did I?'

'Please, Miss Martineau, this is no time to be quarrelling.' Martha interrupted her. 'Let the Captain go. You can stay here with me until he returns.'

'Thank you, ma'am,' Duncan said.

Molly, who did not want to return to Stacey Manor and her dull life there, realised that it would be the best solution. 'Very well,' she said. 'I know we cannot go to London until you have rescued Mr Upjohn, so it seems to me the sooner you set off the better.'

He did not stop to argue about going to London but turned on his heel and left the cottage. They went to the door and watched him galloping away.

Molly, who had done nothing but quarrel with him, even when he had been so kind to her and bought her a whole trunkful of fine clothes, felt suddenly bereft and miserable. Whatever he was and whatever he did, he had been her saviour and protector and if she never saw him again she would be sorry, very sorry indeed.

'Take care!' she called after him, but by that time he was out of earshot and did not hear her.

Chapter Four

'Now, Miss Martineau,' Martha said, taking hold of Good Boy's reins. 'Bring your horse round to the back of the house, if you please, then we will go inside and I will have your version of the story. You can tell it to me while I prepare something to eat. It will while away the time until the Captain returns and, please God, with Frank.'

They put the horses side by side in the makeshift stable, rubbed them down without speaking, after which Martha drew a bucket of water from the trough in the yard and gave them a drink. 'There's hay over there,' she said, nodding towards a small stack. 'I can see these poor beasts have been long on the road and deserve some petting.'

Molly, doing as she was told, reflected that she had been long on the road herself and was in need of pampering, but it was evident she would not get it, not from Mrs Upjohn, nor the Captain, who had ridden off without a backward glance. And now she had to explain herself to this woman and she had no idea how much she ought to tell. She wished the Captain had rehearsed her in it, but no, off he had gone, assuming she would know what to say.

Once the horses were settled she followed Martha into the kitchen of the tiny cottage where Martha bade her be seated. 'I've little enough in the house to eat,' she said. 'But you are welcome to share what there is. What Frank wants to be doing, racketing round the countryside with the Captain just as if he was still in uniform, I do not know. And how come you to be with them?'

'It was only meant to be a little adventure,' Molly began, sitting on one of four chairs set round the table, and watching Martha moving about with saucepans and vegetables and a large fish which she set about boning and skinning. 'I was so bored at Stacey Manor; there was nothing to do but go for walks and ride and read. I have read everything my godmother—that's Lady Connaught, you know—had in the house several times over…'

'Yes, yes, but how did you meet Captain Stacey and my husband? Frank never said anything about Stacey Manor, nor no Lady Connaught.'

'I do not think Mr Upjohn was ever at Stacey

Manor. Captain Stacey came to visit Lady
Connaught alone. When he left, I followed him.'

'Why?'

'Why?' Molly considered the question with her
head on one side, smiling a little. 'I was curious about
him. And he was so set on riding off long before it
was daylight and that seemed very mysterious to me.
And though he bears the family name of Stacey he
did not appear to be one of the *haut monde*.'

'Is that all? Just curiosity?'

'Yes. I followed him and he heard me and he said
I had to go back to Stacey Manor, which I was not
at all wishful to do. He slapped my horse and made
it bolt into the trees and I fell off and bumped my
head so he was obliged to put me on his horse and
we rode to the inn and went to bed.'

'To bed?' Martha asked, shocked to the core.

'Not together; of course not. It was at breakfast
time there was a commotion about a robbery.
Captain Stacey came in while everyone was discussing what to do about it. The constable questioned
him, but I vouchsafed he had been with me all night.'

'But everyone must have thought…'

'I said I was his wife.'

'He allowed that?' Martha, in spite of wishing her
guest would come to the point and tell her about
Frank, was intrigued.

'He could hardly deny it once I had said it.'

'And where was Frank while this was going on?'

'I saw Mr Upjohn when he passed through the dining room but he was not questioned and he did not speak to us. I did not meet him until much later in the day after Captain Stacey had hired the curricle. He was waiting for us at an inn near Norwich, a long way from the scene of the robbery. It was then we discussed how I could be got to London without a scandal…'

'London?'

'Yes. I wished to join my mama, and Captain Stacey thought of you and the plan was contrived that we should all travel to London together…'

The fish had been put in the pot and Martha began peeling potatoes. 'But that does not explain why Frank was suspected of being a highway robber. Are you sure you have left nothing out?'

Molly hesitated and decided not to voice her conviction that the two men had had a hand in the hold-up; it would only upset her hostess and if Captain Stacey brought Frank safely back nothing need be said at all, but what he wanted to tell her himself. 'No, except the description the witness gave of one of the robbers said he had a scar beneath his eye— but Captain Stacey said many men have scars. After all, there has been a war and men were wounded.'

'That is true. Frank took a sabre thrust saving the life of the Captain at the battle of Ciudad Rodrigo. But that was some time before they were both taken prisoner.'

'They were taken prisoner? Oh, do tell me about that. I know so little and I am sure it must have been very exciting. Sometimes I wish I were a man and could go to war and ride about the countryside having adventures.'

Martha, who had labelled Molly as a hoyden at best and a strumpet at worst, began to revise her opinion. The girl was a simpleton. No, not even that; she was a grown-up child, which, she supposed, was the most dangerous of all. The Captain had obviously been captivated and she didn't think Frank had been so unaffected as he had pretended when he had inveigled her into going with him in the curricle. And what a farrago that had been!

'War is not an adventure,' she said. 'It brings out the worst in men as well as the best. It is bestiality and dirt and hunger and forced marches and danger of being blown to bits or cut to ribbons. And for what? Simply so that a man may say he has done his duty and not let his companions down. And I know, for I have been there…'

'To war?' Molly queried in surprise.

'Yes. I went with them. Two years I spent in Portugal and Spain, following in their wake, cooking and cleaning and looking after my man until he was taken prisoner along with the Captain.'

'Oh, I am sorry. It must have been hard for you.'

'It was better than being left behind in England with no means of support.'

'But when he was captured? What did you do? You did not go to prison with him, did you?'

'No, I waited. There was nothing else I could do. There was no way I could come home to England. As far as the army was concerned, I did not exist. It was hard. I had to find work to put food into my mouth…'

'How?'

'Cooking and cleaning for the single men. There were other ways but I did not stoop to those.'

'What other ways?'

'If you do not know, it is not my place to enlighten you, miss. I wish you would not ask me.'

Molly, who was used to being fobbed off when she asked questions, did not insist on being told. 'But you managed and the men escaped? Oh, do tell me they escaped.'

'Yes. Frank went back to his regiment but the Captain was put on special duties. I did not see him again until today.'

'You did not know the Captain and Mr Upjohn had met again?'

'Oh, yes, Frank told me they had met by chance

in Norwich. He had gone there looking for work, but he had been unlucky and was just making up his mind to return home when he chanced to run into Captain Stacey. The Captain offered him a job but it was not the kind of work where he could take me because they would be moving about the country-side a great deal. And yesterday he came back and told me the Captain had a job for me too and we could be together again. I should have known it was all too good to be true.'

'But it is true. They are going to escort me to London to my mama, only the Captain said it was not at all proper for me to travel without a lady companion and he thought of you. When they come back, we shall still go. We shall be safe once we are out of Norfolk.'

'Safe?' Martha looked up in alarm. 'What do you mean?'

'Safe from all these robberies,' Molly said hastily. 'There have been so many, no traveller can be anything but anxious.'

Martha appeared satisfied with that explanation, much to Molly's relief, and they sat down to dine together. Molly regaled her new friend with the story of their shopping expedition and all the things the Captain had bought for her, which had sadly been left behind at The Bell, and Martha told her more about life as a camp follower in Spain and Portugal which had Molly's blue eyes round as saucers.

'And I thought riding in the dark was an adventure,' she said with a sigh. 'Why, that is nothing at all compared to what you have done.'

'You should be thankful that you have never had to endure it,' Martha said testily. 'You have never been hungry, never heard big guns and been afraid for your life, never eaten dog…'

'Dog?' Molly repeated, thinking of her mother's pet pug. 'Oh, no, I refuse to believe that.' She looked with distaste at her plate of food, though she had seen Martha put the fish in the pot.

'It is true. When I came home, I swore I would never let my husband go to war again. We would live in quiet seclusion until the end of our days. But Frank could not settle and when Captain Stacey offered him a chance to travel…' She shrugged. 'How could I hold him? He is a man, after all, and a soldier.'

'I think it was wrong of the Captain to tempt him. I shall speak to him about it.'

Martha smiled wearily; the girl spoke so confidently, as if she had some influence over the Captain, but she was sure that was not so. She could not imagine Captain Stacey under the cat's paw. 'I wish you would not. Knowing both men, I know it would do no good and might very well have the opposite effect. Frank will come to it in his own time.'

'How long do you think it will be before they are back?'

'I don't know, but I am sure it won't be tonight. I will make a bed up for you in the parlour. I think you will be comfortable there. Let us pray they come back safe and sound tomorrow.'

Molly could do nothing but echo her plea as she helped Martha clear away their supper and wash the pots, then she was given a blanket and a pillow to make herself comfortable on the sofa and Martha bade her goodnight and climbed the ladder to the upper room.

It seemed a long night to Molly, although she was tolerably comfortable and very tired. Never before had she been kept awake by worry and fear. Her childhood, though hardly privileged, had been serene, with nothing but the prospect of a scolding to trouble her. Now she was beset by thoughts of what might be taking place in Cromer.

If anything happened to the Captain, what would she do? Already her life had become so entangled with his she could not imagine living without him, bad temper, mocking smile, gambling and all. Was that love? She was not such a ninny as to believe that, but it was a feeling she had never experienced before, this concern for another human being, and she supposed it meant she was growing up.

She fell asleep at last and dreamed of the Captain brandishing his sword at windmills which turned into constables. The horse he was riding became a green dragon breathing fire. And the fire, orange and yellow and pink, licked about his feet and set his clothing alight. She saw him smiling as the flames consumed him and in her dreams she screamed.

She sat up suddenly, her mouth open, her eyes clouded by the memory of a dream so vivid she thought it must be real. The flimsy curtains to the room flapped in the breeze, revealing a huge red and pink sunrise. The shadows on the curtains made it look like tongues of flame. She breathed a sigh of relief.

She looked up to see Martha hurrying down from above. 'What is wrong? Why did you call out?'

'I had a bad dream. I thought the Captain was on fire.' She laughed shakily. 'I expect it was the sun through the curtains. I'm sorry if I woke you.'

'You didn't wake me; I could not sleep.'

'You are worried?'

'Naturally I am worried. And so should you be.'

'I am, but the Captain is a resourceful man and he will do his best for your husband.'

'But I cannot help feeling it might be too late.

What will they do to Frank? Will he be sent to prison? Or hanged? Highway robbery is a hanging offence, is it not?'

'I do not know. But Captain Stacey will avow his innocence, an' if he is not believed I will repeat what I told the constable in Aylsham. The Captain was with me all night and Mr Upjohn slept in the next room.'

'Is that true?'

'It is not so very far from the truth, for we did not arrive at the inn until nearly dawn and though the Captain procured a bed for me I slept no more than an hour or two.'

'Not long enough for them to hold up a stage-coach?' Martha wanted desperately to be reassured.

'No, of course not. Put it from your mind. They will be back by the time we have breakfasted and you will have been worrying for nothing.'

But the men did not return. Martha and Molly sat about alternately talking and watching the road from the gate all day long and at dusk they had a silent meal before making ready for a second night of wakefulness.

Neither would voice the fear that was growing in their breasts that something bad had befallen them, that both men had been taken and would never return, though privately Molly vowed that if they had not arrived by noon the following day she would set off on Jenny to find out what had happened. Her longed-for journey to London was entirely forgotten.

Duncan pulled his galloping horse up in the shelter of some trees to wait for Frank to catch up with him. Caesar was a strong stallion and had carried him well all day but he was tiring and they must soon stop to allow both horses to rest, especially as the mare Frank was riding was more used to pulling a curricle than having a man on her back. The night before Duncan had come upon the prisoner and his escort just short of Cromer. It had been late at night and, concluding that there would be no one awake to receive them, the constables had decided to light a camp fire and cook a meal before going into the town at first light. There was a skinned rabbit on a stick being turned over the flames by one of their number and the appetising smell had reminded Duncan he had not eaten since the midday meal he had shared with Molly at The Bell. They had been very lax in setting guards, for all three were grouped around the fire, while Frank was tied to a tree nearby. The horses were tethered on a line a little way off and were quietly cropping the grass. He had left his horse and crept forward to assess the strength of the opposition and, if possible, to alert Frank to his presence without being seen.

'We'd have got into town before dark if he had been more of a horseman,' one said, jerking his head in Frank's direction. 'How anyone could keep slipping off a gentle creature like that is beyond me.'

'Well, I suppose he had the right of it when he said it was a draught horse and not used to a rider,' another said, staring into the flames. 'And he had no saddle.'

'We should have let him fall. Being dragged along the ground at a gallop might have taught him to keep his seat.'

Duncan, crouching in the darkness not a dozen yards away, smiled to himself. Frank had evidently been employing delaying tactics, hoping for rescue, because he was almost as good a horseman as Duncan himself.

'I wonder he has never been caught before if his seat is so bad,' the second man commented.

'It cannot be that bad,' the third man said. 'He was working in Sir John's stables for three weeks afore he piked off. I recognised him when he held up the coach, for all he was masked, and I saw him ride off.'

'I told you,' Frank put in from behind them. 'You've got the wrong man. I couldn't ha' done it for I can't ride, never could. When I was young we were too poor to own a horse and we lived in the city; how could I learn?'

'In the army. You were a soldier, weren't you?'

'In the infantry. The infantry march, they don't ride.'

'I saw him,' the valet persisted. 'And so I shall vouchsafe in court.'

'If he ever gets to court,' another mumbled, confirming Duncan's fears.

They turned back to their fire as one of their number drew the rabbit from it and began to cut it up and hand the pieces to the others on the end of the knife. 'What about him?' one asked.

'Oh, let him go hungry. It might help him to remember where he was when Sir John had his gold snaffled.'

They were obviously relaxed and confident and Duncan, keeping a close eye on what they were doing, risked crawling up to the tree where Frank was tied.

'Don't speak,' he hissed. 'It's me.'

'Yes, I saw you.' The answer was a whisper spoken through closed teeth. 'Get a move on, will you?' Then, remembering his place, he added, 'Sir.'

Duncan busied himself with the knots. 'Are they armed?'

'One has a pistol and another a musket.' He nodded towards the horses where there was a musket propped against one of the saddles. 'The third one is Sir John's valet. He recognised me.'

Duncan undid the last of the knots. 'Go for the horse and get going,' Duncan whispered, pulling his cravat over his mouth and nose. 'I'll hold them off.'

Frank was stiff from his cramped position, but he managed to hobble to the mare, untie her and set the others loose before throwing himself on her back. Although he moved swiftly and silently, it was enough to alert his captors. They did not see Duncan and assumed their prisoner had managed to free himself. One tried to catch the horses, while another ran for his musket, only to be beaten to it by Duncan who blocked his path, threatening him with his own weapon.

'Lie on the floor!' he commanded.

The man did not hesitate; he sprawled face down. The third man tried to come at Duncan from behind but he whirled round and hit him with the butt of the musket, sending him reeling. The valet did not see heroics as any part of his duty and simply sat staring at the scene with his mouth open and a piece of meat on the end of a knife halfway to it.

Duncan whistled up Caesar who came obediently and the next minute he was galloping after Frank, with the shouts and curses of the men ringing in the darkness behind him as they tried to recapture their mounts.

Frank was waiting half a mile up the road. 'You took your time,' he said. 'I was beginning to think we'd be in Cromer before you. It would have been devilish awkward to defend myself if I couldn't tell the truth about that traitor.'

'I was delayed. Now, let's be off before they come after us.'

'Where to?'

Duncan had been asking himself that question and there was only one safe place that came to mind. 'Stacey Manor.'

They took a roundabout route in order to put followers off the scent, but were there in less than half an hour.

It was half an hour in which Duncan began thinking about what he would tell his grandmother. She would want to know where Molly was and why he had returned without her and he had no idea what he could say. He had promised to protect Molly and take her to her mother; instead he was riding about the countryside at dead of night pursued by constables.

And supposing everyone had retired and there was no one to admit them? They could hide in the stables, but he did not think that would serve. The area might be searched. What they needed was a cast-iron alibi provided by someone no one would dare to disbelieve and that was his grandmother. And would she give them that, considering her poor opinion of him?

Not wishing to alert the servants, they rode up to the house as quietly as possible and dismounted outside the stables. Silently they led the horses into the stall and unsaddled them, then found hay and water for them. That done, they went back to the house.

There was a side door which was sometimes left unlocked to allow Brunning, her ladyship's butler, to return after a night out in the village. Duncan had discovered the man's secret quite by accident when he was no more than an adventurous stripling and had promised to keep it from his grandmother, demanding in return the right to use the door himself whenever he liked. The arrangement had always worked very well, but he wondered if Brunning still went out at night or if the practice had been discontinued.

He beckoned Frank to follow and found, to his delight, that the door gave when he tried the handle. They crept inside and along a corridor. Duncan, who knew the way, found no difficulty in the dark, though Frank stumbled now and again. In the large reception hall, they found that two lamps had been left burning and, picking up one of these, Duncan led the way upstairs to the room he always occupied when he was staying there.

'Now, we'll settle down for the night,' he told his friend. 'Tomorrow, we will convince everyone we arrived this afternoon.'

'I would rather we had ridden straight home,' Frank said, looking round at the huge well-furnished room. 'Martha will be beside herself with worry.'

'She knows we cannot return tonight. She has Molly with her. They will be company for each other.'

'I wondered what you had done with her. But I hope the chit will say nothing to Martha.'

'Molly knows nothing.'

'Give me leave to doubt that. She's a downy bird and not easy to gull. And I'll wager Lady Connaught ain't either.'

'You are probably right,' Duncan said morosely, stripping off his coat, waistcoat and cravat and sitting on the edge of the bed to pull off his hessians. 'But we shall see tomorrow. There's a truckle in my dressing room next door. Make yourself comfortable. I am for my bed.'

'I don't know how you can sleep,' Frank grumbled as he went to obey. 'We are in the devil of a coil.'

They were both awakened before dawn by a loud banging on the outside door. Frank was all for escaping down the ivy outside the window, but Duncan refused to allow it. It was as well he did, because a peep from the window revealed constables covering any escape from the rear of the house.

'What'll we do?' Frank asked. 'Will they insist on searching the house?'

'I doubt it. Grandmama can be very formidable, but I must put in an appearance.' He pulled on a pair of breeches and reached for a dressing robe, tying it about his middle before striding to the door. 'You are my valet,' he said over his shoulder. 'Make yourself useful laying out my clothes in case they insist on coming up here.'

'Which clothes?'

'It doesn't matter. I believe there are plenty in the wardrobe.' And he was gone.

Brunning, still half asleep, had answered the door to find the leader of the band of constables standing on the step. The constable was regaling him with horror stories of desperate criminals who were on the loose in the neighbourhood and would murder them all in their beds given half a chance.

He stopped suddenly when he saw Duncan descending the stairs. Brunning turned to see who was behind him. It was as well the constable could not see the butler's face because his expression of surprise was comical.

'I'll deal with this, Brunning,' Duncan said.

The servant recovered his wits with admirable

swiftness. 'Very well, my lord,' he said. 'Shall I acquaint her ladyship?'

'No, there is no need to alarm her.' He turned to the constable. 'I have seen no strangers but if I do I will send for you at once. Tell me, what do they look like?'

The constable was at a stand. It was his opinion that the man who faced him bore a remarkable resemblance to the man who had turned his own musket upon him, but as it had been dark and the man had covered the lower part of his face he could not swear to it. 'Who are you?' he asked.

Duncan glanced at Brunning who was hovering nearby. He had addressed him as 'my lord', a title Brunning knew he had relinquished, but just for today he would resume it. 'I am the Earl of Connaught, which, if you had your wits about you, you would know. Now, tell me about these desperadoes.'

The man stayed only long enough to give a colourful account of the robbers' looks and the dreadful deeds they had perpetrated and took his leave, calling his men from around the house and riding off somewhat chagrined.

Duncan turned away, smiling. Desperado, was he, vicious, a man who would shoot you as soon as look at you? And as for his companion, he was so ugly no one could fail to be terrified by him. They would never be apprehended on that description.

'Duncan!' The voice was imperious and came from the gallery above. 'Come to my boudoir in twenty minutes.' Lady Connaught, disturbed by the commotion, had come out to peer over the banisters. 'I shall need an explanation. And, Brunning, tell Rose to bring my hot chocolate and washing water.' And with that she disappeared into her room again.

Brunning gave Duncan a rueful smile and shrugged his shoulders before going to obey. Duncan went back to his own room to dress and make himself presentable.

The selection of clothes Frank had put out for him was extraordinary. There was a pair of cossacks, a cream shirt, a blue velvet waistcoat and a red satin coat with a huge cut-away collar and tight sleeves. 'Would you have me look like a play actor?' he laughed, picking up the coat and holding it up in distaste. 'I do believe this once belonged to my grandfather.'

He threw it into a corner and fetched out a brown riding coat of Bath cloth and a pair of nankeen breeches, cream stockings, a white shirt and a striped neckcloth, which he had left behind on his last visit for just such an eventuality. He needed no help to dress and Frank sat on the end of the bed in shirt and cord breeches, and watched him. 'They've gone, then?'

'Yes, but there is a greater peril. My grandmother

wishes to see me in her boudoir. It will be like bearding the lion in his den.'

'She would not betray you?'

'Oh, no, but she will no doubt think of a worse fate for me. There is the question of Molly Madcap…'

Frank laughed. 'Who gave her that name?'

'Grandmama, but that does not mean she will not ring a peal over me about the chit.'

'What are you going to tell her?'

Duncan shrugged. 'I'll think of something.'

But when he had presented himself to an irate dowager and been commanded to sit down facing her he was apparently not required to speak.

'I knew you were a scapegrace,' she said, without waiting for an explanation. 'But I never imagined I should have a troop of constables banging on my door wanting to arrest you. I warned you. I told you you were heading for the gallows and now I am proved right. A Stacey hanged for highway robbery! We shall become notorious.'

'Grandmama, I must protest. I did no more than rescue my servant who had been unjustly detained. The constables were exceeding their duty.'

'Could you not let the magistrates decide that?'

'No, for that would have meant revealing my true purpose and I could not do that.'

'And why not?'

'Sir John Partridge is one of the magistrates.'

'What has Sir John to do with it?'

'Everything, ma'am.'

'Then you had better explain.'

He did so and she listened in silence, at the end of which she gave a bark of laughter which told him she appreciated his predicament. 'Does Molly know about this?'

'No, of course not. I left her with Sergeant Upjohn's wife.'

'While you fly about the countryside pretending to be a highwayman.'

Duncan smiled crookedly. 'Yes, but I have done nothing more reprehensible than taking from those who have betrayed their country and become rich by it and giving the proceeds to those who deserve to be looked after and who have been shamefully neglected.'

'So you say, but it is still unlawful. Will the War Department stand by you if you are apprehended?'

He shrugged. 'It was left to me to choose how I went about my assignment.'

'Then find some other way. I want to hear no more of this Dark Knight.'

'He is already superfluous. I have the information I need.'

'I am glad to hear it. Now what are we going to

do about Molly? You have filled her head with nonsense, and no doubt she thinks you are her knight in shining armour.'

He smiled crookedly. 'No, I do not think so. She is forever ringing a peal over me and saying I am not chivalrous. She even tries to teach me manners.'

The old lady laughed aloud at that. 'I'll warrant she does. But I know Molly's character very well and she will see it as a perfect opportunity to indulge in what she calls adventure. And you did not help by keeping her by you when you could have brought her back at once…'

'She would not come. She had her mind fixed on joining her mama and she is very difficult to say no to.'

Lady Connaught smiled. She knew Duncan's difficulty very well but she was not going to let him off the hook so easily. 'You must prove to her that adventure is not what she needs. Take her to London as you planned, make yourself agreeable to her mama and marry the chit at the first available opportunity.'

'But, Grandmama, she is bound to refuse me. She told me I was too old. And, to be honest, I am inclined to agree.'

Even her ladyship's lips twitched at this, but she forced herself to remain severe. 'Fustian! She will do as her mother tells her. Try again.'

'And if I do not?'

'I cannot think why you are being so disobliging,' she said. 'Molly is a lovely child.'

'Yes, she is and that is half the trouble. She is a child and deserves better than me. I said so before.'

'I am biased perhaps, but I am persuaded she could find no one better. You are a man of good education and, until now, of good reputation. You are strong as an ox and could do anything if you put your mind to it. Why, you fought for your country. Wellington himself mentioned you in despatches.'

'It was that report forced me into this coil.'

'Forced, Duncan?'

'I could hardly refuse. I had nothing else I wanted to do and I needed the blunt.'

'You could have come to me. I would always stand buff for you.'

'Thank you, Grandmama, but I'd as lief be independent.'

'So what are you planning to do?'

'I must go to the War Department and make my report and then I have a fancy to buy a small property and breed horses.'

'Good. Go to London as you planned. Take Molly to Harriet and we will see what transpires. Perhaps, after all, you would not suit. I shall not insist.'

'Thank you.' He rose and bowed to her, anxious to make his escape before she added to her diatribe.

'You are a fool, boy,' she murmured to his departing back. 'You are just like your grandfather, as stubborn as a mule, but you will come to see I have the right of it.'

But he did not hear her; he was striding along the corridor to his own room to tell Frank to be ready to leave as soon as they had eaten breakfast.

Now, riding ahead of Frank, he found himself thinking of Molly. Why was his grandmother so intent on marrying him off to her? Molly, when she arrived on the London scene, would have the pick of the eligibles, young men of her own age, with titles and fortunes, who could give her everything he could not. He was too old, too disreputable, too set in his eccentric ways to make a good husband.

Besides, he had no wish to marry. He had tried to go down that road once, believing Beth loved him enough to wait for him. He had been wrong and the hurt he had received when he'd found her married to his brother and the mother of a son was still too raw for him to want to think about anyone else.

'Why the haste?' Frank demanded, coming up alongside him. 'You have been galloping as if the fiends of hell were after you. There is no one behind us and this poor beast will drop if you do not ease up.'

'Very well, we will walk a little.'

They dismounted and walked side by side along the leafy lane in silence until Frank said, 'I own I shall be glad to go home to Martha, but I am hungry. Do you think we can risk stopping at a hostelry for something to eat?'

'I was thinking the same thing, but unfortunately I have pockets to let...'

'That has never bothered you before. We have always contrived.'

'Yes, but after the jobation my grandmother gave me I have undertaken to mend my ways.'

'Did you not explain your difficulty?'

'Yes, and she offered to stand buff, but I told her I have a generous pension from a grateful country and an allowance from my family and I did not need money.'

'Do you? Have an allowance from your brother, I mean.'

'He offered it...'

'Oh, I see. You were too proud to accept it.'

'Something like that.'

'And I am afraid I cannot help. Those constables took every penny I had on me, said it was part of the proceeds of the robbery and must be produced in evidence, but I doubt any of it will go further than their own pockets.'

'Then we must go hungry. It is not the first time we have had empty bellies, is it, my friend?'

'No, but that was in the Peninsula and it was easy to take what we wanted and we were not branded criminals for doing it. Nor did we have two women dependent on us.'

'Then the sooner we rejoin them the better.'

They remounted and continued in silence for some time, each immersed in his own thoughts. Duncan was thinking about Molly, something he found himself doing more and more frequently, and cursing himself for being such a fool as to saddle himself with her. On the other hand, her company was delightful and he felt very sorry for her, having Harriet for a mother and being denied all the things that young ladies of her age should be enjoying.

She had been so happy and grateful when he'd bought her those clothes; many young ladies would have taken everything for granted, would have pouted and cajoled for more, but not Molly. She had been overjoyed when he'd told her she could have that simple ballgown. He could not imagine Beth behaving like that. The difference, he told himself with little conviction, was that Beth was a woman and Molly was little more than a child.

'Do you think the constables will have visited Martha?' Frank asked as they neared his home village. 'Is it safe to go home?'

'Do they know where you live?'

'I do not think so.'

'Then there is no need to worry. And tomorrow we will all four set off for London. We can lose ourselves in the metropolis.'

'You do not mean to return Miss Martineau to Lady Connaught?'

'No, her ladyship has washed her hands of us. We go on as planned.' He said nothing of the difficulty of finding a coach and horses or money enough for their bed and board on the way, though Frank must have been aware of it.

It was evening by the time they arrived and approached the cottage cautiously. Almost immediately the door flew open and Martha ran down the path to greet her husband, crying with relief.

Molly watched them embrace, standing a little shyly in the doorway, wanting to throw herself into Duncan's arms, but knowing it would never do. She smiled as he dismounted and walked towards her. 'You found him, then?' she queried.

'Yes.' She was looking especially lovely, though her eyes were dark-rimmed as if she had not slept, and he wondered whether he had been the cause of her concern and a feeling of remorse tinged with elation filled him, which he quickly stifled. 'All is well.'

'Then put the horses in the outhouse round the back; it will never do for them to be seen. And then you can tell us all about how you rescued Mr Upjohn while we have supper. Martha has been busy all day, cooking for you.'

Both men were ravenous and did justice to the meal they were given and afterwards they sat down to plan their next move, debating whether it was better to go by public coach or to have their own conveyance, concealing from the two women that they had no money to pay for either.

'Frank and I will go into Norwich tomorrow morning and see what is to be had,' Duncan said, rising from the table. 'If you would be so good as to allow Miss Martineau to stay with you again tonight, I will find lodgings.'

'At this time of night?' Molly exclaimed, suddenly realising that the little cottage could not respectably accommodate them all. 'Where will you go?'

'I can knock up the nearest innkeeper.'

'Sir,' Frank said, casting him a warning look which was not lost on Molly who guessed the reason for it. Duncan ought not to draw attention to himself. 'I think you should stay here. If Miss Martineau is agreeable, she can share with Martha while you and I will make ourselves comfortable down here.'

'The sofa is very comfortable,' Molly put in.

'And the hearthrug will do for me,' Frank said.

'Oh, please do stay,' Martha said. 'It is the least we can do since you spoke up for Frank and persuaded the constables to let him go.'

No one disabused her of the idea that Duncan had used reason and influence rather than force to free her husband and so they settled down for the night.

The sofa might have been comfortable for a diminutive figure like Molly, but Duncan, with his broad frame and long legs, found it decidedly otherwise. But it was not discomfort that kept him awake; he had slept in worse places. For the first time, he began to wish he could lead a straightforward sort of life which did not mean lying and subterfuge and living on his wits.

He should have thrown himself upon the mercy of his grandmother but that would have meant falling in with her wishes and his pride would not let him do that. His pride would be his downfall. After all, being married to Molly would not be such a hardship. In fact, it would be no hardship at all, especially if he could cure her of her madcap ways. But her madcap ways were part of her charm.

Charm was not love, he told himself sternly, and

it was not fair to Molly, who deserved to be loved and cherished and looked after, and he was not in a position to do that. If he had still had his titles and estates, that might have been different, but he had denounced them in favour of a life on the road.

He grinned ruefully in the darkness; he was a gentleman of the road which meant he was no gentleman at all but, in the eyes of the world, a ne'er-do-well, a rakeshame, a criminal. And the worst of it was that Molly trusted him and he did not deserve that trust.

Chapter Five

Duncan was not the only sleepless one. Molly, too, had been lying awake thinking. She was sure that Duncan and Frank, innocent or guilty, were wanted by the law and the constables would not give up while there was any chance the men were still in the area. It would not take long for them to discover where Frank lived, considering they had seen Martha and the curricle and would know she did not live very far away. If they came while the men were gone… The horror of that possibility convinced her she did not want to be left behind when the men went into Norwich.

It was while they ate a breakfast of bread and butter that she broached her idea. 'Captain, I have been thinking…'

'Thinking, my dear? I should not if I were you. Thinking will sap your strength.'

'Do not tease me; I am serious. Could the curricle be repaired? It seems to me that if it were repaired we could all leave here together. The sooner we are on our way the better, don't you think?' She paused, waiting for him to comment. He did not speak immediately but sat looking at her with a smile playing about his lips.

'Well?' she asked. 'If you and Frank ride and lead Jenny, I am sure Martha and I can drive the curricle. We would leave nothing behind for anyone to find.'

He had been thinking the same thing, but he could not resist teasing her. 'All the way to London?'

'If necessary.'

'I think, my dear, you would tire of that in half a day and London is two days away, even with a coach and regular changes of horses.'

'You said we might go by coach. You could obtain one in Norwich, I am sure. And we could pick up my trunk…'

'I do believe that trunk is your first consideration.'

'No, it is not, but as you were so generous as to buy it and as the clothes are meant for my Season it would be foolish to abandon it, would it not?'

'Very true,' he said slowly. He turned to Frank. 'What do you think?'

'I think Miss Martineau might be right. If we leave the curricle where it is, it will not be long before someone comes sniffing round it and asking questions in the neighbourhood. It would be wise to remove it and if it turns out to be repairable we might as well put it to use.'

'Why should anyone be interested in you or the curricle, if you have been cleared of any wrongdoing?' Martha demanded.

Duncan and Frank looked at each other, but before either could speak Molly answered her. 'The highwayman's description was so like Mr Upjohn's, others might make the same mistake,' she said quickly, casting a quick glance at Duncan. 'We would be delayed by having to answer questions all over again.'

Martha was not altogether convinced she had the whole story but she allowed herself to be persuaded and while she packed a few of her belongings the men went to inspect the curricle, taking the mare with them to bring it back. They returned in an hour, having discovered that, though the seating and door had been badly damaged, the wheels would still turn. They spent the next hour outside the back of the cottage, banging away with hammer and nails, and by the middle of the day pronounced it could be driven with care.

After eating the remains of the previous evening's supper they set off for Norwich in cheerful spirits.

The day was fine, which was just as well, because the open carriage provided no shelter from inclement weather. Nor was it easy to drive after its makeshift repair and Molly soon relinquished the ribbons to Frank and rode Jenny.

She loved being in the saddle and riding beside Duncan along the leafy lanes of Norfolk was a joy. 'It will soon be time for haymaking,' she said, looking around her at the lush meadows where cattle grazed.

'Yes.' His mind was on other things, such as how to find the means to continue their journey, and was in no mood for trivial conversation.

'You are very quiet.'

'I am thinking.'

'What about? Are you afraid those constables will come back?'

'Why should they? Sergeant Upjohn is an innocent man.'

She laughed suddenly. 'And so, I have no doubt, you told them and I am equally sure they believed you. Mrs Upjohn might be easy to gull, but I am not. I wish you would be honest with me.'

'You know as much as you need to know. And I do not need a jobation from you. It is enough that Grandmama…'

'Lady Connaught?' she queried in surprise. 'You have seen her?'

'Yes.'

'Does she know the truth? Oh, my goodness, no wonder you are so blue-devilled. I'll wager she rang a thousand peals over you and made you promise to reform…'

'You know nothing of it, miss, except what your imagination has painted, and you will oblige me by keeping silent on the subject.'

'Oh, so my imagination painted the robbery, did it? There never was a hold-up, there never was a witness to it who described you and that horse you are riding so exactly, or a Sir John Partridge. You were never questioned by a constable. I never had to stand buff for you…'

'Stand buff? My dear girl…'

'I am not your dear girl and I wish you would not say it in that condescending way. My goodness, it is no wonder you were disappointed in love. No one likes a lover who is a cross-patch.'

'Molly, I do believe I shall strangle you if you do not keep quiet.'

'Then you will add murder to your other offences,' she said blithely. 'Did you promise her ladyship that you would turn over a new leaf?'

'Yes. Does that satisfy you?'

'Oh, then it is no wonder you are in the suds if you cannot have any more adventures.'

'This is adventure enough for me,' he said laconically, wondering why she was so unconcerned. Other young ladies would be in a quake or having a megrim at the mere mention of highway robbery. 'And I would have thought more than enough for a well-nurtured young lady.'

She sighed. 'Perhaps it is, for I should hate to see you confined in prison. That would be even worse than being hanged, I think.'

He laughed at that. She was irrepressible and though he'd said he craved her silence he would be even more depressed if that bright spirit were to be quelled.

Thus they rode into Norwich and headed once again for The Bell, though Duncan, who had been given no opportunity by Molly to think as they rode, had no idea how they would pay for their overnight stay, nor how they would proceed the following day. The curricle was impractical for a long journey and he did not know how long the hasty repairs would last.

Something had to be done, and while Molly and Martha were upstairs in their room attending to their toilette before supper he left Frank to wait in the parlour for them and went into the town where he sold his gold fob and a ruby ring his mother had given him. He regretted parting with the ring but it was the only way out of their predicament. He smiled a little as he walked back. He was a highway-man who stopped short of stealing; Molly might be amused to know that.

He had no sooner returned than Molly entered the dining room and he was struck again by how lovely she was. She was wearing the green jaconet he had bought her and her hair had been brushed until it gleamed like pale gold. She carried herself with all the aplomb of a titled lady—something she had learned from her mother, he supposed. But her glowing cheeks and bright eyes were not those of a Society miss, who might often affect *ennui*, but of a lively, unas-suming girl.

She was followed by Martha, dressed in a plain brown round gown trimmed with cream lace, which he assumed was her best dress, used only for high days and holidays. He supposed that if she was to act as Molly's maid she would have to be kitted out too, with at least one more gown and aprons and caps. Was there no end to the expense incurred in bringing a young girl out?

The two men rose to greet the ladies and escort them to their seats at the table.

'Oh, this is so pleasing,' Molly said as a delicious meal of turbot, chicken and ham, not to mention creamy sweets and fruit, was set before them. 'It is not often I have the opportunity to enjoy good conversation and good food in surroundings like these. Mother would never use a common inn, but always stay with friends.'

'Is that so?' He smiled, knowing that it was not the status of the inn which concerned Harriet so much as the expense. Friends did not need paying.

'Are the inns as good as this in London, Captain?'

'Oh, indeed,' he said. 'Perhaps better, but you are unlikely to see the inside of one, once you are safely with your mama in Holles Street.'

'Then tell us about Society. Tell us about the sorts of things we shall be doing. Whom shall we meet? Shall we see the Prince Regent? And the Queen? And will we ride in the park and flirt a little…?'

'Flirt?' he queried, unaccountably appalled at the thought. 'What do you know of flirting?'

'Why, nothing at all. I am hoping you will teach me.' And she looked in astonishment at Frank when he almost choked on his food.

Duncan grinned. 'I'm not much of a hand at that, Miss Martineau.'

'No, in with both feet, that's you,' spluttered Frank, which earned him a rebuke from his wife and a fierce look from Duncan. 'Well, you were a soldier and unmarried to boot,' he added to justify his remark.

'But I collect you once thought of marriage,' Molly said. 'Did you not flirt then?'

'Did no one teach you it is not polite to ask personal questions?' he retorted. 'Let us talk of something else.'

'Very well. I forgot you found speaking of her painful. What shall we talk of? The battles you have fought?'

'I never met anyone so blood-thirsty. We will not talk of the war. Tell us about yourself.'

'But I am so very uninteresting. Why, I have had more adventures in the last few days than I have had in the whole of my life. Tell me, how shall we go on tomorrow?'

Before Duncan could open his mouth to answer, there was a flurry at the door and an irate man in a cloth coat and nankeen breeches pushed his way past the waiter. He was followed by a constable. 'That's the man,' he said, pointing a pudgy finger at Duncan. 'I insist you arrest him.'

Martha gasped and Molly turned to Duncan, a question on her lips. He shook his head and she sank back into her chair, her heart pounding.

'What am I accused of?' he drawled, addressing the man who was now standing over him in a belligerent manner. 'Is my cravat not tied to your taste?'

'That's my curricle outside—the one with the yellow wheels—and it is my mare in the stables.'

'No one is denying it,' Duncan said calmly. 'You hired both out to me the other day.'

'One day's hire, that's all you paid for.'

'My business took longer than I expected, but I have done with it now.' Duncan reached in his pocket and drew out his purse. 'Another's day's hire should see us right, don't you think? There is no need for constables and threats.'

'What about the damage? It looks as though it was run off the road.'

'That is because it was. You are lucky I am not asking you for damages to life and limb for supplying a deficient vehicle.'

'Oh, please do not argue about it,' Molly said, worrying about the presence of the constable and glad he was not the one who had questioned them in Aylsham. 'Do give him enough to cover his losses, Captain; it is only fair. It was not his fault the coach driver ran us down.'

Once again she had jumped in to back his story, and with admirable swiftness. 'Very well.' He took out several guineas and handed them to the man. 'That should suffice.'

With no more than a grunt by way of a receipt, the man took them and turned on his heel, followed by the constable.

Everyone breathed a sigh of relief but Duncan

was only too well aware that his funds had been seriously depleted. Now how were they to reach London? He did not have enough for the stagecoach fare, let alone the purchase of a coach and horses.

Molly, who had turned to look out of the window as the owner of the curricle departed with it, suddenly exclaimed in delight. 'Oh, just look at that! Did you ever see the like?'

The others turned to see a magnificent carriage pulling into the yard. It was a dark blue colour, its lines picked out in gold. It had a monogrammed door and brocade curtains at the windows and its metalwork gleamed with polish. It was drawn by four matched bays whose coats gleamed almost as much as their harness.

It drew up with a clatter and a flourish and down from its box jumped someone who could only be described as a tulip of the first water. He wore a long coat reaching almost to his heels. It sported three capes and two rows of pockets and enormous brass buttons. The coat flew open as he jumped down and revealed primrose-coloured breeches tucked into highly polished top boots and a black and yellow striped waistcoat. He wore a tall crowned beaver hat with a curly brim and a posy of flowers tucked into its huge buckle.

Another young man emerged from the coach, less

flamboyantly attired, and followed the first into the inn. A third man, in livery, trailed behind them carrying a leather portmanteau.

'Andrew Bellamy,' murmured Duncan with a smile.

'You know him?' Molly queried.

'Only by sight and reputation,' he said. 'He is Lord Brancaster's heir and even more of a scapegrace than I am.'

'Will he recognise you?'

'I doubt it. We have not met in years.'

'Perhaps it is just as well,' she said. 'You would rather remain incognito; is that not so?'

Once more she had demonstrated her perspicacity but before he could agree the new arrivals entered the room and the landlord hurried to be of service. He conducted them to a table while everyone in the room stopped eating to watch their progress, passing close to where the four were sitting. Molly was delighted and smiled unashamedly at the young fop.

He bowed before her with a great flourish. 'Ma'am, your servant.'

Duncan was seething. Molly should not have smiled at him like that; it was almost an open invitation and one which Bellamy had not been slow in noticing. 'You do not need to be taught the art of flirtation,' he whispered fiercely at her. 'You are doing very well without instruction.'

She turned from gazing after the two newcomers and faced him. 'Whatever do you mean? He was perfectly civil.'

'He should not have spoken to you at all. But it is your fault for smiling at him.'

'May a lady not smile at a gentleman? And may a gentleman not acknowledge it?'

'Not in that way, not unless they know each other very well.'

'As you and I know each other, you mean? I may smile at you?'

'As often as you like. I shall not read more into it than you intend.'

'I intended nothing.'

'I know that, but he does not. He would infer that you wanted to further your acquaintance and without a proper introduction…'

'Oh, I see. You are cross with me again.'

'No, of course I am not cross, but it is not a good idea to draw attention to ourselves now if we are to arrive in London in the manner we planned…'

'And how are we to do that? Are you going to hire another coach or shall you buy one?'

'I have not made up my mind,' he said, wondering how either could be achieved. 'Now, I suggest you and Mrs Upjohn retire. We have a long day ahead of us tomorrow.'

The ladies rose dutifully, said goodnight and left the room, leaving Duncan and Frank facing each other.

'It would seem that providence is on our side, after all,' Duncan murmured, with a smile. 'I know Bellamy for a gambler and his father does not stint him. His pockets are deep. We can play our way out of our predicament.'

'We can't do that without a stake,' Frank said.

'I have a little left. Enough for a start.' He smiled suddenly. 'Don't look so Friday-faced; I can beat him easily, but you do not have to stay with me. I absolve you from any obligation.'

'You think I would turn my back on you just because you have lost your head to a petticoat…'

Duncan found himself grinning. 'It is not the petticoat, Sergeant, but what's inside it.'

'Then my advice is to watch out, for I am ready to wager she will turn the tables on you.'

'It is not a wager I shall take on, Sergeant, for I was only bamming. She is little more than a child and my grandmother's goddaughter. I could no more take advantage of her than I could a new-born babe.'

'Then I think you would do well to open your eyes, Captain. I saw no child.'

Duncan was watching Andrew Bellamy and his friend and did not answer. The two young men had finished their meal and were moving into a back room which Duncan knew was set aside for gambling should the clientele require it. He stood up and chinked his purse in his coat pocket. 'Come along, Sergeant, into the fray.'

The owner of the petticoat was sitting in it in front of a mirror, surveying herself with a critical eye, while Martha brushed her hair.

'I wish I looked older,' she murmured. 'No one takes me seriously.'

'I am quite sure Captain Stacey does.'

'Oh, he does not. He is continually roasting me.'

'Only because you provoke him. I wonder he has not sent you home long before now.'

'So do I, but then I can help him and he knows it.'

'How can you help him? You are not still thinking of that robbery they took Frank for, are you? Surely that is all behind us?'

'Of course it is. At least, I hope it is. But people are continually mistaking Captain Stacey for the Dark Knight…'

'Dark Knight?'

'He is a highwayman, a very romantical figure, I have heard, who robs the rich to give to the poor.'

'And you think Captain Stacey is like him?'

'I think he must bear some resemblance to him,'

Molly said, realising she was treading on dangerous ground.

'And does this man have a companion who resem-
bles my husband?'

'I think he must have.'

'And is this Dark Knight a wealthy man?'

'No, I do not think he can be, or he would not need
to take from the rich to give to the poor, would he?
He could use his own money if he had any.'

'And the poor? What manner of people are they?
Could they be soldiers and widows of soldiers?'

Molly swivelled round in her seat to face Martha,
her expression one of dismay. Martha had tricked
her into revealing more than she ought to have done
about the two men and now poor Mr Upjohn would
be in trouble with his wife. 'I do not know. I am only
repeating hearsay, you understand. I am such a
romantic I listen to every whimsical tale that is
going around. Take no notice of me.'

'And do you think Captain Stacey is an honourable man?'

'Oh, I am sure he is, in spite of being the black
sheep of the family. I think he exaggerates about
that. Why, he is looking after me, when perhaps he
would rather not, and he rescued Mr Upjohn…'

'But Frank has done nothing wrong.'

'Of course not.' She stood up and untied the

strings of her petticoat and kicked it off when it fell to her feet. 'Now, I think we should go to bed. It is late and no doubt the Captain will want to leave early in the morning.'

'How? We have no conveyance. The curricle…'

'Oh, he will contrive, you may be sure.' She was not very good at dissembling and she did not want to be quizzed any more. Besides, she was very sleepy. 'Goodnight, Mrs Upjohn.'

Martha sighed, bade her goodnight and left to go to her own bed in the next room.

Molly found a new nightgown in her trunk, put it on and settled down in her bed, but sleep was slow in coming. The more she talked of Duncan, the more she became convinced that he was the Dark Knight. It was both exciting and terrifying. What would happen next? she wondered. How would their journey continue? Was he even now planning another hold-up?

But underlying that was a frisson of fear. She did not want anything dreadful to happen to the Captain as a result and there were many such possibilities. He could be wounded or killed if anyone was so brave as to take a pot shot at him; he could be captured, tried and hanged in spite of her willing-ness to perjure herself for him. It was enough to give her nightmares.

* * *

Holding up coaches was the last thing on Duncan's mind at that moment. He was playing a cat and mouse game with Andrew Bellamy and though his heart was beating very fast and his hands felt clammy he gave no outward sign of it. Not by the tiniest flicker of his eyelids, not by the lightest twitch of his lips, nor the minutest raising of an eyebrow did he betray the fact that he had a winning hand.

It was not the first he had had. Lady Luck had been with him and there was a pile of gold coins at his elbow and several scraps of paper on which Andrew had scribbled his signature against substantial sums. But the pile of coins was not enough to pay for four people to travel to London and the vowels could not be used as currency.

'I'm dished up,' Andrew said, in disgust. 'How anyone can have such luck as you have had, Stacey, I do not know.'

'It can't last,' Frank growled, pretending not to look at Duncan but receiving the secret message contained in the way he moved his hands when sorting his cards.

'No, for I am sure it is about to turn in my favour.'

'Then make your bid,' Duncan said.

Bellamy sighed. 'It will have to be another vowel.'

'No, no more of those.'

'But I have the winning hand.'

'If you are so sure, then back it with something worthwhile. What have you got?'

'You have everything. My ring, my fob, my purse. What more is there, but my watch and the clothes on my back?'

'Oh, I do not think they would fit me,' Duncan said drily. 'And I already have a good watch. But you do have a coach and horses.'

'You can't have those! They are my father's.'

'But you have said you have the winning hand. If you are so sure, you will not hesitate to put them up.' He smiled for the first time since they sat down to play. 'But perhaps you are bluffing.'

'No.'

'Then the coach and horses against all these.' And he picked up the slips of paper and slapped them down again. 'There's two thousand there.'

'As much as that?' Andrew went very white and his hands were shaking. 'Very well. The coach and horses against my vowels.'

Ten minutes later Duncan was the owner of one of the best equipages in the country and the now impoverished Andrew Bellamy was wondering how he was to pay for his night's stay and return to Newmarket from where he had driven that morning.

He was inclined to bluster but his companion counselled him to accept defeat gracefully and the loan of five guineas which would see them safely back.

'I should not like to be in that one's shoes when he faces his father,' Duncan said as they watched the now deflated tulip toil wearily upstairs to his room, followed by his sycophant.

'But he will stand buff for him?'

'Naturally he will.' He laughed. 'He might bluster and threaten but Andrew is his only son and his lordship was a deep player in his young days. He once lost a thousand pounds betting on the colour of the Queen's gown at a soirée. He said it would be rose and it was green. I know because it was my father who won it from him.'

'What are we going to tell the ladies about the coach? I do not think Martha would approve.'

'We shall say Mr Bellamy was kind enough to lend it to us.' He paused. 'And, speaking of the ladies, I think we should be up betimes and on our way by dawn, so give orders for the coach to be made ready and brought round to the front of the house at first light.'

'Very well.'

Frank went to carry out his orders and Duncan went up to the room he had taken opposite Molly's. Ten minutes later, he was deeply asleep.

* * *

Martha, roused by her husband, went to wake Molly long before it was light. The young lady was disinclined to stir and simply pulled the covers over her head and grumbled that it was not fair to disturb her in the middle of the night.

Martha shook her. 'The Captain says we must leave in half an hour, unless you want to be left behind.'

Molly was up like a shot and scrambling for her clothes. 'How are we to travel? What shall I wear? Did he say?'

'Frank told me they have procured the loan of a coach and four. We are to go on in style.'

'Oh, wonderful! Then I shall wear my new carriage dress and the bonnet with the green feather and the kid half boots. Pour my washing water while I find them, please. Oh, I am so excited. How soon shall we be in London?'

She prattled on the whole time she was dressing and while Martha brushed her hair. 'Is the Captain waiting to go or are we to have breakfast first? I must have something to eat and drink for I cannot go the whole day without food. He is surely not in such great haste? Unless, of course—oh, dear, I do hope not.'

'What?'

'That those Cromer constables have not tracked us down.'

'Why should they? I really cannot imagine why you are so afraid of them.'

'I am not afraid of them. I was simply saying that it would be a great inconvenience to be detained by them again.'

'Frank said nothing of them, only that the Captain was in some haste to be in London.'

'Only so he may be rid of me,' Molly said morosely. 'I know he is looking forward to handing me over to Mama, so he may be free. I am an encumbrance.'

'Fustian! I am sure he thinks nothing of the sort. Why, I should not be surprised if he were to offer for you when he sees your mama.'

'Captain Stacey? Offer for me?' Her laughter pealed out as she stood before the mirror and set the straw bonnet on her curls and tied the ribbons beneath her chin. 'Oh, Mrs Upjohn, how can you say that? He is older than me; he did not deny it when I said it. He said he was thirty and, besides, he thinks of me as a schoolgirl; he has said that too.'

'Then more fool he.'

'Oh, you must not call him a fool, Mrs Upjohn, really you must not. He is knowledgeable and clever and brave…'

'That is no guarantee that he is not capable of foolishness, for I believe the contrary is often the case. Now, are you ready? I am sure I heard horses and coachwheels outside.'

They hurried downstairs where they were allowed by an impatient Duncan to drink a cup of hot chocolate and eat some bread and butter before he escorted them outside. Molly stopped when she saw the resplendent vehicle. Jenny and Good Boy were already tied on behind it.

'But this is the coach that came in while we were having supper last night,' she said. 'Surely it belongs to the young gentleman in the big coat and the yellow striped waistcoat? Did you not say his name was Bellamy?'

'Yes,' Duncan said, putting his hand under her elbow and guiding her firmly forward. 'He has been kind enough to lend it to us.'

'Oh, you mean we are to go on together. How agreeable...'

'No, he is going in another direction entirely. We are to have it to ourselves. Now please get in.'

'But I must find him and thank him.'

'There is no need for that. He is still abed.' He opened the door, let down the step and handed her in, allowing her no time to argue. Once she was safely in her seat, Martha joined her, Frank climbed onto the box, Duncan mounted Caesar and thus the little cavalcade left Norwich.

The coach was the height of luxury. It was beautifully sprung and had seats for four upholstered in red velvet, and there was plenty of headroom so that the feather in Molly's bonnet barely touched the roof. And with Martha the only other occupant they could both stretch out their legs in comfort.

They bowled along, drawn by the bays at a spanking pace, hardly aware of the uneven road. But one thing they could not do and that was change the horses. The bays were no ordinary post chaise horses and they had to be kept with the coach. Good Boy and Jenny were not draught horses and, besides, the stallion was very much bigger than the little mare and they would have looked odd between the shafts, so after a few miles Duncan slowed their pace to little more than a walk.

At midday they stopped at an inn at Scole for two whole hours, in which both humans and animals were fed, watered and rested. Molly whiled away the time watching the people coming and going, for Scole was a very important crossroads and the roads in all four directions were very busy with traffic.

As well as public coaches loaded with passengers, who required meals or rooms or both, or to have their baggage moved from one coach to another, there were carts and riders and private carriages pulling in to change horses and the people were as varied as the vehicles.

Molly had something to say about each and her comments were pithy without being malicious, and Duncan, more relaxed than he had been since setting out on the journey, listened to her musical voice and watched her animated face and realised that he could happily do so for the rest of his life. The thought, as it flitted across his mind, shocked him to the core.

From shock he moved to irritation with himself for being such a numbskull. It was unthinkable. Falling in love had not been on his mind when he'd gone to Stacey Manor, only a few days previously. It had certainly been no part of his plan when his grandmother had talked to him about settling down. And even when he had agreed to take Molly to her mother it had simply been a mischievous notion to shock Harriet into being a proper parent to her daughter.

Molly was a handicap, preventing him from doing what he wanted to do. Her trust in him was an embarrassment. Her talk of adventure was simply a wish to escape her humdrum life; she did not understand the life he led and would be horrified if asked to share it. And he could not change. It was not in his power to do so. He had no money, no home, no roots; they had all been swept away by an unkind fate.

'Why are you so silent?' she asked him. Martha had persuaded Frank to go for a walk into the village and they were alone, if one could be alone in a roomful of people. 'You have been sitting there moodily staring out of the window for half an hour. What is out there that has thrown you into the dismals? I can see only another coach and the ostlers leading out fresh horses for it. And they are nothing like so fine as ours.'

He shook himself. 'I am not in the dismals, my dear. How could I be anything but happy in such enchanting company?'

'Now I think you are bamming me again.'

'Not at all. You must learn to accept compliments graciously, Molly. It is part of genteel society.'

'Oh, then I thank you and return the compliment. I am happy to have such an agreeable escort.' She laughed lightly and added, 'Even if he is a little reluctant.'

'Reluctant? I would not say that.'

'Oh, I know you find me a burden. I am quite sure you would rather be the Dark Knight than Captain Duncan Stacey.'

'Really, Molly, you must not say such things. People will begin to believe you and you will have me arrested.'

'I am not such a goosecap as to tell anyone. I have not said a word except when Mrs Upjohn questioned me about how Mr Upjohn came to be arrested, then I told her you must look very much like the Dark Knight for everyone to keep mistaking you for him.'

'And what did she say to that?'

'Nothing except that the Dark Knight must have a companion who looks very like her husband. I do think it was wrong of you to encourage him to deceive her.'

'You don't know what you are talking about, miss, and I wish you would not refine upon it. Mrs Upjohn cannot possibly understand your vivid imagination and your longing for adventure.'

'Oh, she does, and she told me about being at war and how terrible it was. She does not wish for any more adventures, so perhaps it is just as well you promised Lady Connaught you would turn over a new leaf.'

'Did I?' he murmured, but he had ceased to listen to her for he had overheard a new arrival give his name to the landlord. It was Mr Grunston.

The man was fat, loud and overbearing and demanding that his horses be changed at once and food set on the table so that he could be on his way. 'I have important business with the Admiralty,' he said, loud enough for all to hear. 'I must insist on being given precedence.'

'What an unpleasant man,' Molly whispered to Duncan. 'I think we have heard his name before.'

'Have we?'

'Yes, do you not recollect those four men talking about him? Where was it? At Aylsham or Norwich—I forget which. They were saying he was a slaver and I said…'

'I perfectly recollect what you said. Fribble, all of it.' He looked up as Frank and Martha came into the room. 'Ah, here they are. I think we have rested the horses long enough. Come, Miss Martineau, back to the coach.'

It was while they were proceeding at a gentle canter towards Bury St Edmunds that Mr Grunston's coach came up behind them. The coachman was evidently in a hurry for he gave a blast on his horn to warn Duncan to give way before coming up alongside.

'Shall we give him a run for his money?' Frank asked as Duncan rode up on his nearside.

'No, my friend. Your wife would skin me alive, and as for Miss Martineau, she would likely be so excited she would be all over the place. Better let him go.'

Reluctantly Frank pulled the carriage up in a gateway and the slaver's barouche rushed past in a whirl of dust.

It was after it had passed that Duncan told Frank what he had heard about the man. 'It makes my blood boil,' he said. 'When our soldiers and sailors are without work and forced to beg, that fat pig lives in luxury. And, what is worse, it is condoned by the Admiralty. They provide him with ships.'

'He needs to be taught a lesson.'

Duncan smiled. 'Yes, but not by us.'

They stopped at The Angel in Bury St Edmunds for the night, only to find Mr Grunston there before them. He had eaten well and imbibed freely of claret and brandy, and was, in Frank's words, top-heavy, so much so that he was loudly calling for his coach to be brought round so that he might drive through the night.

'I do not like that man,' Molly said, after Duncan had procured rooms for them all and they were sitting down to supper. 'That is the third time he has crossed our path.'

'Possibly because, like us, he is going to London,' Duncan said.

'I hope we do not meet him again or I shall be constrained to tell him what I think of men who buy and sell human beings. Do you think that black man he had dancing attendance on him was a slave?'

'Undoubtedly.'

'I wish we could free him. Could we not buy him and set him free?'

'I doubt his master would part with him, and freeing one man would not solve the problem, would it?' Duncan said. 'What would the man do with his freedom? How would he live in a strange country where there are already thousands of men without work?'

'Your sensitivity does you credit, Miss Martineau,' Martha said as tureens of food were brought to their table. 'But the Captain has the right of it. Freeing one man is not the answer.'

'It is a job for the Dark Knight,' she said, then added meaningfully, 'Whoever he is.'

'Whoever he is,' Duncan repeated with a smile. 'Come, let us enjoy this meal and retire early. I am exhausted.'

They finished their meal without mentioning Mr Grunston again and afterwards the ladies went up to their rooms.

As soon as they had disappeared, Frank turned to Duncan. 'What do you say to one more jaunt? It seems to me that providence has taken a hand in this or why else would we have run into the man again and him so anxious to gallop through the night?'

'No, Frank. What we did, we did for a reason. That does not mean we are above the law, nor that I will allow you to fall back into your old ways.'

'But he is a sitting duck. There was only an old coachman and a black footman with him and I doubt he would lift a finger to defend his master. The ladies need never know, though I doubt Miss

Martineau would turn a hair if we invited her to come with us.'

'Heaven forfend!' Duncan laughed.

'One more time, then you may go to London and act the gallant with the best of them.'

'No, my friend. We are already being pursued by the constabulary, and the last thing I want is for us to be apprehended for a whim of yours.' He stood up, yawning. 'I am off to my bed. I will see you at breakfast.'

'Yes. Goodnight, Captain.'

Duncan retired to his room, leaving Frank to follow more slowly. He was busy thinking about ways to replenish his funds and forgot all about Mr Grunston.

Chapter Six

At breakfast the next morning, both men appeared in very good spirits. Frank was smiling secretly to himself and Duncan seemed to have found a new lease of life; his tiredness had left him and he was bright-eyed and cheerful.

'You are in high gig this morning, Captain,' Molly said. 'You must have slept well.'

'Tolerably, my dear, tolerably.'

'That is more than Frank did,' Martha put in. 'He did not come to bed until cockcrow.'

'I told you,' Frank said, refusing to look at Duncan. 'Good Boy had the colic. I sat up with him.'

'Oh, does that mean we cannot go on?' Molly asked.

'No, he has recovered.'

The waiter came and refilled their coffee pot. He was obviously bursting with news. 'The Dark Knight has been at work again,' he said. 'The

Newmarket mail has just come in and the passengers are full of it.'

'Oh, do tell us what happened,' Molly said, leaning forward eagerly.

'A private coach was held up between here and Newmarket last night.'

'Oh, dear. Was Mr Gr—?' She gave a little cough to cover her slip. 'Was anyone hurt?'

'No, though I fancy the gentleman's pride was injured. By all accounts, he was stripped of his fine clothes and arrived in Newmarket wearing his footman's livery. You may remember the gentleman, ma'am, he had a black man for a servant.'

'Oh, you must mean Mr Grunston. But surely the servant was much smaller than his master?'

'So he was. I believe Mr Grunston's arrival in Newmarket was a comical sight; his breeches hardly covered his knees and would not meet about his waist and his coat was so tight, he could not move his arms. The passengers on the mail were still laughing when they arrived here.'

'Oh, it is unkind to laugh at another's misfortunes,' Molly said, though she was laughing herself. 'And what was the black man wearing?'

'He has disappeared in his master's togs. Mr Grunston has offered a reward for the apprehension of the high toby and the return of his servant. But they will need better luck than they have had so far. The Dark Knight is as elusive as a ghost, here one minute, somewhere else the next.'

'Every Tom and Dick of a highpad scamp is labelled the Dark Knight,' Duncan said dismissively. 'It is nothing but rumour. 'Tis my belief there is no such person.'

In the face of Duncan's scepticism, the waiter left them to attend to new customers and Molly sat back in her seat and surveyed Duncan with eyes shining with laughter.

Martha looked from one to the other. 'I beg you share the jest with me.'

'Oh, it is only the thought of Mr Grunston bursting out of his slave's clothes,' Molly said.

'But being robbed is not a laughing matter, Miss Martineau. I am beginning to regret my decision to make this journey for ten to one we shall be the next victims, what with travelling in Lord Brancaster's coach and having so many fine horses with us. We shall be mistaken for Quality.'

'Oh, I do not think there is any fear of that,' Molly said. If Martha refused to go on, then the Captain would not take her to London and her whole adventure would come to an end. 'Why, we have the Captain and Mr Upjohn to defend us. No highwayman would dare to stop us.'

Duncan, watching Molly's performance with a mixture of admiration and fury, was startled when he found himself the recipient of a conspiratorial wink. It was the outside of enough!

Discomfited and irritable, he paid the innkeeper and hustled them all out to the coach which he had ordered up to the door. Frank was busy checking the equipage and refused to meet his eye. He strode over to him. 'Why, Frank, why?'

'I wanted to see the devil squirm,' the sergeant said, knowing perfectly well what he meant. 'I didn't take his valuables, only made him change clothes with the black man. It was Miss Martineau talking about the Dark Knight...'

'You were surely not influenced by Molly's madcap ideas?'

'Well, she had the right of it. It *was* a job for the Dark Knight.'

'Damn the Dark Knight!' he said fervently. He had laughingly invented the name when Sir John Partridge had demanded his identity; the night was dark and he had said the first thing that came into his mind. He had never expected the pseudonym to become so popular. Nor that Molly would find it so appealing. Somehow or other he must stop her mentioning it again. He left Frank and went over to where she was about to step into the coach.

'Ride Jenny, Miss Martineau,' he commanded. 'I wish to talk to you.'

The tone of his voice was ominous but she refused to be cowed and obediently allowed him to help her into the saddle. Hoping she might be given the opportunity to ride some of the way, she had dressed in her riding habit. Martha, disliking travelling inside alone, climbed on the box beside her husband and they set off again with Good Boy tied on behind.

'I am surprised we are taking this road,' Molly said as they turned towards Newmarket, slightly ahead of the coach. 'Surely it was down here that Mr Grunston was held up? Are you not afraid the same thing might happen to us?' Her laughing eyes were full of mischief.

His responsibility for her was weighing heavily on his mind. She deserved his total commitment, or as much of it as he could give her, considering neither Mr Grunston nor Sir John Partridge would take their losses with equanimity. If the latter ever discovered his identity he would send someone after them to retrieve his belongings and that might put everyone in peril.

The worst of it was he could not tell Molly the truth and she, as usual, was jumping to conclusions. To her it was all a great frolic and not dangerous at all. He could not disillusion her without frightening her. She was looking at him now, her lovely head on one side, waiting for a reply.

'Frank and I are a match for any high tobies.'

'I am sure you are,' she said, giving him an ingenuous smile. 'But I would have expected you to take a more direct route.'

'I never undertook to go the shortest way.'

'No, I concede you did not,' she said. 'But the sooner we arrive in London, the sooner you may be rid of me, and that is what you want, is it not?' There was a tiny note of wistfulness in her voice.

'Did I say I wanted to be rid of you?'

'No, but your whole demeanour proclaims it. I do believe you find me a hindrance to your calling, which is very disappointing, for I should love to be a highwayman. A female high toby would take the country by storm, would she not?'

'Certainly she would,' he admitted drily.

'What is the feminine equivalent, by the way?'

'I have no idea; I should not think there is one.'

'Highwaywoman is much too long, don't you think? Why, she would be a dozen miles away before the victims were able to utter the word.'

'I should think they would die of shock before that.'

She laughed, thoroughly enjoying teasing him. 'I would not want to be the cause of anyone's death. There is nothing for it but I would have to dress as a boy. Do you think I would make a good boy, Captain?'

'No, I do not,' he snapped.

'You are in a very disagreeable mood,' she said. 'And I had thought you would be in the best of spirits after last night. Indeed, when we met for breakfast, you were positively smiling, which is something you do not do very often.'

'If I am in a disagreeable mood, it is because you will persist in talking nonsense. It is enough to give me an earache.'

'Then I will be silent.' She spoke huffily and he was immediately sorry. He reached across and put his hand on hers.

'I beg your pardon, Molly. I am a crosspatch, I admit it, but the truth is I am not used to being responsible for someone like you.'

'It is a heavy burden, I know.' She was aware of the pressure of his hand on hers but chose to ignore the sudden fluttering of her heart and the tingling feeling in the pit of her stomach; she was not experienced enough to connect one with the other. 'It is no wonder Mama was disinclined to take me to London and Aunt Margaret used to despair of me.'

'I am sure she did not. She spoke of you very affectionately.'

'Did she?' Molly brightened. 'But she often said

the sooner I found a husband to knock some sense into me the better.'

'He would have a very hard time of it, I am persuaded.'

'Oh, no, for I am willing to learn. But I should not like him to beat me.'

She spoke so seriously, he burst into laughter. 'Oh, Molly, my sweet, he would be an unutterable cur to raise a finger to you.'

'Not even if he were provoked?'

'Not even then.' He turned to look at her and his heartbeat quickened. He would almost be sorry when they reached London and he had to part with her. A life on the road was beginning to be a far less attractive prospect than it had been two or three days before. 'But that does not mean I will allow myself to be provoked and do nothing. There is more than one way to skin a cat.'

'What a dreadful maxim. I beg you find a less distasteful image. I am very fond of cats.'

By this time he had completely forgotten what it was he wanted to scold her about, or, if he remembered, set it to one side. It was much more agreeable to listen to her chatter, even though he pretended he did not like it. He was almost sorry when they drew up at the Greyhound in Newmarket in the late afternoon.

Once they had procured rooms for the night, they were able to take a stroll round the town. Duncan had been there before and he was able to point out the important buildings and tell them about the stables and racehorses, some of whom they saw cantering on the heath in training for races the following day.

'Oh, do you think we might go to the races?' Molly asked as they walked together a little ahead of Frank and Martha. 'I should so like to see the horses running. Do they have lady riders?'

'Good heavens, no!' Duncan exclaimed.

'I do not see why not,' she said. 'Ladies are lighter than men and if they ride well that would surely give them an advantage.'

He grinned at her. 'Now I suppose you are day-dreaming about being a lady jockey?'

She laughed. 'I'll wager I could ride as well as any of them.'

'And that is one wager I will certainly not accept.'

'What a pity,' she said, without rancour. 'But you will take me to watch?'

'Perhaps. If you promise to behave.'

'Oh, I will. I will be the epitome of decorum, the very stiffest, most upright lady you can imagine.'

'I shall look forward to seeing that,' he said with a smile which told her he did not expect it to happen. 'Now I think it is time to return to the inn for supper.'

* * *

Molly was delighted with the races. She loved the colourful crowds, the magnificent horses, the diminutive riders and all the tipsters and racegoers making bets, sometimes for thousands of pounds. Duncan gave her a few coins from those he had won at cards the previous evening. There was always a great deal of gambling in Newmarket and not all of it on the race course; it had been easy to find a game, which was his intention when deciding to come.

'I'm going to put it on that one,' she said, pointing to a chestnut filly.

'You will lose,' he said. 'She might as well have three legs for all the winning she will do.'

'Fustian! She is a lovely animal; she has such beautiful eyes.'

He laughed, thinking of Molly's expressive eyes. 'A horse does not run with its eyes. Look at its legs, its haunches, the depth of its chest.'

'Oh, that goes without saying,' she said. 'But the eyes show the spirit. She wants to win; you can see it there.'

'And like all females she gets what she wants— is that what you mean?'

'Yes. Please put a guinea on her for me.'

He smiled and took the coin from her outstretched hand and strolled over to lay the bet, adding several guineas of his own. He had no idea why he went against his own advice; the filly had no form and he should not gamble foolishly when his funds were so low, but if Molly fancied her, who was he to argue? Besides, she was called Brancaster's Bright Belle and that seemed a good omen.

They crowded as closely as they could to the edge of the course as the horses thundered past. Molly forgot her promise to act with decorum and jumped up and down in excitement, shouting the filly's name as it took the lead. To everyone's surprise, Bright Belle won her first heat and then her second. Everything depended on the last run. Molly hardly dared breathe as the horses lined up and took off.

This was a much harder race, for the runners had all won previous heats, and though Bright Belle kept with them for half the distance she began to flag. At the end of the second furlong, she was lying third and falling behind; it looked as though she had given her all. 'Come on, Belle,' Molly shouted. 'Show them what you're made of. You can do it.'

It seemed as though the filly heard her, or perhaps her jockey did and he wanted to please the vivacious young lady he had seen out of the corner of his eye. Whatever it was, Bright Belle put in an extra effort and passed the horse in front to run neck and neck with the leader. Molly was becoming hoarse with shouting and even Martha was caught up in the excitement and clasped her hands in front of her, muttering, 'Come on, Bright Belle,' as they approached the finishing line.

The crowds were going wild, urging one or the other horse on, and as they passed the finish with Bright Belle winning by no more than a nose there was a concerted sigh and then Molly grabbed Duncan by both hands and danced him round and round until both were dizzy. 'We won! We won!'

He tried to slow her by releasing his hands and putting them on her shoulders. Giddy, she stumbled and fell against him. He held her fast, feeling her heart beating rapidly against his chest, and smelling the fresh scent of her hair just below his chin. He wanted to go on holding her, to tip her head up and kiss her lips, to go on kissing her, to make love to her.

But it was only a momentary weakness. He allowed his lips to brush her hair before pulling himself together and holding her at arm's length. 'Steady, my dear; it is not a fortune you have won, you know.'

'Oh, but I do not care about that. It is the pleasure of seeing her win, when you said she had no hope…'

Reluctantly he released her. 'Oh, so it is your victory over me you are crowing about.'

'Yes. No, I did not mean that. It is the victory of the underdog which pleases me. You should understand that.'

'Should I?' he queried.

'Yes. I am persuaded you like nothing better than to fight for those who cannot fight for themselves.'

'Gammon! What evidence have you of that?'

'None but my eyes and ears…'

'Captain, I think you should collect your winnings.' Frank interrupted them. 'I fancy the fellow is about to depart.'

This was indeed true. The man who had taken a large number of bets besides Duncan's, and had obviously lost a great deal of money, was not going to pay up if he could avoid it. He was scurrying away through the crowds. Duncan and Frank went after him.

They were soon lost in the crowds who were milling about waiting for the next race to start. Molly, left with nothing to do, watched the people around her, some excited at winning, some disconsolate. She looked on in fascination as one finely dressed gentleman's pockets were picked and the thief made off with a watch, a fob and a purse. The man did not even notice his loss.

She walked over and tapped him on the shoulder. 'Sir, I believe you have just been relieved of the contents of your pockets.'

He swivelled round to face her. She gasped when she realised it was Mr Bellamy, but he did not notice as he patted his pockets and realised they were empty.

'I saw the man do it. He went that way.' She pointed. 'You will know him; he has a ginger beard and a long black cloak. Very thin fingers, which is why, I suppose…'

He did not wait for her to finish but dashed off in the direction she had pointed. 'Oh, dear,' she said. 'I wanted to thank him for lending us his coach.'

'He did not remember you,' Martha said. 'You should not have spoken to him.'

'Not told him I had seen his pockets rifled? Oh, that would have been very uncivil of me.'

They became aware of a scuffle breaking out a little way off and saw him tackling the thief, who was putting up a spirited resistance. It seemed that Mr Bellamy was having the worst of it, when Duncan and Frank, returning with their winnings, intervened. They held the struggling thief while Andrew went through his extraordinarily large pockets and retrieved several watches and purses.

'These are mine.' Andrew held up his belongings, while other victims hurried forward to reclaim their stolen property. 'I am in your debt, Stacey.' He smiled at Molly who was making her way towards them. 'And to the young lady.'

'Molly?' Duncan queried, looking at her. She was smiling back at Bellamy as if they were the best of friends and he felt a sudden stab of jealousy. Bellamy had everything in his favour: youth, looks, and the prospect of inheriting Brancaster's title and wealth. There was no cloud of rejection and dishonour hanging over him. He was what Society called one of the eligibles.

'I saw it happen,' she said, coming up to them and allowing Andrew to take her hand and put it to his lips. 'The thief was very deft, for he had the things out of Mr Bellamy's pockets in a trice.'

'You have the advantage of me, ma'am,' he said. 'You know my name but I am in ignorance of yours. Indeed, I do not think we can have met, for I would surely have remembered so delightful an encounter.' He bowed towards her, smiling in a way that infuriated Duncan.

'That is because you have not met,' he said coldly. 'Miss Martineau does not go out in the society you frequent.'

'But she has done so today and for that I give thanks.' He paused. 'Miss Martineau, you say?'

Duncan had no alterative but to present him. 'Miss

Martineau,' he said, turning to her, determined to be formal, 'may I present Mr Andrew Bellamy?' To Andrew he said, 'Miss Margaret Martineau.'

He bowed with a flourish. 'Your servant, Miss Martineau, and a very grateful one, for I should have been penniless again if you had not seen the knuckle at his business.'

'Penniless again?' she echoed.

'Why, yes. Did my friend, Stacey, not tell you?'

'No. I am indeed sorry to hear it has happened before.'

'The circumstances were different,' Duncan put in quickly. 'It is getting late, Miss Martineau; I think we should be going. The racing is over for the day and I am sure you must be hungry.'

'Then please join me for supper,' Andrew said. 'It is the least I can do to show my gratitude.'

'I do not think so,' Duncan said coldly. 'Miss Martineau is fatigued.'

'Indeed I am not,' she contradicted him. 'Is there any reason why we should not accept Mr Bellamy's invitation? Besides, I wish to thank him for being so kind as to lend us his coach and horses.'

'Lend them?' Andrew queried, turning towards Duncan with a slightly puzzled frown. And then he gave a laugh that was mischievous if not downright malicious. 'Oh, yes, of course,' he said, speaking to

Molly. 'It was my pleasure, ma'am. I hope you found it comfortable.'

'Indeed, yes. But it must have inconvenienced you a great deal to part with it.'

'I have other means of conveyance, ma'am. Think nothing of it.'

'It will be returned to his lordship,' Duncan said, stiff-lipped.

'Is that so? I wonder why you see the need?' He seemed suddenly more cheerful. 'But I had rather it were returned to me.'

'I am sure that can be arranged,' Molly said, while Frank and Martha looked on, Frank with secret amusement and Martha in bewilderment.

Duncan was feeling a little like a cornered animal, which was a state of affairs he was certainly not used to. And it was all because of Molly. Never before had he had to prevaricate to please a woman; they either took him as he was or they did not take him at all. Molly was different. He wanted Molly's good opinion even though he knew he did not deserve it, and he did not want her to know he had won the equipage in a game of cards.

'How about it, Stacey?' Andrew asked. 'You owe it to me to give me the chance to…' He paused and smiled. 'To express my gratitude to Miss Martineau for saving my purse.'

'But that is cancelled out by our debt to you for lending us your coach,' she said.

'Then that is the end of the matter,' Duncan said, snatching at this with relief. 'Come, Miss Martineau.' He took her arm and almost propelled her away, followed by Frank and Martha and the sound of Bellamy's laughter.

'That was most uncivil of you,' she scolded him when they were sufficiently far away for him to slacken his speed. 'Mr Bellamy was being polite.'

'Was he?'

'I begin to think he did not lend us his coach at all. I begin to think you held him up and took it from him at pistol-point.'

He grimaced; this was even worse than being accused of winning it at cards. 'He would not have stood there bowing and smiling if I had, would he? He would have shouted for help and had me arrested.'

'True,' she admitted. 'But perhaps he forbore to do that because I told him his pockets had been rifled and you helped him to overcome the knuckle.'

He smiled at her use of the slang word, which he was sure she had only just learned from Andrew's lips. 'The value of a purse is far inferior to the value of a coach and four matched horses. Frank will return them to Lord Brancaster after we have arrived safely in London. Now we will say no more of it.'

She opened her mouth to speak again, but desisted when she saw that he had set his mouth tight shut and was looking decidedly grim. If he was going to be a crosspatch, then she would not walk beside him. She slowed her pace to walk beside Martha. Frank took the opportunity to accompany Duncan.

'It was bad luck running into Mr Bellamy again,' Frank said to him.

'It is of little consequence. He would not renege on a debt of honour and force us to return the coach.'

'But he wants the chance to win it back. And he doesn't seem the kind of man to take no for an answer. If he makes a noise about it, he will have everyone on his side, baying for you to accommodate him.'

'If he comes looking for us, then naturally I shall comply, but I did not want to take him up on it in front of the ladies.'

'Forgive me for saying so, sir, but it seems to me you are paying altogether too much attention to Miss Martineau. It will end in tears. Hers, if not yours.'

'And I'll thank you to keep your thoughts to yourself.'

It was an answer which convinced Frank that his employer had lost his head, if not his heart, and he had better tread warily. He said no more and they arrived back at the Greyhound in time to change for supper.

* * *

Molly dressed in one of the gowns Duncan had bought her in Norwich, a froth of pink lace over a darker pink satin slip, and then sat down for Martha, who had already changed into her one good dress, to arrange her hair. 'Put it up,' she told her. 'Make me look a little older, if you please. The Captain is constantly calling me a child and I do not like it.'

'Perhaps it is not your looks but your behaviour which prompts that,' Martha suggested. 'You are as bright and eager as a child and speak before you think. You would do well to watch that.'

'Oh, do you think so?' She was thoughtful for a moment. 'I think you must be right, for Mama has said the same thing. She is always telling me I should hold myself aloof, that ladies never betray their feelings.'

'I know nothing of Society ladies,' Martha said. 'But it is wise to hold a little of yourself back. You must keep the gentlemen guessing; it is the only way to engage their interest.'

'Really?' She was astonished. 'You mean I must pretend indifference, even when I am far from in-different?'

'Especially then.'

'How strange.' She looked at herself in the glass, turning her head this way and that and putting on a haughty expression which did nothing but make Martha smile. 'You see,' she said. 'No one takes me seriously.'

'Oh, I am sure the Captain does. Now, are you ready?'

Molly picked up her fan and they went down to the dining room, where the men were waiting for them. Duncan, who had very little in the way of baggage with him, had changed his coat and put on a fresh cravat, and Frank, apart from washing and brushing his dark hair, was wearing the same breeches and coat he had been wearing all day.

They had hardly begun their meal when Andrew Bellamy strolled into the dining room. He was attired in a green silk coat, white breeches and white cravat, exquisitely starched and tied so that its froth of lace filled the neck of his pointed shirt collar. His coat was open to reveal a pink and red striped satin waistcoat. His companion looked positively drab in a black tailsuit.

Molly caught sight of them first. 'Why, here is Mr Bellamy,' she said, with a delighted smile.

He saw her almost at the same moment and hurried over to make his bow. 'Miss Martineau, your obedient.' He turned to Martha. 'Ma'am.' And to Duncan and Frank. 'Good evening, gentlemen. I did not know you were staying here.'

'Yes, what a coincidence,' Molly said. 'Captain, do ask Mr Bellamy and his friend to join us.'

Duncan, forced into a corner, could do nothing but comply. Andrew accepted with alacrity.

'Let me present my cousin, Mr George Lampson, Miss Martineau.'

'Mr Lampson.' She bowed towards the black-suited man as he took his place at the table. 'This is Mrs Upjohn and her husband, Mr Frank Upjohn— my friends and travelling companions.'

'Mr Upjohn I have already met,' Andrew said, seating himself next to Molly, to Duncan's annoyance. 'Mrs Upjohn, it is my pleasure.'

Martha did no more than incline her head and Molly gained the distinct impression that she did not like the newcomers. Nor, she realised, did Duncan, which was very strange when Mr Bellamy had been so generous to them. Forgetting all Martha's advice to be more restrained, she set about redressing what she perceived as a slight.

For the rest of the meal, Molly's happy chatter and Bellamy's amused responses drove Duncan into silence. Occasionally he made a low comment when appealed to but most of the time he watched and seethed. He would not admit that the little green god was sitting on his shoulder.

'We are going to London for the Season,' Molly told Andrew. 'I am so looking forward to it.'

'The Season?' Andrew queried in surprise. 'But it is half over.' He looked at Duncan. 'I am surprised, Stacey, that you did not set out earlier.'

'Oh, it was a spur-of-the-moment decision,' Molly explained before Duncan could reply. 'But I shall soon catch up.'

Andrew smiled broadly. 'Oh, I do not doubt you will. Just when everyone is becoming fatigued and bored by it all, you will arrive and stir them into life again.' He paused, looking from her to Duncan. 'But I am puzzled. Stacey is no more than a soldier; he has no entry into the *haut monde*, so who will sponsor you?'

Duncan knew very well what the man was thinking. Molly was not a real lady and must belong on the fringes of Society; no self-respecting unmarried young lady would be travelling in such a fashion with a couple of ex-soldiers and a woman of no importance long after most of them were already in town. She was probably what was euphemistically called a 'little bit of muslin' and therefore fair game.

'Look here, Bellamy,' he began angrily. 'If you think…'

'Doesn't matter what I think,' Andrew put in. 'It's what the world thinks.'

'The world can go hang.'

'Dear me, so defensive! I assure you it is not in the least necessary. I understand.'

'It is more than I do,' Molly said.

'He is using you,' Andrew said, answering her and nodding towards Duncan. 'He is using you to gain entry into London's drawing rooms. But he will find it will take more than a pretty little nobody to accomplish that.'

'Oh, that is unfair!' Molly cried. 'He did not want to take me. I insisted. And besides, he is only my escort. I am going to stay with my mama. I do not need a sponsor.'

He bowed. 'Then I beg your pardon.' But he did not look in the least repentant. 'But if you are on your way to London, why delay your journey to go to the races?'

'Because I wanted to see the horses,' she said. 'And Captain Stacey was kind enough to agree. I was vastly amused. Do you know, I won several guineas?'

'Beginner's luck,' Duncan put in. 'A freak result.'

'Is that so? Or is the little lady a better judge of horseflesh than you are?'

'It was Brancaster's Bright Belle,' she told him.

He smiled knowingly. 'What made you choose that one?'

'She liked the filly's eyes,' Duncan said laconically. 'And who was I to argue with a lady?'

'You said she might as well have only three legs,' Molly reminded him. 'It is not my fault if I won and you lost.'

'Oh, I did not lose.'

'You backed her to win?'

'Yes.'

Her laughter pealed out, making one or two of the other guests look round to see the source of the amusement. They saw a lively young lady in the company of four very different young men, chaperoned by a drab woman who looked decidedly uncomfortable. If she had been their daughter she would have been locked in her room for her own safety, not let out to frequent coaching inns.

'How ironic!' she said. 'You expected to lose and you still backed her. Why?'

He shrugged. He did not know why. 'Sometimes you have to back your hunches. It felt like a lucky day. Mr Bellamy understands that.' He appealed to the young man. 'Is that not so?'

'Yes, indeed. And I backed her too, but it wasn't a lucky hunch; the filly belongs to my father and I have seen what she can do, if stretched.'

Molly clapped her hands. 'Then this is a celebration. Everyone is happy.'

Andrew grinned and Frank smiled and even Martha's lips twitched at her pleasure. Only Duncan seemed downcast. She could not understand it, but she did not mean to let it spoil her evening.

'Do you live hereabouts, Mr Bellamy?' she asked.

'No. My father's country home is in Huntingdonshire,' he said. 'I have lately been visiting there.'

'On a repairing lease, no doubt,' Duncan murmured.

Andrew threw him a look of pure venom. 'Unlike some, I have no need to flee the capital. I am never out of funds.' He smiled at Molly. 'I think you have not chosen your company wisely, Miss Martineau. Allow me to take over and escort you to the capital.'

Molly heard Duncan's quick intake of breath but he did not speak. She smiled at Mr Bellamy. 'I thank you, sir, but I am quite content with the escort I have. My godmother has entrusted Captain Stacey to take care of me and deliver me safely to my mama.' She paused and added, 'Besides, the Captain has your coach.'

Duncan, who had a glass of wine to his lips and was about to sip from it, spluttered into it, choking.

She looked from him to Andrew Bellamy who had lost his urbane smile and was glaring at Duncan, and decided it would be better to change the subject quickly. If the Captain had obtained the coach by deception… 'I do thank you, sir,' she said, pretending she had not noticed. 'Perhaps when I am settled in Holles Street we shall meet again. My mama no doubt will be taking me to all the right places.' She stood up and the men scrambled to their feet. 'Now, if you do not mind, I shall retire.'

She accepted their bows and murmured good-nights with what she hoped was cool aplomb and left the room, followed by Martha.

'Enchanting,' Andrew murmured to her departing back. 'Quite, quite enchanting.'

'And out of reach,' Duncan growled. 'Keep your grubby hands off her.'

'Grubby?' he queried, displaying perfectly mani-cured hands for inspection. 'Is it not a question of the pot calling the kettle black? What is your interest in her? Mama one of the *ton*, is she? No, that is not possible; no mother worthy of the name would have sent her off to London with a discharged soldier for an escort and without a conveyance, and little in the way of baggage.' He surveyed Duncan's thunderous face and smiled knowingly. 'You know, I do believe you are bamming her into believing you are taking her to her mama. You are not, are you?' He paused. 'Unless that air of innocence is all a sham and she knows exactly what she is doing.'

Duncan's fist caught him full on the jaw and he toppled sideways, taking the tablecloth and the contents of the table with him.

There was a moment of stunned silence from everyone in the room and then pandemonium as everyone crowded round. Andrew scrambled to his feet, wiping blood from his cut lip, and faced a furious Duncan, who stood with his feet apart and his hands clenched at his sides, ready to raise them should Bellamy attempt to retaliate.

'You have given yourself away, Stacey,' Bellamy said. 'No true gentlemen would resort to fisticuffs.' His emphasis on the word 'gentleman' conveyed his contempt.

'The Captain is a gentleman,' Frank put in, while everyone else in the room stood agog with curiosity. 'He is a Stacey.'

'So he is, though not one the family acknowledges. I am persuaded the connection is so remote as to be disregarded.'

Frank opened his mouth to speak again, but Duncan put a hand on his arm. 'Leave it, Frank. If our friend chooses to use my lack of breeding as an excuse not to challenge me, then let him. I have no wish to hurt him.'

That was too much for Bellamy to swallow. 'You will hear from my representatives, Stacey.'

'After we reach London and I have seen Miss Martineau safely reunited with her mother, I shall be delighted to oblige,' Duncan said, still angry, but fully aware that he could not take the risk of duelling with Bellamy while he was responsible for Molly. 'Come on, Frank; the company here is not to my liking.' And with that he walked from the room, followed by the sergeant. The spectators murmured among themselves and then, realising nothing more exciting was going to happen, dispersed.

Molly lay in her bed looking up at the ceiling, her head too full of images to sleep. It was less than a week since she had first set off after the Captain and inveigled him into being her escort and so much had happened it seemed like a lifetime.

It was an adventure of the first magnitude: coaches being held up by highwaymen; shopping and sightseeing; betting on the horseraces; pick-pockets and Mr Bellamy joining them for supper. He was a real gentleman, handsome, well-dressed, polite, so why didn't the Captain like him? He had been as prickly as a hedgehog all evening. He was a strange man, was the Captain. One minute he was laughing and being the best companion in the world, the next he was growling and getting on his high horse over some little thing of no significance.

She was afraid it was her behaviour that brought on these strange moods, but as she didn't know how else to behave she could not do anything about it.

She was still pondering on this when she heard a crash coming from downstairs and then a babble of voices. Curious, she crept from her bed and opened her door a crack to listen. There was silence. And then she saw Duncan and Frank come out of the dining room and begin to climb the stairs. Neither looked very pleased with life. 'What happened?' she asked. 'I heard a crash.'

'Nothing to worry about,' he said. 'I fell against a table. Very clumsy of me.'

Why did she think he was lying? 'Are you hurt?'

'No, of course not.' They had reached the landing and Frank gave her a nod and continued on to his own room. Duncan stopped and looked down at her. She was looking especially lovely with her hair flowing about her shoulders and the wrap she had put on over her nightgown falling open. He could see the outline of her firm young breasts and felt his loins stir uncontrollably. 'It is very late and we have a long day tomorrow. Go back to bed.' With an effort he resisted the temptation to kiss her. 'Goodnight, my dear.'

She bade him goodnight and watched from the doorway as he went along the corridor to his own room. He walked with a heavy tread, his head bowed, as if he was exhausted, and she supposed he was. He had all the responsibility of their journey on his shoulders and she had not made it easy for him. They were nearing their destination and he would be free of her; she was very sure he would not remain in London once his escort duty had been fulfilled; he would be off on the open road again, footloose and free of all encumbrances. And she would miss him.

No one could be so gallant one minute, so uncivil the next, so handsome and valiant and yet so infuriatingly condescending. Sometimes she longed to beat her fists upon his broad chest, to wipe the smile from his face with angry protests that he should see her for what she was, a young lady with sensibilities, not a child to be scolded or indulged as the fancy took him.

It just proved how far apart they were, not only in age, but in temperament. And though she had seen flashes of humour and light-heartedness he was, for the most part, a serious-minded man who did not suffer fools gladly. And she had been a fool. She had made it impossible for him to refuse her request for an escort without giving a thought about how inconvenient it might be for him. Was it possible to be more empty-headed? It was time she grew up. She fell asleep, promising herself she would try to be more understanding.

Chapter Seven

Molly was woken by Martha long before dawn.
'Dress quickly. The Captain is leaving as soon as it
is light enough,' she said.

She dressed in her green carriage dress and set a
feather-trimmed bonnet on her fair curls then
hurried downstairs to find the others already there.
Duncan looked grim and she realised that he was in
no mood for her banter. She ate her breakfast
quickly and then they went out to the coach, which
was in the yard ready and waiting for them.

This time Caesar was roped on behind with the
other horses and Duncan sat in the coach with
Molly, while Martha climbed up beside her
husband. It wasn't long before Molly realised that
they were going at a cracking pace, much faster
than on any previous days when Duncan had been
careful not to overtire the horses.

After several minutes of being thrown about quite violently as the vehicle swayed from side to side, she turned to look at him, but he was staring straight out of the other window as if he could not bear to look at her. She was puzzled. Even when he was angry with her, he had never ignored her like this. What had she done?

'I am not at all flattered that you are in such haste to be rid of me that you will risk the horses in this fashion,' she said.

He was still smouldering over his confrontation with Andrew Bellamy. Never in all his life had he backed down from a fight. Bellamy would undoubtedly spread the word that he was a coward and had refused to meet him. That would hurt more than any physical pain. He was so tense, he could feel the muscles in his jaw twitching and his hand was gripping the leather strap on the door as if his life depended on it. Her voice only served to exacerbate his feelings of frustration.

'On the contrary,' he said, tight-lipped. 'You should be pleased that I am doing it for your sake.'

'It is not for my sake.' She rounded on him. 'You have some deep game of your own.'

'If I have it is one that you started, riding off after a man at dead of night like some common camp follower.' He did not know why he said it; it was cruel and untrue. What was the matter with him? Had he been so long out of feminine society he did not know how to treat a lady?

The pain in her expressive blue eyes and the way she shuddered told him clearly he had hurt her and he cursed himself for a fool. It was the unaccustomed responsibility for someone so vulnerable, his own ramshackle way of life which he had realised could not go on that had put the words into his mouth. And his pride. He had no cause to be proud. He reached out and laid a hand on hers. 'I am sorry, Molly. I did not mean that.'

She pulled herself away from him, curling up in the corner of the carriage like a wounded animal. 'Yes, you did. You have been saying so all along. And it is my fault, for I insisted on you taking me to London. Now I wish I never had. I am such a mopstraw and so ignorant, I am persuaded I should make a dreadful cake of myself in Society. It is no wonder Mama did not want me with her.'

'Humbug!'

She turned to look at him, puzzled by the expletive, but before either of them could speak again they heard galloping hooves and shouts and two riders suddenly appeared from nowhere and rode into the road in front of them. Frank was forced to pull the coach to a halt.

Moments later, a rider appeared at the door and, leaning down, opened it, pointing a pistol at them. 'Out! Get out!'

Molly gasped. The man was masked and wore a black riding cape. Silently Duncan got out and turned to hand Molly down. Neither spoke.

'Over there.' The man jerked his head to the side of the road. The other man had his pistol trained on Frank and Martha who sat on the box, perfectly still.

Molly looked at Duncan but all he did was nod. She stepped to one side and he followed her.

'Your money and your jewels,' the man demanded.

Molly found her voice. 'I have none.'

'Do you take me for a flat? Come on, hand them over or…'

'She is telling the truth,' Duncan said, realising that the men were probably ex-soldiers and not professional criminals. 'I have but lately taken her up. She is nothing, a nobody…' He ignored Molly's gasp. 'A ladybird not worth risking a hanging for.'

'No? Then perhaps you are, my lord. Turn out your pockets, if you please.'

Duncan complied, pulling out a purse containing a few coins and his watch.

'I hope you don't mean to persuade me that's all you have.'

'It is.'

'Lord Brancaster is known for being high in the stirrups, and he wouldn't stint his son and heir.'

Molly stole a sideways glance at Duncan but his expression was inscrutable.

'It is also known that his heir is a gambler,' he drawled. 'At this moment, he has pockets to let.'

The man received this news with incredulity. He bade his companion to keep them all covered and proceeded to pull the trunk and other baggage from the boot, which he emptied out all over the road. Molly watched in horror as all her lovely clothes were scattered in the dust. 'I told you so,' Duncan said when this search revealed nothing.

The man did not reply but turned to the interior of the coach and pulled out all the squabs, peered under the seats and behind the back-rest, even examined the roof. Nothing in the way of money or jewels was discovered. He forced Frank and Martha down from their perch at gunpoint and subjected them to a humiliating search.

'Now you,' he said, advancing on Molly.

'Please,' Molly pleaded. 'I give you my word I have no valuables. His lordship spoke the truth. He picked me up.' She smiled. 'And you are known for a chivalrous man…'

'Am I?'

'You are the Dark Knight, are you not? It is said he never robs ladies.'

The man looked at Molly and laughed. 'Then they say wrong, don't they?' He reached out to pull Molly forward.

'No, you don't.' Duncan stepped in front of her. 'You lay a finger on her and…'

'Thrash me? I should like to see you try.'

Duncan was still smarting from the humiliation of refusing Andrew Bellamy; he could not be seen to back down again. He launched himself at the man, knocking the pistol from his hand and pulling him in front of him so that the accomplice dared not shoot. When the second robber turned to see what was happening, Frank seized his chance to dive for his legs and pull him to the ground. In a moment he, too, was disarmed.

Molly, quicker-thinking than even Duncan would have credited her with, picked up the pistol and handed it to him. 'Thank you, my dear,' he said calmly, pointing it at the robber. 'Now, put everything back in the carriage as you found it.'

Reluctantly they obeyed, bundling Molly's clothes back into her trunk and forcing the lid shut, then replacing Martha's few belongings in her portmanteau. They looked round when they had done this but Duncan was still watching them. 'And the rest. And the cushions.'

When they had finished Duncan strode over and pulled the masks from their faces. 'So that I remember what the Dark Knight looks like,' he said, smiling. 'Now it is your turn to empty your pockets for me.'

This revealed a purse of coins, a ring, a watch and a gold cross on a chain which Duncan took and put into his own pocket.

'What are you going to do?' the man asked, trembling.

'What do you think I should do?' Duncan was affable. 'It might be quite a feather in my cap to be the means of apprehending the Dark Knight, don't you think?'

'Yes, but…'

Duncan turned to Molly. 'What do you say, my dear? Shall we take these two incompetent snafflers to the law?'

Molly was so relieved to learn that Duncan was not the Dark Knight after all, she was inclined to be lenient. 'Not if they promise to turn over a new leaf. I should hate to be the one to bring them to the gallows.'

'Oh, thank you, miss. God bless you.' The second man spoke for the first time.

Duncan smiled at Molly. 'I think you are too kind-hearted, but as we are in some haste to continue our journey and I have no wish to waste time answering questions I shall do nothing.' He used the gun in his hand to point to the bank at the side of the road. 'Now, stand over there.'

They shuffled back, looking chagrined. 'Further,' Duncan commanded.

They retreated another pace and fell backwards into the stream. There had been no rain for some time and there was more mud than water in it. While they scrambled to their feet, covered in stinking slime and weeds, Duncan ushered Molly back to the coach. Not until they were on their way again did he sit back and roar with laughter.

'It is not funny,' she said, realising she was trembling all over now that the danger had passed.

'Oh, it is; it certainly is. You will never know how comical it is. To be held up by the notorious Dark Knight in broad daylight and best him. Oh, that is the greatest entertainment I have had in years.'

'Entertainment!' She could hear Frank, on the box, chuckling too and Martha protesting. 'I begin to think you are both a little touched in the attic. We could all have been killed.'

He attempted to be serious and for a moment stopped laughing, but then the thought of those two men set him chuckling all over again.

'You *are* mad,' she said. 'You should be giving thanks for our deliverance.'

'Oh, I do, I do.' He chinked the man's purse in his pocket. 'In more ways than one.'

'You can't keep that; it should go back to the poor man from whom it was stolen.'

'And you know it was stolen, do you?'

'Of course it was. So was the ring and the crucifix. You should hand it to the watch at the next place we stop.'

'They would not pass it on, even if they knew who had lost it, and I had as lief it was in my pocket as theirs.'

'That man thought you were Mr Bellamy.'

'I rather fancy he did, but it is hardly surprising; we are travelling in the Brancaster family carriage.'

'And you are not the Dark Knight,' she murmured pensively.

'Did I ever say I was?'

'No, I allow you did not, but…'

'You thought I was and now you are disappointed.' He spoke softly, not laughing now. 'Captain Duncan Stacey is no more than he claims to be—a half-pay officer with as little romance in him as a tin kettle. I am afraid, my dear, I am no Don Quixote, not a bit of good at tilting at windmills.'

She smiled suddenly. 'You defended me very well when that man threatened to lay hands on me.'

'Oh, that was nothing.'

'He could have shot you.'

'No, my dear, I do not think so. But you are shaking.' He put his head out of the door and shouted up at Frank. 'Stop at the next respectable hostelry, Sergeant. We'll rest the horses and have something to eat and drink before going on.'

There were several people in the dining room of the inn they chose in Saffron Walden, but they were quickly served. Frank and Martha finished their meal first and went to the stables to see that the horses were being well looked after and made ready again for the road, leaving Duncan and Molly talking to a clerical gentleman and his wife.

The Reverend was as thin as his lady was fat; he wore generous side whiskers but was otherwise quite bald and he was holding forth to all who would listen about the evils of travelling in a country that was rapidly going to the devil.

'Beggars and thieves everywhere,' he said, waving his spoon about. 'A man of the cloth should be able to travel freely in his own coach without fearing for his life. Forced from our carriage at pistol-point, we were, and all our belongings taken.'

Molly looked at Duncan, but he was concentrating on the plum duff on his plate. 'Sir, I am sorry for your misfortune,' she said. 'Tell me, when did this happen?'

'Early this morning,' he said. 'On the way here from Cambridge. We had set out early because I wished to make one or two pastoral calls on the way. We had just left the town behind and were making good progress over the Gog Magog hills when the two men sprang out at us. They took everything we possessed—my purse and watch, my wife's betrothal ring with a fine ruby in its centre. Even my crucifix.'

'It is a very frightening experience, I know,' Molly said. 'We, too, were stopped on the road by two such evil-looking characters as you are likely to meet in a twelve-month.'

'Why, ma'am, it sounds very much like the same two,' he said. 'I am a man of peace and I expected my cloth to protect me. I begin to wonder what the world is coming to, when no one has any respect for a man of God.'

'No, it is to be deplored,' Duncan said. 'We were stopped, 'tis true, but the rogues took nothing. We were able to turn the tables on them.'

'Then you were indeed fortunate,' the Reverend said. 'I should have put up some resistance, but they threatened to harm my wife if I attempted it.'

'You lost a crucifix and a watch, you say?' Duncan asked.

'Yes, the crucifix was of solid silver on a silver

chain. The watch was presented to me by grateful parishioners when I left my last living and is inscribed.'

'I do believe we have them safe,' Molly said. 'The Captain relieved the robbers of them when he retrieved our own belongings.'

Duncan took the watch from his pocket and examined the inscription. 'Be so good as to tell me your name, sir.'

'Josiah Appleby.' He called the landlord over to him. 'Gilpott, tell this gentleman my name, if you please.'

Mr Gilpott looked startled, but furnished the information, adding that he had known the Reverend gentleman some years and he was a regular customer of the inn. Duncan smiled and handed over the watch together with the money and the other items he had taken from the highwaymen. 'One cannot be too careful,' he said.

'Oh, thank you, sir!' Mrs Appleby exclaimed as the landlord went to look after a new arrival. 'How very fortunate we met up with you.'

'Let me recompense you,' the Reverend said, opening the purse and extracting two guineas.

'No, not to be thought of,' Duncan said. 'Glad to be of service.' Though he was speaking to the Reverend he was not looking at him, but at a man in a frieze coat and a shallow hat who had just entered the room. He was accompanied by the innkeeper who brought him across to where the parson sat.

'This 'ere's a Bow Street Runner, Reverend,' the landlord said. 'He's investigating this 'ere Dark Knight on behalf of Sir John Partridge what was 'eld up by 'im some few days ago. I told 'im you could, like as not, furnish 'im with details.'

'Indeed I can, and so can these people here, for we have both been victims of that gentleman and his accomplice.'

'Is that so?' The Runner looked at Duncan.

Duncan cursed inwardly but produced a lazy smile. 'Yes, but they took nothing from us and I can tell you no more about them than the Reverend. I fancy they rode off towards Newmarket.'

'One of them admitted to being the Dark Knight,' Molly put in.

'Are you sure they were both men?' the Runner asked. 'There is some doubt that one might be a female. There was a woman at the inn in Aylsham who turned up in the middle of the night, bold as you please.'

'Gammon!' Duncan said, ignoring Molly's splutter as she tried not to laugh. 'Two men, you may depend upon it.'

'And did one have a scar on his face?'

'I saw no scar,' Duncan said, praying that Frank

would not enter the room just then to tell them the carriage was ready for departure.

'I wonder,' the Runner said thoughtfully. 'Can there be more than one Dark Knight?'

'I shouldn't be surprised,' Duncan said. 'The country is full of scamps.'

'May I ask your business, sir? Where you came from and where you are bound?' And, seeing Duncan's frown, he added, 'My duty, you understand, sir; no wish to pry. Discretion's my name. Little lady's name will not be mentioned.'

Molly held her breath, but Duncan simply changed his frown to a benign smile. 'It is no secret, sir. I am escorting Miss Martineau to her mama in London from Stacey Manor, at the request of Lady Connaught, her godmother. You may check with her ladyship if you wish.' He stood up and turned to Molly. 'My dear, we shall be late arriving at your mama's, if we do not leave at once.' Bowing to the parson's wife and bidding her husband good day, he hurried Molly from the room, giving her no time to protest that she had not finished her meal.

'That was very uncivil of you,' Molly protested as she was bundled into the carriage and Duncan climbed in behind her. 'You could have described those two ruffians much better than the Reverend, for you pulled the masks from their faces.'

'If we had stayed we would have been there until supper time answering questions,' he said as they moved forward with the riding horses tied on behind. 'The episode has already delayed us.'

'But you could have helped the Runner to catch the Dark Knight.'

'So I could,' he said, a quirky smile playing about his lips. The two robbers were an unexpected blessing; they would keep the Runner busy for a good day—long enough for him to deliver Molly to Holles Street and report to the War Department. 'But I did not choose to. He will manage well enough.'

'I wish I knew what deep game you are playing,' she said. 'You are not at all what I expected of a romantic hero.'

'And I never expected to be obliged to play the role,' he retorted.

She sighed. 'I know that for you are singularly ill fitted for it.'

'I am a soldier—or I was until Boney decided to throw in the sponge. Now I am a common man with pockets to let. Mayhap when you find yourself in among the *ton* you will meet someone who fits your bill.'

'Oh, do you think I will?'

He shrugged, unwilling to admit that he envied whoever it might be. 'I do not know, for it is years since I was in Society. But I will tell you this. It is no good puffing a man up in your imagination and then complaining when he don't live up to it. We are all human with human frailties, whatever those novels you read say to the contrary.'

'No, I can see if I did that it might cause disappointment,' she said, so seriously that he found himself smiling. 'You think I should be a little sceptical?'

'It might be wise. But tell me, Molly, exactly what are you anticipating?'

'I do not know. To be introduced into Society, to go to routs and soirées and to the theatre. Above all, I should like to go to a ball and have all the eligibles at my feet.' She sighed. 'But I know that is only a dream because I am not at all beautiful and I do not know how to converse with all the latest *on-dit*, and the ballgown you bought for me is so dirty and creased where those men trampled it in the dust that I have nothing to wear. But it would be so gratifying if just one gentleman paid me a little attention.'

'Only one?' he queried a little pensively. 'Such modest expectations! But I collect he would have to be rich and have a title, or the prospect of one?'

'No. It is not at all necessary, though perhaps Mama might think so.'

'Oh, undoubtedly your mama would think so,' he agreed.

'But that would be unrealistic, don't you think? I have no fortune which, I am persuaded, would make up for all the other deficiencies.'

'It might indeed,' he said. 'It seems you must settle for a man of no particular importance, without a fortune or a title—in short any tulip who pays you his addresses.' He stopped when he saw the distress on her face. How could he be so insensitive? Was it because Bellamy had been so particular towards her and she had obviously been delighted by him? Or was it because they were so near to Foxtrees, his ancestral home? Not five miles from here, his brother enjoyed what should have been his and which would have made him someone of conse-quence, able to pay his addresses to any lady he fancied in the proper manner.

But it was grossly unfair of him to take his disap-pointment out on his young companion. He turned to her, speaking softly. 'Molly, I am sorry. I had no right to speak like that. I was simply trying to point out the pitfalls of being too trusting. I am not the only rakeshame you are likely to meet.'

'No, but I am not such a sapskull as to think you are. And I am not at my last prayers yet.' Which, without her realising it, put him firmly in his place.

'Captain,' Frank called down from the box. 'I

fancy we are being followed. There have been horses behind us for several miles.'

Duncan put his head out of the door and looked back. 'Slow down and see if they pass.'

Frank did so and two horsemen rode up alongside them. One doffed his hat and grinned at Duncan as he came level with the door of the coach.

'Bellamy!' Duncan exclaimed.

'I shall be waiting for you,' he shouted as he galloped past. 'That is if you can find the courage.' His last words were carried on the wind.

'What did he mean?' Molly asked.

Duncan made a valiant effort not to betray his fury. 'I expect he is just making sure we do not damage his carriage or spoil his horses.'

'I am sure he has no need to worry on that score, though you have been galloping the cattle very hard today.'

'For heaven's sake, can you not keep quiet about anything?' he demanded. 'You must have your say and state your opinion on every subject from high-waymen to horseflesh and I am sick of it.'

'I am sorry,' she said. 'I will not say another word.' And this time she meant it. He had never spoken to her like that before, however annoyed he had been, and she was confused and hurt.

The nearer they came to their destination, the more

gloomy he seemed to become. Perhaps he was anticipating a jobation from her mother or perhaps he had realised he ought to do something about his ramshackle life. He had been very quick and brave when the highwaymen had held them up and he was used to taking command—anyone could see that—so why could he not find useful employment? Surely it was not so difficult for officers as it was for the men?

They travelled in silence until they arrived in Bishops Stortford, where they pulled into the yard of an inn. Duncan bespoke rooms for them and they went up to change for supper.

When Molly returned downstairs, he was waiting to escort her into the dining room. He smiled at her, his ill humour apparently forgotten, and opened the door for her to precede him. They were followed by Frank and Martha.

'Why, here is Mr Bellamy and Mr Lampson!' Molly exclaimed, spotting the two men at one of the tables.

Andrew rose, smiling, and took her hand to raise it to his lips. 'Miss Martineau, what a great pleasure it is to meet you again so soon.' He held onto her hand and looked into her eyes, making her blush. 'You are still in the same bad company, I see.'

'Now that is very unkind of you, sir,' she said. 'What has the Captain done to deserve such animosity?'

'He knows. But we will not speak of it in company. Please join me.' He indicated seats at his table.

Duncan was silent and she looked round for him. He was making his way to another table. 'Thank you, Mr Bellamy, but not tonight,' she said. 'We are all very tired from travelling and shall undoubtedly retire early.'

He bowed. 'Another time, perhaps, when you are not so constrained.'

'I am not constrained,' she said. 'But yes, perhaps another time.'

She turned and walked slowly over to where Duncan, Frank and Martha had settled themselves and were ordering food.

'You could at least have been civil to him,' she said to Duncan, taking her place next to him. 'He has been very obliging, after all, and it is not fair to take your dismals out on him.'

'Miss Martineau, you do not know the truth of it,' Frank put in. 'The Captain…'

'Sergeant, be silent!' Duncan commanded.

Molly had never heard Duncan speak to Frank like that and she felt very embarrassed on his behalf, though he said nothing, but subsided into his seat and concentrated on the mutton chop and sausages on his plate.

It was a very silent meal, fraught with tension, and

Molly was glad when it was over and she could retire to her room.

'Do you know what all that business with Mr Bellamy was about?' she asked Martha as they climbed the stairs.

'No, I don't. It has something to do with what happened in the past, I think. But it has certainly put Captain Stacey into a bad temper. I shall be glad when we are on our way again. I believe the Captain means to reach London by nightfall tomorrow.'

Duncan and Frank were finishing off the wine, before retiring themselves, when Bellamy strolled over to them. 'Well, sir,' he said, addressing Duncan. 'How does it feel to hide behind a woman's petticoats? I'll wager you won't feel so comfortable about it when you reach London. News of your cowardice will go before you. What excuse will you have then for refusing to meet me?'

'There will be no excuses,' Duncan growled. 'Now, if you will allow me.' He stood up and made to leave.

Bellamy seized the sleeve of his coat to detain him. 'You call yourself a Stacey. No Stacey I ever heard of backed away from a fight.' He laughed and pulled a glove from his coat pocket and flung it into Duncan's face. 'Refuse again, if you dare.'

Slowly Duncan stooped and picked up the

glove, while the other diners looked on, their faces alive with interest. 'I shall look forward to receiving a visit from your seconds,' he said. 'Come on, Sergeant.'

'Now you've done it,' Frank said as they left the room and climbed the stairs. 'You should not have allowed him to taunt you into accepting his challenge.'

'I can't not accept it. I did it once before for Molly's sake, but now I must act for my own sake.'

'There were several witnesses in the dining room; someone is bound to send for the watch or a magistrate and there'll be hell to pay. And if you should kill him...'

'I have no intention of killing him. I merely wish to teach him that he cannot, with impunity, insult my good name or the honour of a lady who is under my protection.'

'What do you think Miss Martineau will say when she hears of it?'

'She need not know.' He realised, as he spoke, that keeping Molly out of it was going to be very difficult, if not impossible. He had no idea what her reaction might be. Was her love of adventure such that she would be excited, rather than frightened, by the prospect? After all, she spoke gaily of highwaymen and holding up coaches, but then that was fantasy. She had no experience of death or severe injury and he did not know what she would do when faced with reality. 'You do not have to stay.'

'Captain, if you think I will leave you now when you need me, then you must have a very poor opinion of me. Who else will you find to act for you?'

Duncan grinned. 'Thank you, my friend. Now, see if you can procure someone else to make a second. I do not think Mr Bellamy will delay in sending his men.'

He was right. He went to his room to prepare himself for what he knew was a highly risky and illegal undertaking, and in a few minutes Frank returned with a scrawny youth he had found in the tap room, followed by Andrew Bellamy, his valet and George Lampson.

'You have the choice of place and weapons,' Lampson said.

'Pistols,' Duncan said. 'At dawn. In the clearing in the wood on the London road. It is about three miles from here. Far enough away not to attract attention.'

Bellamy smiled, though now the challenge had been accepted he was looking decidedly shaky and rather pale. 'Until tomorrow, then.'

'Why did you choose pistols?' Frank asked, when the others had left. 'You are the best swords-man I ever met.'

'I don't have my sword with me and, besides,

pistols will have it done more quickly. One shot each and it will all be over.'

'And you might be lying dead or mortally wounded.'

'I do not think so. It is not so easy to look a man straight in the eye and fire a pistol at him with any accuracy. Not in cold blood. Especially if your opponent has deliberately missed. Bellamy is a young pup; I'll wager he has never fired a shot in anger. He will be shaking so much he will miss.'

'That is a monstrous gamble.'

'I have taken bigger risks.'

'Are you coming back here afterwards?'

Duncan smiled. 'If I survive, you mean?'

'I didn't like to say it, but yes.'

'We have no choice. I cannot abandon Molly and I know you will not leave Martha.'

'No, but there will be a hue and cry and if Mr Bellamy is wounded this is the first place anyone will look.'

'You can come back for the ladies alone and bring them to me and we can go on as before.'

'And if…?'

'You can still come back for them. Take Molly to Holles Street as planned. It is only one day's ride from here. You should have no trouble.'

'Very well, though I could wish this business had never been begun.'

'You expect me to take that young pup's insults?'
'No, of course not, but…'
'Let us get some rest, then. It will soon be dawn.'

Molly was woken from a deep sleep by voices in
the room next door, the one occupied by the
Captain. Curious, she rose and put her ear to the
wall, but the voices were too low for her to hear
more than a single word here and there. She heard
the murmur of the Captain's voice and this time her
own name came to her clearly through the
woodwork, then Mr Upjohn's voice, raised in
protest. Pistols; she heard that word very clearly. If
someone was going to shoot off a pistol, she hoped
no one would be hurt by it. More than anything she
hoped it would not be the Captain. The thought of
him lying bleeding, perhaps dying, was more than
she could bear.

A door was opened and shut with a soft click. She
scrambled out of bed and opened her own door. The
Captain and Mr Upjohn, dressed for outdoors, were
disappearing down the stairs; she could just see the
tops of their heads in the light from the lamp left
burning on the landing.

She scrambled into the breeches she habitually
wore under her old habit, pulled on a shirt and
stuffed her hair under her riding hat. Picking up her

boots, she tiptoed from her room and down the stairs. Pausing on the step to pull on her boots, she heard, rather than saw, two horses leave the yard and gallop off down the road.

It took only a couple of minutes to saddle Jenny and then she was galloping after them, digging her heels in and urging Jenny to go faster.

It was a clear moonlit night and it was easy to see the ribbon of road winding ahead, but there was no sign of the horses in front of her. Already the horizon to the east was tinged with pink. Soon it would be day and then everyone would be astir, going about their business. Why had the Captain and Mr Upjohn left the inn in such a hurry, abandoning her and Martha? It did not seem the sort of thing they would do voluntarily. If she had not known that he was not the Dark Knight, she would have thought he was going to hold up a coach.

Galloping along the empty road, she could easily believe the whole adventure was fantasy, a dream from which she would soon wake to find herself in bed at Stacey Manor with the sun shining through the window and the birds twittering in the eaves. But that would mean the Captain was a figment of her imagination too and she did not want to believe that. She wanted him to be real. He was becoming a necessary part of her life. Without him she would be lost.

The road ahead disappeared into the gloom of a copse of trees and she was forced to slow down. It was as well she did, for she heard the unmistakable snuffle of a tethered horse among the trees to her left. She pulled up sharply and dismounted. Leading Jenny by her bridle, she walked slowly forward, eyes and ears alert.

There was a clearing in the trees and in the clearing were six men, standing in a circle. Molly gasped as she recognised the Captain and Mr Upjohn, Mr Bellamy and his cousin. The other two she did not know, though she thought one of them had been with Mr Bellamy the first time she had seen him.

She watched as the Captain and Mr Bellamy took off their coats. Mr Upjohn offered Mr Bellamy an open box from which he extracted a pistol. Duncan took another from the same box and the two men moved to the centre of the clearing and stood back to back. They were going to fight a duel!

She stood, hidden by trees, clinging to Jenny's bridle as the two men paced away from each other while Mr Upjohn counted: one, two, three… It seemed to take an age, but could only have been seconds before they reached twenty, turned to face each other and raised their weapons. She plunged her fist into her mouth and looked away as two shots echoed in the morning air, one some seconds after the other.

They were followed by a deathly silence and then she heard Andrew Bellamy laugh. It was a shaky kind of laugh, a laugh of relief, a laugh that told her he had not been hurt.

She swivelled round to see Duncan on the ground where he had fallen. She forgot her fear, forgot she was supposed to be asleep in her bed, as she ran out from her hiding place and sped across the grass to where he lay, tears streaming down her face.

'My, the filly was here all along,' Bellamy drawled. 'Such devotion!'

She ignored him and flung herself on the ground beside Duncan. He was still as death and there was a great deal of blood seeping into the ground beside him. 'Captain! Oh, you must not be dead. Oh, please God, don't let him be dead.'

'Touching,' said Bellamy.

'Get out!' Frank snarled. 'Get out of here. Think yourself lucky he did not put a bullet through your heart.'

Molly, intent on feeling for a heartbeat through the blood-stained shirt, was hardly aware of the young man's going, but soon the echo of several sets of hoof-beats faded and she realised that only Frank remained. She looked up at him with a tear-streaked face.

'He could have fired,' he said, kneeling beside Duncan and carefully cutting away his shirt to reveal the wound. 'He could have picked his spot, easy as eating pie, but he didn't. He fired into the air and waited.'

'He did it on purpose? Why? Did he want to die? Oh, Mr Upjohn, what was he thinking of?'

'He's not dead,' he said, looking up from his examination into blue eyes that no longer sparkled with mischief but with tears. 'Winged. The bullet passed right through his shoulder, which is a blessing, but it is making him bleed like a stuck pig.'

'Then we must get a doctor to him.'

'And have him arrested? No, miss, I think not.'

'But he will die if he is not attended to. I have never seen so much blood.'

He forbore to point out that she was inexperienced in such matters whereas he had seen worse— a great deal worse. 'At least you are not swooning at the sight of it,' he said, prepared to concede that much, just as Duncan stirred and moaned.

'Captain, thank God. But lie still, do, for you are bleeding badly.'

He opened his eyes and grinned lopsidedly at her. She had wiped her tears away with blood-stained fingers and her cheeks were smeared with dirt and blood. And the expression of tender concern in her eyes made his heart leap. 'It is only a flesh wound,' he murmured. 'I shall be as right as ninepence in no time.'

'You should never have had the wound in the first place,' Frank put in, his concern for his friend making him speak more sharply than a servant ought. 'Why in creation's name did you not wing him? If you had only put a ball in his pistol arm, he could not have shot you. But to stand there and invite him to do his worst…'

'His worst was not so bad. And now he has to live with his conscience and I have no such problem. How could I take Molly to London if the law was on my heels?'

'I thought it already was,' Molly put in as Frank stood up and went over to Caesar's saddlebag where he knew Duncan always kept a clean pad and bandage—a practice he had started while in the Peninsula. It had saved more than one life and he had made it part of his baggage on this particular mission.

'No one is on my heels, little one, not on Duncan Stacey's heels. Unless it be you. How come you to be here? Did you follow us?' He was making a valiant effort to speak normally, but it was obvious he was in pain.

'Yes. And it is as well I did. You need a doctor…' She started to rise, but he reached up with his good hand and pulled her down again. She almost fell on top of him. His lips were on hers before she could even draw breath.

Unwilling to hurt him, she did not struggle, and then she realised she did not want to. His mouth was warm and sensuous on hers, making her insides stir with a strange uncontrollable heat, which spread from her fluttering heart to her belly and down, down to her groin. She had never been kissed like that before, had never been kissed by any man that she could remember; neither of her stepfathers would have dreamed of kissing her, except perhaps an affectionate peck on the top of her head when she pleased them.

This was different—so different, she was lost to time and place. There was no hard ground beneath them, no blood-stained shirt between them, no onlooker in the shape of Frank Upjohn, no horses snuffling impatiently nearby, nothing but their two selves, floating on a cloud.

He released her at last. 'My poor sweet, what have I done to you?'

'Me?' she queried, her voice thick with the sensuality of what had happened. 'You have done nothing to me. It is you who are wounded, but Mr Upjohn will not fetch a doctor.'

He smiled. There had been no histrionics, no protestations of outrage, no maidenly blushes. She ought to have been scandalised; she ought to have been angry. Instead she was looking at him with loving, innocent eyes. He was a cur and deserved to be whipped. But somehow he could not form the words to apologise; apologies would spoil the moment, make it sordid and wrong and it had been neither. It had felt so right.

'I should hope not,' he said cheerfully to cover the depth of his emotion. 'I have Frank. He's a great one with wounds, is Sergeant Frank Upjohn. It will not be the first time he has bound me up.'

Frank came back with the bandage and began staunching the fresh flow of blood and securing the pad over the hole. 'Raise him up,' he commanded Molly. 'I have to get this round him.'

She did as she was told, putting her arm about Duncan and helping him to sit up, while Frank bound him tightly. 'There! That should hold it.'

'Good. Now help me up, old friend.'

'You think you can ride?'

'Well enough to reach Foxtrees.'

'Good idea. They will look after you.'

'Oh, I do not intend to go up to the house and embarrass them all,' Duncan said, grunting with pain as Frank stooped and lifted his good arm to put it round his shoulders and haul him to his feet. 'There is a deserted gamekeeper's cottage in the grounds. It is almost derelict but it will serve until I have recovered a little…'

He was standing now, but leaning heavily on his friend. His face, beneath the early morning stubble, was grey, his eyes too bright. He forced himself to stumble towards the horses. 'Get me up on Caesar, Frank, then go to your wife. When she wakes and finds we have all disappeared, there is no telling what she will do. The last thing we want is a hue and cry made of it.'

'Later. First we must find that cottage you spoke of.'

'It is only a five-minute ride. I can manage.' Mounting his horse set his shoulder bleeding again and he was all but fainting. 'Come,' he said, gritting his teeth and turning his horse deeper into the wood, followed by a watchful Frank.

Molly ran back to Jenny, hauled herself without decorum or elegance into the saddle, glad that Jenny was a good-natured beast and stood still for her. Her heart was racing and her hands trembling. This had been a night to remember, when she had been kissed for the first time. Oh, it had been magical. Nothing had prepared her for the sensations it had caused in her body, sensations over which she had no control—the tingling, the trembling, the warmth washing over her, the virile smell of him, the taste of his mouth, her own involuntary response. At that moment, nothing on earth would have prevented her from following him.

Chapter Eight

He turned in his saddle and gave her a quirky smile, as if to reassure her, before facing forwards and plodding on. His back was ramrod-straight, but she could guess the effort it was costing him to remain in the saddle and half expected to see him thump to the ground with every step the horse took.

She followed, every sense heightened by what had happened. It was as if the sun had exploded into a million pieces which were showering down on her in brilliant splinters of exquisite pain. She was vibrantly alive. If he had not been wounded and if she had not been so worried about him, she could have sung with joy.

Was she in love? But it was nothing like the love she had read about in the romantic novels she devoured. Indeed, if a man had tried to kiss the heroine of those pages in that way, she would have flown into the boughs, shouted for help, considered herself ruined. Was that why Captain Stacey had smiled? He was undoubtedly experienced in these matters and she was not.

On the other hand he was injured and only half conscious, that was it—he had not known what he was doing. When he recovered he would be ashamed, apologise, swear never to let it happen again. And she would be the poorer. How confused she was and yet how unbelievably happy.

A five-minute ride, he had said, but that was five minutes for a healthy man who could canter. They had been riding slowly along this woodland path for at least ten.

And then suddenly the trees thinned out and there was another clearing in front of them. The sun had come up while they had been in the wood and now it bathed a little flint and stone thatched cottage in its light and warmth. It was a haven, even though all the windows were broken and weeds choked the flowerbeds.

Duncan slipped from the saddle and was caught by Frank who had dismounted as soon as they stopped. 'He's out again,' he said, picking the heavy man up and staggering with him into the little house. Molly followed.

Most of the furniture had been taken out; there

was nothing but a broken chair and a slatted bed. A cupboard door stood open to reveal empty shelves. Frank lowered his burden onto the bed.

'Now go,' Duncan commanded, coming to his senses. 'Molly will look after me.'

'That I doubt. She is a young lady, unused to such things, and it is hardly...'

'Fitting?' Duncan finished for him. 'This is not the time to worry about decorum. Molly will do very nicely. And think of your wife, waking up in a strange inn all alone. She will be frightened or angry or both—you know better than I which it will be—but either way it ought to be avoided. Take my purse from my saddle and pay our dues and bring her back here. We will decide our next move when you return.' The effort of speaking left him breathless.

Frank turned to look at Molly. 'You think you can manage him? The ride has started him bleeding again and he needs a fresh bandage and something to drink, though heaven knows where you will find either without going to the house. And don't let him roll about, especially if he gets feverish...'

'Frank, go!' Duncan commanded. 'That's an order.'

As soon as his friend had gone, the wounded man sank back onto the bed and closed his eyes. Molly watched him fighting insensibility and knew he would succumb before long. She knelt beside him and took his good hand. 'Captain, what do you want me to do?' 'I want you to cease calling me Captain. My name is Duncan. Haven't we been together long enough for you to know that?' It was said slowly and breathlessly. 'Yes, Ca… Duncan. But where am I to find bandages and food and drink?'

'You have a petticoat under that skirt, haven't you?'

'No. Breeches.'

He gave a short laugh which turned into a grunt of pain. 'I might have known.'

'I can tear the hem off my habit. It is too long anyway, but I fear it is not very clean.'

'There is a well outside. Find a bucket. There's a drinking cup in my saddlebag…'

She ran outside to do as he suggested and was soon back with a bucket of sparkling, cold water. 'Here it is…' She stopped. He was unconscious again.

She tried to tear the hem off her skirt, but it was well stitched and she could not make a start. Looking round, she saw a shard of broken window glass and used that like a knife. Once the tear was begun it was the work of a moment to rip the rest. She stood there with her skirt barely reaching her calves and smiled. Indecorous or not, she was better without it.

She took it off, tore it into strips and immersed

them in water. While he was still unconscious she peeled off the old dressing and washed the wound, trying not to notice his bare chest, with its dusting of dark hairs. The wound began to bleed again as she worked but she made a pad of damp material and bound it tightly with dry strips.

He moaned a little and murmured incomprehensibly. 'Be still,' she said, trying not to sound frightened. It would not do for him to think she was afraid of a little blood. 'I have nearly finished.'

She left him to throw away the pink-tinged water, clean the bucket and draw more from the well. She fetched his saddlebag from Caesar and found the drinking cup which she filled with fresh clean water and took to the bed.

'Here, drink this.' Putting her hand under his head, she raised it to help him to drink.

'Thank you.' He sank back again, but he looked more alert. 'My ministering angel.'

'Oh, no, for I am entirely ignorant of what to do. I still think you should have a doctor.'

'Why?' He smiled, touching the bandage. 'He would do no more than you have done and dose me with some foul concoction which would do nothing but make me sleep. And he would demand excessive payment for keeping his mouth shut. Duelling is illegal.'

'Oh.' She paused. 'Then why did you do it?'

'Sometimes a man has no choice.'

'He impugned your honour?'

'Not mine. I could have waived that without too much regret, but when someone I hold dear is insulted...' He stopped, fidgeting to make himself more comfortable. 'This bed is devilish hard.'

She rolled up what remained of her habit and put it gently behind his shoulder. 'A lady?'

'Never you mind. It is not for you to know.'

'And I think it is very uncivil of you to have secrets from me. Especially after...'

He reached out and took her hand. 'After I kissed you? Does that make a difference? Has the world stopped turning because of it? Am I no longer your reluctant escort?'

'You cannot escort me anywhere now,' she retorted, stung into retaliating. 'But perhaps that is what you wanted, though it seems to me a risky way of ducking out of it. Asking to be shot!'

He chuckled suddenly. 'That's what Frank said.'

'You should have listened to him. And if you are in pain, then you are well served. I have no sympathy.'

He looked at her for several seconds, his eyes moving over her face as if reading the expressions that flitted across it: perplexity, because she had not meant to be so acerbic, worry, anger, concern. There was real anxiety in her blue eyes. A tear glistened on her lashes and she blinked hard to dispel it, making it roll slowly down her grubby cheeks.

He lifted his good hand and wiped it away with the back of his finger, making her shiver. 'I am sorry, my dear. I have not served you well, have I? I have dragged you about the countryside, compromised you, taught you to prevaricate and gamble, and now this.' He looked about the tumbledown hovel. 'Is this adventure enough for you?'

'More than enough,' she said crisply. 'Adventure is all very well, when it is no more than a lark and no one is hurt by it. But this is altogether more serious. I was afraid you would die…'

'It will take more than a pinprick to kill me, Molly.'

'It is more than that, and if it should fester or you develop a fever, what must I do?'

'Neither is likely.'

'You said something about a house…'

'Did I? I must have been dreaming.'

'No, you were wide awake. And Mr Upjohn thought we might obtain help there.'

'No. And I forbid you to go. I need you here.'

'But you need proper bandages and food and drink.'

'Not so much that I cannot wait until Frank returns. He will bring all we need.' He looked quizzically at her. Even with her dirty, blood-smeared face and her hair in a tangle, she was beautiful, and the breeches she wore outlined her firm young thighs and tiny waist. It was as well that every movement was painful or he would be tempted to take her in his arms again and declare his love for her. 'Are you afraid I will kiss you again?'

She felt the colour flare into her cheeks. 'No, I think you were not yourself and did not know what you were doing.'

'Oh, I did, believe me. The temptation was too much to resist, but I apologise unreservedly. It will not happen again.'

Which was not at all what she wanted to hear.

A silence fell between them and a few minutes later he fell asleep. She sat on the edge of the bed, watching the rise and fall of his chest, the twitching of his nose and lips, as if he was dreaming, and decided he was not about to die. The terrible tension she had been feeling ebbed away, leaving her exhausted. She could not keep her eyes open. For want of anywhere else to lay her head, she stretched out beside him and in seconds was slumbering.

That was how Frank and Martha found them, her arm flung across him, her head nestling in the crook of his good arm.

'Disgraceful!' Martha said, but Frank only smiled knowingly and bent down to touch Molly's arm.

She woke instantly and sat up, looking round, wondering for a moment where she was. 'Oh, Mr Upjohn, you are back.' She scrambled from the bed, her face on fire with embarrassment.

'Yes. How is the patient?'

Molly turned to look at Duncan and a slow smile lit her face. 'I think he will do. I think he will do very well.'

Duncan woke at the sound of her voice. Forgetting his injury, he tried to sit, and winced when it hurt him. 'Damn this confounded shoulder; it is as stiff as a board.' He looked up at Frank. 'Any trouble?'

'If you mean did I see Brancaster's son and heir, no, I did not, though I do not doubt you have made an enemy there. You humiliated him in front of his cousin and his valet and he will not easily forget it.'

'I am quaking in my boots.'

'It is not a matter for jest. You might not be so lucky the next time.'

'At the moment we have more important matters to deal with.' They must reach London before that Runner caught up with them.

'I've brought food and drink and Martha has some salve in her bag which will help your wound.'

'Good. And the carriage?'

'Outside.'

'Then the sooner we are on our way again the better.'

'Not today, surely?' Molly protested. 'You are not well enough…'

'I say when I am well enough and my first concern is to see you safely into the hands of your mama. We have dallied too long.'

Molly was disappointed. He really was wishful of being rid of her, after all, and she had hoped… She pulled herself up short; she did not know what she had hoped. 'You are singing a different tune from the one I heard the other day,' she said tartly. 'Nothing would serve then but we must go to Newmarket. You said you had not undertaken to go by the shortest route.'

'I have changed my mind. It is wonderful how a ball through the shoulder concentrates the mind. The sooner you are with your mama, the easier I shall be.'

'Amen to that,' Frank said, with feeling.

While they had been speaking, Martha had been taking the salve and some fresh bandages from her bag. She handed them to her husband and while he set about re-dressing Duncan's wound and putting the useless arm in a sling she fetched out a parcel of food: cold roast chicken, half a loaf and some little fruit tartlets.

Molly sat on the only chair and watched these proceedings. She was feeling rather glum but she could not explain why. Perhaps it was because Frank and Martha had taken over looking after her patient and there was nothing she could do for him, or perhaps it was because Duncan had made it very clear he did not want her and, if that were so, it had not been at all fair of him to kiss her.

What had the duel been all about? Someone else's honour, not the Captain's. A lady perhaps? The lady the Captain had spoken of, the one who had not returned his love? Had he, in the weakness caused by the wound, thought he was kissing her? Oh, how mortifying if that were so, for she had responded in a way which, thinking about it now, made her go hot and cold all over.

But he had seemed perfectly alert. Oh, she did not understand. She wished with all her heart he had not kissed her; they had been perfectly at ease with each other before that, and now there was a constraint between them and he did not seem to want to look at her.

After they had shared a frugal meal, the ladies went to the coach while Duncan changed his torn and blood-stained clothing for the biscuit-coloured pantaloons, blue superfine coat and canary-yellow waistcoat which he kept in his bag for those occasions when he needed to give the impression of being a man of means. Then Caesar and Jenny were roped on behind and Duncan joined her in the coach and they set off again.

Their progress was slow but that was to the good because Duncan, while pretending all was well, winced with every jolt.

'I wish I knew what you were duelling about,' Molly said.

'No need for you to know.'

'Was it about the carriage? Mr Bellamy didn't lend it to you, did he?'

'Yes, he did. Not willingly, I agree, but he did allow us to borrow it.'

'Then what was it about? You could have been killed.'

'That's what a duel is,' he said. 'One man trying to kill another.'

'Do you always reduce everything to the commonplace?' she demanded. 'You make light of even the most serious situation. I cannot believe it is not all a sham to cover your true feelings.'

'I have no feelings.'

'She must have hurt you very much to make you so bitter.'

'She?'

'The young lady you loved once. You said it had come to nothing.'

'Do you always store up things people tell you so that you may bring them out later to discomfit them?'

'I was not trying to discomfit you. I wish you to be

perfectly comfortable. If you did not want me to speak of it, you should not have told me in the first place.'

'You are right. I must remember to hold my tongue in future.'

'But perhaps talking about it might help.'

'No.' He was very firm.

'What do you suppose has happened to Mr Bellamy?'

Her sudden change of topic startled him. 'Bellamy? I do not know. You saw what happened. He rode away.'

'Yes, and I am persuaded he was the one who stole the woman you loved. That's why you duelled with him, that's why you would not shoot him. It would have made her so unhappy and she would not have been persuaded to return to you. Why, I do believe it might have the opposite effect and drive her into Mr Bellamy's arms. On the other hand, if she thought you had desisted from firing at Mr Bellamy and put yourself at risk on account of her happiness, she would think more highly of you. She would know you were ready to die for her.' She stopped speaking suddenly. 'You are laughing again.'

'Oh, Molly, you are priceless. I do believe you could make a living as an author.'

'Do you?' she asked, diverted. 'Do you really?'

'Such an imagination! Such romantic notions!'

'Now you are bamming me.'

'No, not at all. I am full of admiration. Nothing seems to put you in a taking, not duels nor hold-ups, nor my grumpiness. You follow my lead, and pick up on everything I say, with the quickest wit imaginable. You have lied for me and you did not contradict when that scamp mistook me for Bellamy, you picked up the gun without the least distaste, you have dressed my wounds, and all that without quaking.'

'Oh, I was quaking, but I knew I must not let it show. The Colonel, one of my step-papas, always told me to stand firm and face my fears. He said it often when he was teaching me to ride.'

'And I collect you are a fearless rider.'

'I would not say that, but I enjoy riding and do not baulk at a fence unless it be very high.'

'Then how did you come to be thrown from a cantering mare?'

'When?'

'Why, the night we met. Jenny was hardly bucking, was she?'

'It was dark. The shadows of the trees…'

'And perhaps you were gulling me into believing you were hurt. I have seen no signs of it since.'

'I believe you are determined to quarrel with me,' she countered. 'It is not gentlemanly to question a lady's honesty.'

He laughed. '*Touché*, my dear. I apologise, for I would not for a second have been deprived of your delightful company since.'

She was confused. The compliments rolled easily from his tongue, almost as if he meant them, but he was also quick to upbraid her, to tell her she had no idea how to go on. He had kissed her as if he meant that too, but he had not denied the suggestion that Bellamy was the man who had stolen the woman he loved. And she did not know how she felt about that.

She did not think there was any hope of reaching London that day, but she did not mind. All at once it did not seem such a delightful prospect. She had forgotten how sharp her mother's tongue could be, how she disdained to notice her offspring unless it was to run errands or mend a tear in a petticoat or listen to the many difficulties she had had to contend with all her life. As if it were Molly's fault her father had died and her two stepfathers after him, and left them without a feather to fly with!

It would be much more fun to be a lady high toby and ride with the Dark Knight, taking from the rich to give to the poor and laughing at every attempt to bring them to book. Except, of course, that the Captain was not the Dark Knight; she had been glaringly abroad in thinking that. He was, as he had always maintained, nothing more than a scapegrace and a gamester. But there was more to it than that. Much, much more.

The memory of that kiss still warmed her. She was drawn to him, wanted to be close to him, to learn more about him, but sometimes he angered her so much she disliked him intensely. He was an enigma—a man with strange ideas about honesty, not averse to breaking the law and yet she knew instinctively that he was an honourable man.

She risked a peep at him from beneath the brim of her bonnet. He was sitting with his eyes shut, but the corners of his mouth were turned down as if he was in pain, which he probably was. He ought to be in bed, not racketing about the countryside.

He was not unaware of her scrutiny and wondered what she was thinking. Trying to decide when he spoke the truth and when he was hoaxing her, he supposed. But he didn't know that himself. He said things he did not mean, gave way to impulses that were far from gentlemanly and generally behaved in the rakeshame manner his grandmother had deplored.

But how could he change? He could not make himself into a man about town overnight. Or could he? Did he want to? What had he to offer someone like Molly? Adventure palled in the end and there was nothing else, no income worth the name, no title because he had relinquished it. Would he have done that if he had known Molly at the time? It was no good tormenting himself with that question; it was done and he had to live with the consequences.

How long would it be before retribution caught up with him? How many other Dark Knights were there riding about the countryside? They would all be tarred with the same brush. It was time he abandoned his scapegrace ways. His grandmother had offered him a way out, but was that fair on Molly, even if he did love her to distraction? It was because he loved her that he must part from her.

He must take her to her mother and quietly fade out of her life. He wished her happy. More than anything in the world, he wished her happy.

By the time they arrived in Great Chesterford his injury was hurting like the devil and he was more exhausted than he could ever remember being, except perhaps when he had been wounded and taken prisoner during the war. He was glad to abandon his earlier intention of reaching London that night and stop at the first coaching inn they came to, procure beds for them all and tumble into his.

'I advise you to do the same,' he said to Molly, bidding her goodnight on the landing outside her room. 'You look done in and you must not arrive in Holles Street looking not quite the thing.'

'Tomorrow?'

'Yes, my dear.' He was swaying on his feet. 'Tomorrow, your journey will be over.'

She did not know why the prospect of that depressed her. It was what she wanted, wasn't it?

She rose next morning and hurried downstairs. Frank was pacing up and down the parlour with a worried frown on his face. There was no sign of Duncan.

'Where is he? What has happened?' she asked breathlessly. 'Is he worse?'

'He started a fever in the night...'

'Then he must have a doctor, whatever he says to the contrary.'

'No, for I watched over him and the fever broke about an hour ago. He is sleeping now. I did not have the heart to wake him.'

'No, let him sleep as long as he can. There is no hurry.'

He did not agree. That Runner would tumble to the truth before long and they had to hand the evidence over to the War Department before Sir John caught up with them. Nor did he trust Bellamy to leave well alone. Duncan had tried to persuade him to go on ahead, but he would not leave him. He could only wait and hope. None of this could he explain to Molly; he had been sworn to secrecy.

She looked at him. 'You are exhausted, Mr Upjohn. You go and rest. I will watch over him.'

She went to Duncan's room and sat by his bed, watching him hour after hour, praying for his full recovery. He was breathing evenly and his colour was normal, so she was hopeful. But he must be an extraordinarily strong man to sustain a wound like that and still get up and travel for hours and then overcome a fever in so short a time. 'Let him get well,' she prayed. 'And I will never provoke him again.'

She dipped a cloth in a basin of water on the table by the bed and bathed his brow. He flung an arm out and muttered to himself but the words were unintelligible.

'Hush,' she said. 'Rest easy. You are safe and going to get well again.'

He opened his eyes slowly, smiling when he recognised her. 'All this for a kiss,' he murmured.

She felt her face go hot. 'It has nothing to do with that and it is unkind of you to remind me of it…'

'So it is. And I beg your pardon. Perhaps I was hoping…' He stopped suddenly.

'Hoping what?' she demanded.

'Nothing. What time is it?'

'Two o'clock.'

'Two!' He sat up with a jerk and winced when it

hurt him. 'We must be on our way. Why did you let me sleep so long? Leave me, girl. Let me get dressed.'

'You ought to stay in bed at least another day.'

'Don't be foolish. I am perfectly well. Go on. Tell Frank to get the horses harnessed and saddled. I will join you in a few moments.' He had flung back the bedcovers and she fled in embarrassment.

Half an hour later, they were on their way again on the last lap of their journey. Frank had strapped Duncan's arm to his chest so that it would not be jolted, but apart from that he would not allow anyone to help him. He was pale and obviously in pain, but pretended it was nothing. Molly began to wonder what it was that was so urgent; she was sure it had nothing to do with taking her to her mama. He had been content with their leisured pace until the day before yesterday. But she had, at last, learned when to keep silent and leave him to his thoughts, and so she sat looking out of the window at the countryside as they passed, not speaking.

The excitement of the previous days and nights and her lack of sleep began to tell as the carriage rolled on, and, though she tried, she could not keep her eyes open. Her chin dropped and her head lolled. Duncan put his good arm round her shoulders and, with a little sigh, she nestled her head against his chest and slept.

For mile after mile he cradled her head, not even moving when his arm went numb. A little cramp was a small price to pay for her proximity, for the sweet smell of her hair in his nostrils, for her innocent trust. He would savour it while he could, for in a few hours he must relinquish her.

It was dark when the carriage pulled up outside the house in Holles Street and he woke her gently. 'We are here, Molly.'

She sat up with a start and tried to straighten her bonnet which was askew over one ear. 'Oh, dear, have I been asleep?'

'Yes. Come, we have arrived.'

'Already?' She peered out of the coach window at the house. There was a lighted flambeau at either side of the door and a light in an upper window, which was a relief for she had suddenly wondered if her mother might be from home.

He jumped down to open the carriage door and let down the steps, showing very little sign of his injury, except for the sling which held his arm to his chest. He held out his good hand to her, smiling reassuringly. 'Come, my dear, let us surprise your mama.'

Leaving Frank and Martha to wait with the carriage, he took her elbow to escort her to the door and knocked firmly. A moment later, the door was opened by a manservant who stared at him in surprise as if he had been expecting someone else.

'Please tell Mrs Benbright her…' Duncan stopped. 'No, tell her there is someone who urgently wishes to speak with her.'

'Mrs Benbright is preparing to go out.'

'She will see me. I have come from Stacey Manor with a package for her.'

Molly, who had come up behind him, chuckled at this, but he reached back and took her hand, squeezing it so she lapsed into silence.

'Your name, sir?'

'Stacey.'

The man knew the name of Stacey, for who in London did not know of the Earl of Connaught and his pretty Countess, though they had never graced the portals of Holles Street before this, it being on the unfashionable side of Oxford Street? Why they should choose to come visiting at this hour, it was not his place to enquire, though his curiosity was almost eating him alive.

He conducted Duncan and Molly to the withdrawing room, where he left them to go in search of Mrs Benbright. Duncan stationed himself in front of the firescreen, while Molly wandered about the room looking at the furnishings and ornaments.

There were two sofas upholstered in green

brocade which matched the curtains at the long windows. Several small tables were set against the walls upon which were arranged small china ornaments. There were several high-backed chairs with spindly legs and, in an alcove, a shelf full of books, which was a surprise to Molly, for she had never known her mother to read anything but the *Lady's Magazine* and the *Ladies' Monthly Museum* which were full of gossip, fashion and serialised novels. She was inspecting the titles when the door opened and her mother came into the room.

Molly's first impulse was to run to greet her, but the sight which met her eyes made her stop where she was. Harriet was dressed in costume. Her pink gown had the most enormous hooped skirt which was caught up at intervals with ribbon bows, revealing a pale blue satin underskirt, white stockings and red satin shoes. The bodice of rose-pink and amber stripes was so tight, Molly wondered how she could breathe. Indeed, she must have been having difficulty in the direction because she almost fell out of the low *décolletage* with every rise and fall of her bosom.

She was wearing a white wig of gigantic proportions interlaced with ribbons, beads and feathers over her dark hair and there was a great deal of jewellery round her neck and upon her arms and fingers. A lace handkerchief peeped from the end of her ruffled sleeves and a quizzing glass and a fan dangled from her wrist.

'Tony!' she exclaimed. 'Is it really you? I thought when Perrins said it was Stacey he meant the Earl.'

'I thought you might,' he said, moving forward lazily to take her hand and bow over it.

'They said you were dead. We all believed you were dead.'

'I know.'

'You have given me quite a turn. I declare I shall have to sit down.' She fell into a chair and began vigorously fanning herself. 'Where have you been all this time? What have you done to your arm?'

'A slight accident, no more.'

'Does Hugh know you're back? Oh, what a mull that will make. Beth won't like it by half. Oh…' She stopped.

Molly looked from one to the other. Clearly her mother knew the Captain very well, but why had she called him Tony? And what did her mama mean about him being dead? He looked very much alive and in command of himself.

'Hugh does know and so does Beth, so you may rest easy,' he said. 'I ain't here to ask you to break the news to them.'

'Oh, thank heavens, for I should not like having to do that, and indeed should feel obliged to refuse.

But what is to be done? Are you going to turn them out? You know they have a son?'

'Yes, I know, and I have no intention of throwing them out, no intention of appearing at Foxtrees at all. I am a ghost.'

'You look very substantial to me. I would go so far as to say very agreeably in countenance.' She stopped. 'Why are you here? Perrins said something about a package from Stacey Manor. There is nothing wrong there, I hope? Lady Connaught is not ill? Or Molly? Oh, do not tell me the tiresome child has caught measles or some such.'

'No, her ladyship is in plump currant,' he said, nodding towards Molly, who stepped away from the bookcase which had been half concealing her. 'And so is Molly, as you can see.'

'Molly!' her mother gasped. 'What are you doing here?'

Molly came forward and kissed her mother's cheek, aware that it was heavily rouged and powdered. 'I have come to visit you, Mama. It was so dull at Stacey Manor and the Captain was so good as to escort me here and we have had such adventures…'

'Dull? Escort? Adventures?' she repeated faintly, wafting her fan ineffectually. 'What are you prosing on about?' She stopped to look suspiciously at her daughter. 'You have not run away from Stacey Manor, have you? Oh, what will her ladyship think of you, you ungrateful wretch? Tony Stacey, I am surprised at you conniving in this. I knew you for a scapegrace, but this… Have you run quite mad?'

'It is not the Captain's fault,' Molly put in quickly. 'He was a most reluctant escort but I persuaded him that Aunt Margaret would not mind. And now I am here he will leave me with you.'

'And what am I supposed to do with you?'

Molly was very near to tears; this was not the welcome she had hoped for. But it was her own fault; she should not have arrived unannounced. 'I hoped you would let me stay with you,' she said. 'I should be no trouble. I should so like to see something of the town and go out and about with you.'

'Trouble! Trouble is nothing to it. You are enough to give me a seizure, arriving on the doorstep like a stray kitten. Look at you! Such a bedraggled chit I never did see. I cannot take you out looking like that and I certainly cannot afford to tog you out.'

'Captain Stacey has been so good as to provide me with a wardrobe.'

'Stacey?' She went into peals of laughter. 'What does he know of ladies' fashion? He is a single man and a soldier to boot.'

'I think they suit me very well.'

'So they might, for you will not be going out into Society…'

'But, Mama…'

'No more. I told you months ago that it would not be possible until next year. I explained it very carefully, so why did you have to throw away the only chance either of us will have on some cork-brained idea that I would welcome you?'

Molly choked back a sob. 'I should not be any trouble, Mama.'

Duncan could stand silent no longer, though he had promised himself he would not interfere but await developments. 'Miss Martineau, please do not distress yourself. Our arrival was untimely, that's all. Your mama has been taken by surprise.'

'That is the least of it,' Harriet put in tartly. 'I am going out. A long-standing engagement I cannot cancel. Nor will I for a wilful child who thinks she may order the world to suit herself.'

'Madam, I would as lief leave her with a dragon as you, but it is late and I suggest you give orders for a room to be made ready for your daughter and talk about it tomorrow,' he said. 'No doubt your escort will be here directly…'

The mention of her escort decided Harriet. She rang the bell for Perrins and instructed him to have Betty make up a bed for Molly in the green room.

'Tomorrow we will decide what is to be done with you,' she said. 'But not before the afternoon, for I do not expect to be home much before dawn and shall sleep late.'

Her orders had barely been given before they heard a knock on the street door and a few moments later the butler returned and announced the Marquis of Tadbury. If Harriet intended to tell Perrins to conduct him to another room to wait, she was thwarted because the gentleman himself followed the servant into the room and executed an exaggerated leg, sweeping his feather-decked hat off and bowing before her.

He was dressed as a cavalier, with a blue satin coat and a darker blue silk sash. There were frills at his throat and at his wrists and he wore a full-bottomed curly black wig. But what surprised Molly more than his costume was the fact that, in spite of being rather portly, he was so young. Why, he was younger than Captain Stacey!

'My love, you are in looks tonight,' he said, surveying Harriet's heaving bosom with more than a little interest. 'I shall be the envy of the whole *ton*.'

Molly's stifled laugh betrayed her presence and he looked round in alarm to find himself being subjected to the scrutiny of two merry blue eyes and two sardonic brown ones. 'You are not alone?'

Harriet sighed. 'May I present Miss Margaret Martineau? Molly, this is my friend, the Marquis of Tadbury.'

Molly curtsied demurely, conscious of her bed-raggled appearance and wishing she could have been spared the encounter until she had been able to refresh her wardrobe. She supposed that was why her mother had not introduced her as her daughter.

He bowed. 'Miss Martineau, your obedient. I do not think I have come across the name before.'

'No, you would not,' Harriet said quickly before Molly could reply. 'She has lately come up from the country with my cousin, Captain Stacey.'

Duncan inclined his head in a curt nod. 'Your servant, sir.'

'Stacey,' the man repeated. 'Not one of the Connaught Staceys?'

'A distant connection,' Duncan said laconically.

The Marquis turned to Harriet. 'I did not know you were related to the Staceys, my love.'

'It is only very distant,' she said, her cheeks flaming beneath the *maquillage* she wore. 'It hardly signifies. I really think we should be leaving or Lady Bonchance will think we are not coming. It is excessively impolite to arrive after everyone has gone in.'

'You are right. Let us be off. My carriage is only a pace or two down the street—couldn't bring it to the door for the barouche standing outside. Is that yours, Stacey? Damn fine set of bloods in the shafts.'

Duncan smiled. 'Yes, aren't they?'

'Take them off your hands if you ever think of selling.'

'I have had numerous offers for them, but they are not for sale,' Duncan said. 'But you have reminded me that they have been standing too long. I will take my leave of you.'

Harriet turned to Molly. 'Bid the Captain goodnight, Molly, and then go to bed. You look done in.'

Molly would have liked Duncan to stay for a little while and talk to her. She was feeling confused and unhappy. Nothing was as she had expected but then when she asked herself what she had expected, she had no answer. The one she had given the Captain when he had asked the same question seemed trite and foolish.

She smiled a little wanly. 'Goodnight, Captain. I am much obliged for your escort.'

He took her hand and raised it to his lips, looking into her sad little face and wishing he could put the smile back on it. 'It was my privilege, Miss Martineau. Perhaps I may give myself the pleasure of calling on you tomorrow?'

'Not before three o'clock at the earliest,' Harriet put in. 'In fact, I would as lief you did not come at all tomorrow. I shall not rise before noon, I am engaged for tea, and in the evening I go to Almack's, and I cannot allow you to visit Molly unchaperoned.'

'I am sorry, Captain,' Molly whispered. 'Perhaps another time?'

'Yes, of course,' he said, though he could cheerfully have strangled Harriet. She had been less than pleased to see her daughter and he would not be at all surprised if she packed her back to Stacey Manor on the next available coach. How disappointed Molly would be! She had set her heart on seeing something of London Society and finding the husband of her dreams. He was not that man, he told himself. She was looking for someone younger and more in keeping with her romantic notions.

Having discharged his duty as the reluctant escort, he should put her from his mind. He smiled at her, a secret smile of sympathy. 'Goodnight, my dear.' And then he said, in a whisper only she could hear, 'Keep your ginger up. Tomorrow, I am sure all will be well.'

She watched him leave with her mother and the Marquis, heard the front door slam and both carriages driving away, and she was alone. She sank onto one of the sofas, realising that her mother had not offered the Captain any refreshment, nor her either, but Mama must have been so taken by surprise, the proper civilities had quite deserted her.

She looked up when the door opened and a young woman in cap and apron came into the room. 'I'm Betty, miss,' she said. 'I'm to take you to your room.'

'Thank you. But I am very thirsty and a little hungry. It was a long journey...'

'Bless you, miss, I thought you must have dined long ago, it being so late. There ain't much in the house, for Mrs Benbright don't eat in very often, but I dare say I can find some cold chicken and some bread and cheese, though I don't think you should eat cheese late at night, miss, on account it will give you nightmares.'

'The chicken will do very nicely, if you please. And perhaps a dish of hot chocolate?'

'I'll tell Cook and bring it up to your room. Now, if you'll follow me, I'll show you where that is.' She led the way up a second flight of stairs, chattering all the while. 'Goodness knows why her ladyship should put you in the green room, it being right at the back of the house, so far from her own, and such a sickly colour. But there, you won't be disturbed by the traffic in the street, nor Mrs Benbright coming home in the early hours, so like as not you'll sleep well there.'

'Her ladyship?' Molly queried.

'Mrs Benbright.' She giggled. 'That's what we call her behind her back, but like as not we'll be saying it to her face before long if the Marquis comes up to the mark…'

'I am not sure you should be calling her anything behind her back,' Molly said. 'It is disrespectful.'

'Oh, well, if you are going to be stiff about it, I'll say no more,' Betty said. 'But there's only the three of us and if you're to work here we must all get along and be friends.'

'I did not come here to work,' Molly said. 'Mrs Benbright is my mama.'

'Your mama?' Betty repeated incredulously. 'We never knew she had a daughter. She never said so.'

'There is no reason why she should,' Molly said. 'I do not imagine it is the done thing to discuss one's private business with servants.'

'Beg pardon, miss, I'm sure,' Betty said stiffly. 'Is there anything else you need?'

'No, thank you.'

Molly was so bewildered and exhausted and the candle the maid had left with her was so feeble, she saw very little of the room, except the bed. But her trunk had been brought up and stood against the wall, and she found her nightgown, undressed and slipped between the sheets. By the time Betty came up with the food and hot chocolate, she was already asleep.

Chapter Nine

Duncan, having watched the Marquis's ornate town coach drive away, turned to give Frank instructions to see that the carriage and horses were safely stabled and then find lodgings for himself and Martha. 'Meet me tomorrow morning at eleven at Stephen's Hotel in Bond Street,' he told him.

'Where are you going, Captain?'

'Home, Frank, home.' He untied Caesar and hauled himself one-handed into the saddle and picked up the reins. 'We will decide our next move tomorrow.'

'Are you fit to ride, sir?'

'Yes. Don't worry. It's not far. Goodnight to you both and my grateful thanks for all your help.'

He rode slowly towards Bond Street, glad to be alone. He was unaware of his surroundings, and the late-night traffic on the road; his mind was full of Molly. She had been delightful company, enjoying her adventure, teasing him with her seriousness one minute and her merriment the next, unconscious of the peril she was in. She had been cheerful and stoical, putting up with his temper and never complaining when he left her to play cards, nor when he insisted on travelling through the night. She had accepted whatever food he provided and was inordinately pleased with the few fripperies he had bought for her and seemed to thrive on risk. All for the sake of a Season.

But would her mother grant her wish? And if she did not, what madcap scrape would Molly get herself into? The capital was full of unsavoury characters and not all of them among the lower orders. She would never be able to distinguish honesty from treachery, gentleman from rogue, unless there was someone with her to point out the pitfalls. He found himself envying the young bloods who would be sure to flock about her once she had been seen about town. It wouldn't hurt him to stay for a few days to see how she fared.

His grandmother was right; it was time to put the past behind him and make a new life for himself. Now his mission had been accomplished, he could not go back to being a ne'er-do-well. He was not a criminal. But he ought to tell Hugh of his plans. They might meet socially and the last thing he wanted was to embarrass his brother and sister-in-law. He did not know how he felt about seeing Beth again, but he could not hide himself away for the rest of his life. He had done no wrong. He grinned ruefully; if you didn't count highway robbery, of course.

He turned Caesar towards Berkeley Square and five minutes later was sitting outside Connaught House, looking up at its façade. He was almost relieved to discover the knocker off the door. The family, so he was informed by an astonished Mr Birtwhistle who admitted him, were still in the country and not expected until later in the Season and there was only himself and the housekeeper in residence.

'No matter,' Duncan told him airily. 'Not stopping. Came for my mail. It has been kept for me?'

'Yes, sir…my lord.' The butler was clearly agitated.

'Captain,' Duncan corrected him. 'Captain Stacey will do very well.'

'My lor… Captain,' he amended. 'I didn't rightly know what to do about the mail; some of it came from the War Department. I left it in the library for the Earl to… Oh, dear… We thought you were dead.'

'Yes, I know. But as you see…' he spread his good arm '…apart from a slight injury, which is healing well, I am in the best of health.'

The man made an effort to recover. 'Would you like some refreshment, my lord?'

'Captain,' Duncan corrected him again. 'Yes, I should like something to eat and a glass or two of wine, while I go through my correspondence.'

He made a good meal and drank half a bottle of claret which he owned was very good; his father had always kept a good cellar and it seemed Hugh was following in his footsteps. He was feeling decidedly mellow by the time the butler came to clear the table and put a bottle of the best French brandy and a fresh glass in front of him.

'Tell me, Birtwhistle, how is everyone? In plump currant?'

'Yes, sir, very well. The young viscount is a delightful child.'

'Oh, yes,' Duncan mused. 'I had forgotten him for the moment. Viscount Stacey, the son and heir.'

'Sir, may I ask a question?'

'Fire away.'

'What do you intend to do? I mean, should I inform the…um…Earl that you are back and have been here?'

Duncan smiled. 'My brother knows I am back, Birtwhistle, and as for what I mean to do I am not exactly sure, but I'm not about to upset the apple cart if that's what's worrying you.'

'Thank you, sir. Will you be staying, sir?'

He could not resist the prospect of spending at

least one night in a comfortable bed in his old home, and as his brother was not in residence he could see no harm in it.

Later, lying on a feather mattress in the big four-poster in the second best bedroom, he took stock of his situation and the euphoria left him.

This large, fashionable house should have been his London home and, if he liked to kick up a dust, it still could be. He could bring Molly here as his countess. It was ironic that if it had not been for that trick of fate which had deprived him of his inheritance he would never have been sent to Norfolk, never become the Dark Knight, never met Molly, never known the sweetness of a single kiss, the music of her inconsequential chatter, never succumbed to her scolding. That bullet had expunged all his old bitterness, leaving him cleansed of acrimony, a new man. Beth was not the woman for him, but Molly was.

She had come to London with the express purpose of finding the romantic husband of her dreams, though he was sure she had little idea of what that really meant. The thought of anyone else enlightening her filled him with helpless fury. He did not want her to marry anyone unless it was himself. But could he ask her to marry him when he was not the hero of her fantasies and had neither title nor wealth to offer her? He could not force his way back into Society now, could not take back what he had freely given. Would she settle for less? Had he the right to ask it of her?

The next morning, in his best uniform, he entered the imposing portals of the War Department and spoke to the man on guard. 'Captain Stacey to see Colonel Gadsby.'

The man disappeared along a corridor and returned to conduct him to the Colonel's room, where he flung open the door and announced him in a strident voice.

'Tony!' The Colonel, a huge man with long dark curls and a pointed beard, left the desk behind which he had been sitting and hurried forward, hand out-stretched. 'I did not know you were back in town.'

Duncan grasped the hand. 'Arrived late last night, sir.'

'Sit down, Captain. How did it go? I see you sustained an injury.'

Duncan sat in a chair near the desk and the Colonel resumed his seat behind it. 'Oh, that came later, sir. It is nothing but a scratch.'

'But you did obtain the proof we need?'

'Yes, sir, though the man was no flat; he was suspicious of everyone. His house was like a fortress and his servants close-lipped. I could not have done it without Sergeant Upjohn. He obtained a position as a groom and managed to get into the house—something I could not have done because Sir John was bound to recognise me. Frank learned there were documents kept in a chest, but he could find no opportunity to search for them.'

Duncan had met Sir John Partridge when working as an agent in France. The man had come over from England in the middle of a war, as bold as you please, to negotiate the sale of guns and ammunition to the French army. At the time, Duncan had been pretending to be a sympathetic American and was serving as an interpreter in the French intelligence service. He could do or say nothing without blowing his own cover, but as soon as he'd returned home he'd reported what he knew.

As a result, he had been asked to find documentary proof, a task he was more than happy to undertake, even without the added inducement of a reward. It was fortuitous he had run into Frank when he'd tracked the man to Norwich. Frank's help had been invaluable and if, at the same time, it had saved his sergeant from a life of crime, then it was a double blessing.

'Just when we began to think we were at a stand,' he went on, 'my sergeant learned he was making a journey to Cromer and taking his strong box with him.' He paused and then chuckled. 'We became high tobies.'

He reached in the pocket of his frockcoat and withdrew a bundle of documents which he handed to the Colonel. 'I think this is what you are looking for: letters, bills of lading, receipts. There is enough evidence there to convict him a hundred times over and the beauty of it is that he does not know he was robbed for those. He thinks it was the gold the scamps were after and has been making strenuous efforts to have the doers of the deed caught and brought to book before they realise the significance of what they have.'

The Colonel spent a few moments scanning the contents of the documents, before looking up and smiling at Duncan. 'You have done well, Captain. It will give me a great deal of personal satisfaction to see the traitor hang.'

'Indeed, sir. Publicly, I hope, so that everyone knows his treachery.'

'There will be a trial. We must allow him that. But what happened to the gold? I gave no orders for anything else to be confiscated.'

'No, sir, but if we had left him with his blunt he would have twigged what we were about. It was put to good use. We distributed it among needy ex-soldiers. It seemed a kind of rough justice.' He said nothing of Mr Grunston, the slave trader; that episode had been well outside his remit and just showed how far he had gone along the road of the ne'er-do-well.

'Did it indeed? I think perhaps I will conveniently forget you told me that. If there is a fastener out on you, I do not want to know about it.'

'Oh, I do not think anyone will make the connection,' he said, smiling. 'There are so many scamps about these days calling themselves the Dark Knight.'

'Quite so. What are you going to do now? Ain't it time you found yourself a filly and settled down?'

'I doubt anyone would have me,' he said with a wry smile. He was no nearer finding a way of making a living that did not involve gambling and though, for the most part, he was very successful at it, it was no way for a man wishing to marry to go on.

'I wish you luck, whatever you do,' the Colonel said. 'There is, as I told you at the outset, a considerable reward. I will make sure a draught is taken to your bank by the end of the week.'

'Thank you, sir, but I wish half of it to be sent to Sergeant Upjohn. If possible I would wish him to be absolved of complicity in any illegal acts while acting under my instructions in this matter.'

'I think that can be arranged.'

Duncan thanked him, bowed and took his leave. He met Frank and Martha as arranged, paid them what little money he had and sent them home in Lord Brancaster's coach. 'Take it back to him,' he said. 'Thank him for its use and tell him I will compensate him for any inconvenience. And you will hear from Colonel Gadsby yourself.' He smiled. 'It will be enough to start you off in a little business of your own.'

He brushed aside their gratitude and watched them go. It was too early to call on Holles Street and as Caesar needed exercise he set off for Hyde Park. Avoiding the carriageway and the ride, he made for the wide area of grass beyond the lake and allowed the stallion to have its head. An hour later, he slowed to a walk and turned back to skirt the southern shore of the lake, making for the Curzon Gate.

The idea he had mentioned to his grandmother, that he might breed horses, had been growing slowly in his mind. After all, horses were always wanted for every kind of use—for riding, for carriage work, for the army; there was always a ready market for top quality animals. He knew a little about the subject and if he employed experienced help he felt sure he could make a success of it. Would Molly consent to be a farmer's wife?

* * *

It was daylight when Molly woke and the sun was shining through the curtains. She rose and drew them back to look out on a small back garden which had been untended for some time, judging by the length of the grass and the weeds in the borders among which a few flowers struggled to survive.

She had no idea of the time, but she was wide awake and anxious to explore her surroundings. There was water in the jug on the wash-stand and she washed quickly and dressed in the turquoise muslin gown Duncan had bought for her, brushed her hair and tied it back with a matching ribbon before leaving the room to find her way downstairs.

The house was very quiet and she supposed her mother would be as good as her word and would not rise before noon. Not wanting to disturb her, she crept along the upper corridor towards the stairs. Once in the hall, she opened all the doors one by one and peeped into the rooms. There were not many for it was not a big house.

There was the drawing room she had been in the night before, where a tray containing an empty bottle and two used glasses told her that her mother had invited her escort into the house on their return. On the other side of the hall was a bookroom which was so tidy and smelled so musty, Molly was sure it was never used. Towards the back of the house was a breakfast parlour and another small sitting room.

She was standing, undecided what to do, when she heard voices on the other side of the door which evidently led to the kitchen. She opened it shyly and saw three servants sitting round a table—Betty, Perrins and a red-faced woman in a large apron whom she took to be the cook. They sprang to their feet when they saw her.

'We didn't know you were awake, miss,' Betty said. 'Mrs Benbright don't rise afore noon.'

'No, I know. But it is such a lovely day, I wanted to be up and about.'

'You will be wanting your breakfast.'

'A little tea and toast, if you please, and I will take it in the breakfast parlour. I see the table is laid up.'

She had just begun her meal when her mother wandered into the room in a puce silk peignoir which did nothing to enhance a pasty complexion brought about by too many late nights. Her hair was loose about her shoulders and her eyes were heavy.

'Good morning, Mama,' Molly said brightly, and noticed her mother wince. 'I did not think you would be awake yet.'

'Well, I am not sure that I am,' her mother said, sitting down opposite her. 'I am not at all sure this is not some horrible nightmare.'

'What is?'

'You arriving like that without a by-your-leave. And with Tony Stacey too. There will be the most prodigious scandal, especially when the *ton* learns that his lordship is not dead at all...'

Before Molly could comment on this, Betty came in with a tray containing a pot of chocolate, a plate of buttered toast, a dish of hard-boiled eggs and a jar of conserve. She set it all on the table. 'I didn't you know were up, ma'am,' she said, addressing Mrs Benbright. 'Do you want me to fetch you anything else?'

'No, this will suffice, thank you.'

Betty disappeared reluctantly. 'Now I suppose they will have a fine time of it, discussing our affairs in the kitchen,' Harriet complained. 'As if I do not have enough to contend with.'

'What do you mean, "his lordship"?' Molly demanded. 'Whom were you speaking of? Not Captain Stacey surely?'

'Captain Stacey, as you call him, is an earl, or he would be if his brother had not usurped the title, thinking him dead. He has always been called Tony to distinguish him from his father for whom he was named and who died two years since. He is Duncan Anthony Stacey, Earl of Connaught.'

'Duncan is an earl?' Molly queried in astonishment.

'But he never gave me even the smallest hint. Nor did Aunt Margaret. She introduced him to me as Captain Stacey and she called him Duncan, not Tony…'

'She always did.'

'Oh, dear, I wish I had known. I have not always been civil to him and I never addressed him as anything but Captain.'

'You referred to him as Duncan just now.'

'Did I?' Molly felt her face flush. 'Oh, that is because he told me to use his given name.'

'Did he, now? And what else happened on this highly improper journey to London? I collect you mentioned adventures.'

'Well, there were,' Molly said. 'But nothing unseemly occurred.'

'The whole escapade was unseemly,' her mother said irritably, taking a slice of toast and looking at it as if it might poison her. 'I wonder at Stacey embarking upon it. Unless he don't care for his good name any more.'

'I don't suppose he does, if his brother has been too hasty in taking it over. Is it any wonder he prefers to be an adventurer and pretend to be the Dark Knight, which I know now he is not?'

'Is that what he said he was?' Harriet asked, barely following the gist of what her daughter was saying.

'The Dark Knight? No, he denied it, and later

when we were held up by the high toby ourselves and one of them as good as admitted he was the Dark Knight I knew he could not be. I do not know if I was glad of it or not, for the Dark Knight has a romantic reputation, but I should not like the Captain to be hanged for a scamp…'

'Molly, what are you saying?' her mother asked weakly. 'I begin to think all those romantical books you read have turned your head. Such a Banbury Tale I never heard.'

'I am sorry, Mama; I did not mean to displease you, but there is so little to do at Stacey Manor, and when the Captain came to see Lady Connaught and rode out in the middle of the night…'

'Middle of the night? You left in the middle of the night?' Her mother's voice was almost a squawk.

'Yes, but I had no thought of coming to you then; it was only later, when my horse threw me and the Captain took me to an inn to recover, it came to me that it would be a prodigious adventure to come to London.'

'He took you to a common inn?'

'Yes, but he behaved very properly. After that we travelled in a coach with four beautiful bays and were never without a night's lodging though I own he sometimes had to play cards to pay for it. And he insisted on Sergeant Upjohn's wife travelling with us…'

'Sergeant Upjohn's wife! You think a common soldier's wife is an adequate chaperon, do you? My life! You might as well have had none at all.'

'Mrs Upjohn is clean and respectable and very polite and...'

'Oh, that is the outside of enough! Captain Stacey, as you call him, has cut himself off from his family and left himself without a feather to fly with, so how could he afford to hire a coach and four?'

'He did not hire it, he borrowed it. It belongs to Lord Brancaster.'

'Lord Brancaster? Where does he come into it?'

'He doesn't, but we met his son, Mr Andrew Bellamy, and he was kind enough to lend us the carriage.' She was very careful not to say anything about the duel.

'If I had known this last night, I would certainly have called him to account for it. He has quite ruined your reputation and mine along with it. What Tadbury will say when he hears of it, I dare not imagine.'

'What has it to do with the Marquis?'

'Are you a sapskull, girl, that you can say that? I had all but got him to the point of proposing, but he will think twice of it when he realises what a scapegrace I have for a daughter.'

Molly found it difficult not to smile at the idea of the Marquis of Tadbury becoming her third stepfa-

ther. Why, he was nearer her age than her mother's!
'Surely there are others just as eligible?' she said.
'He looks so…so young.'

'I am tired of being married to old men, Molly;
they have a tendency to die on me. And the Marquis
is very rich and very careful of me, which so many
men of the *haut monde* are not. And I fancy myself
as a marchioness. You would not ruin it for me,
would you?'

'Of course not. But I do not see that we have to tell
the world how I came to London. You need only say
your daughter has come to keep you company…'

'My daughter!' Harriet wailed. 'No one knows I
have a daughter—or if they do they think she is no
more than a child.'

'You will have to tell the Marquis some time,'
Molly said with perfect logic. 'You cannot deny my
existence if you mean to accept his suit.'

'Yes, I know, but I was going to lead up to it when
I was sure of him. Now he will hear of it from
Stacey, you may be sure.'

'The Captain won't say anything. My goodness,
he was a most reluctant escort.'

'Not so reluctant as to refuse,' Harriet said with
heavy irony.

'No, but the circumstances made it difficult for
him. There was all that business when the stage was

held up and being questioned by the watch and there not being another stage until the next day. And I persuaded him that it would be better if he travelled with a wife…'

'Wife!' shrieked Harriet. 'You mean to say you have been passing yourself off as Stacey's *wife*?'

'Only for one night, and he did not come to bed…'

'Enough!' Harriet said weakly. 'I do not want to hear any more of this. You have given me a megrim and I shall have to go and lie down again.' She left the room, the back of her hand to her forehead.

Molly sighed and took Miss Austen's latest novel from the shelf, thinking to take it out to the garden, then changed her mind. She went to the kitchen and asked Perrins to send the potboy round to the mews to have Jenny saddled and brought to the door.

Returning to her room, she scrambled into the new habit which Duncan had included in his purchases in Norwich, pulled on her boots and set her feather-trimmed riding hat on her fair curls. Ten minutes later, having asked Perrins for directions, she was riding her mare down Oxford Street towards Hyde Park, completely ignoring the fact that she ought to have had an escort.

It was a lovely summer day, the sort of serene day when everyone should be happy. Indeed the faces of those about her seemed cheerful enough as they went about their daily business. An errand boy was whistling, a young man and a girl were deep in a conversation which was making them smile, a bird sang from its perch on a railing, ignoring the cat that was sunning itself on a step.

The shops were open and people passed in and out of their portals, carrying packages; phaetons and tilburys and curricles went up and down the busy street; a stagecoach rattled along, the guard tooting his horn to let the next stop know they were coming. Even the barefoot beggars called cheerily. Molly's spirits lifted as she rode. How could she despair when the world was such a lovely place?

She turned in at the gates of the park which was crowded with people in carriages of every description, all dressed in the latest mode, going at a sedate pace, nodding to acquaintances, stopping every now and again to exchange pleasantries and the latest *on-dit*. Were they talking about her? Her mother seemed to think they would be and it had worried her more than a little. According to Mama, reputations could be lost with a single word, or even no word at all, if someone of importance were to cut one dead.

The carriageway was divided from the ride by a fence. She found her way round it and set off at a trot to try and dispel the image of her and her mother being the subject of everyone's gossip. It was foolish, she told herself after a few minutes; no one knew who she was; her mother had taken care of that.

Her thoughts occupied her so completely she was unaware of the rider coming towards her until he pulled up in front of her, forcing her to stop. 'Why, I do believe it is Miss Martineau,' he said, doffing his curly-brimmed beaver and bowing from the waist.

'Mr Bellamy.' She inclined her head in acknowledgement, while controlling Jenny, who objected to being reined in so unexpectedly.

'All alone?' he asked, looking about for her escort.

'As you see.'

He was dressed in a single-breasted coat of bath cloth and buckskin riding breeches tucked into tasselled topboots. His starched muslin cravat fell over the top of a yellow and black striped waistcoat, reminding her of a bumble bee. He was, she supposed, what was called a pink of the *ton*.

'Then please allow me to accompany you.'

'I am sure you have other things to do.'

'Nothing of more importance, my dear. I am at your service.'

Molly wasn't at all sure she liked him addressing her as 'my dear' but she did not comment. The Captain did it all the time and she assumed that was how young men went on in the *haut monde*. 'Thank you, sir, but I was thinking of turning back.'

'Not yet, surely? Riding is a pleasure on a day such as this; we should take advantage of it, for tomorrow it may well be raining. Do you not agree?'

'Yes,' she said doubtfully, wondering whether she ought not to give him a set-down. But how could she do that when he had been so good as to allow them the use of his family coach? 'I did not thank you properly for lending us your carriage,' she said as he turned and walked his horse beside hers.

'Think nothing of it.'

'Oh, but I do! And for the Captain to call you out was not at all the thing.'

'How is the gallant Captain? No permanent damage done, I trust?'

'He was recovering well when I last saw him. But it was unkind of you to shoot him when he had re-frained from firing.'

'One of us had to do something; we could not stand facing each other for the rest of the day. And I only winged him.'

'Why did he call you out?'

'Do you not know?'

'No, he would not say.'

'Then neither will I.' He smiled. 'Where is he? I am surprised he is not with you today.'

'I don't know where he is. He was only my escort for the duration of the journey to London, you know. I do hope you will not put any other interpretation on it.'

'If you say that was all there was to it, then of course I will not.' He reached out for her reins and drew both horses to a stop. 'Shall we walk a little?'

He jumped down and held out his hands to help her dismount. She looked about her, wondering whether she ought to comply, but none of the riders who were hacking up and down was paying them the least attention, so she slid from the saddle and stood beside him.

'There, that is better,' he said. 'We cannot converse properly across the backs of our horses.'

They walked side by side, leading their mounts, but she felt uncomfortable about it and wished she had given him the right about when he had first approached her. What would her mother say if she knew where her daughter was at that moment? Would she put it down to another of her embarrassing scrapes or would she be pleased that someone was fixing an interest in her?

'Miss Martineau, may I call on you?'

She pondered this for a moment. Calling meant no more than paying respects, after all. 'If you wish. Mama will want to thank you for the use of the carriage, I am sure. But I do not know how long I shall remain in town.'

'Not remain! Oh, how could you be so unkind as to give the world a glimpse of your loveliness and then disappear again? I declare it is cruelty of the most severe.'

She laughed at this piece of nonsense and answered lightly. 'Oh, sir, you put me to the blush.'

'And a very pretty blush it is,' he said, caressing her cheek with his finger.

'I think we should mount again,' she said, turning away in confusion.

'So soon?' He took her shoulders in his hands and turned her to face him. 'We have hardly had a chance to converse at all.'

She refused to look up and he put a finger under her chin and raised it so that she was forced to look into his eyes. She shivered apprehensively and he, aware of it, smiled. 'Are you afraid of me?'

'No. Should I be?'

'Not at all.' He lowered his mouth to hers but he had hardly touched her lips before she realised what was about to happen and pulled herself away. 'Mr Bellamy, I must go. Mama will be concerned.'

'Very well.' He sighed melodramatically. 'Another time perhaps, when we can contrive to be alone and you have learned to relax in my company.' He stooped and cupped his hands for her foot and in a moment she was in the saddle again where she felt more at ease.

They had almost reached the gate when she saw Duncan approaching on Caesar and her heart suddenly seemed to beat twice as fast as usual and her hands to shake. He was riding leisurely, as if he had all the time in the world. He could not have seen what had taken place, could he? Oh, she prayed he had not!

He reined in when they met. He looked very impressive in the uniform of a hussar and she wondered if he had rejoined his regiment. Did that mean she would not see him again? The thought made her suddenly sad.

'Miss Martineau, I hope I find you well?' he said, searching her face, trying to read she knew not what, but she felt the colour flare in her cheeks and it put her on the defensive.

'Very well, thank you, Captain.'

He turned to Andrew, forcing himself to be polite for Molly's sake. 'Bellamy. I did not know you were in town.'

'How could I resist, when this lovely lady is here? We have been having quite a coze, you know. Delightful.'

'I am sure.' Not by a flicker of the eye did he betray his deep concern. 'Molly, allow me to escort you home.'

'I have Mr Bellamy to escort me,' she retorted.

'And I do not remember giving you permission to call me Molly.'

'It seems you have been given your congé, Stacey,' Bellamy said with a wide grin which made Duncan want to hit him again. 'I should accept it with a good grace, if I were you.'

'Miss Martineau?' Duncan appealed to her.

In spite of feeling uncomfortable with Mr Bellamy, Molly objected to being treated like a child by Duncan and so she smiled and picked up her reins again. 'Please do not trouble yourself, Captain. Mr Bellamy will see me safely home.'

He could not insist and was obliged to withdraw. She was still chasing her dream, still looking for her romantic hero. Did she think she would find him in Bellamy? He was sure marriage was not on the young man's mind, not to Molly, who had neither pedigree nor fortune, and he was afraid he was more likely to offer her carte blanche. Would Molly have sense enough to realise what was happening before it was too late? He doubted it.

There was nothing for it; he must join the *haut monde* and set out to try and win her hand in the way she dreamed of. But if he stayed in town, who was he to be? Not the Earl of Connaught; that was no longer possible. He supposed that Molly's assumption that he was a distant cousin of the Staceys was as good an identity as any and one which would be easier to maintain than a complete fiction, especially as he had always been known as Tony as a child to distinguish him from his father. Duncan Stacey was not a name anyone in today's *haut monde* would recognise, except Harriet who had known him since he was in leading strings, and she was too busy furthering her own ends to spread tattle about him.

Molly's escort chattered inconsequentially all the way back to Holles Street in spite of the fact that she was, for the most part, silent. She had been very rude to the Captain and she was burning with shame. Did he really think she preferred Mr Bellamy's company to his?

He helped her dismount at the gate and escorted her to the door. 'Thank you for your escort, Mr Bellamy,' she said, holding out her hand.

'Oh, you do not mean to send me away without introducing me to your mama, do you? I have been looking forward to meeting her.'

'I am not sure she is at home.'

'I understand,' he said, grinning. 'You do not wish her to know you were riding out alone. Your secret is safe with me.' He took her hand and bowed over it. 'But I shall expect to be rewarded.'

'Rewarded? But I have no money…'

He laughed. 'It was not money I was thinking of, my dear, but the opportunity to ride with you again. I shall call on you and suggest it. Adieu, my fair beauty.'

He turned and mounted his horse, just as the door was opened by Perrins. She hurried inside and up the stairs to change out of her habit.

'Molly, where have you been?'

She looked up, startled to see her mother at the head of the stairs. As she was obviously dressed for riding, there was nothing for it but to tell the truth. 'For a ride, Mama; it was such a lovely day I could not resist it.'

'Alone?'

'I set out alone, Mama, but I met Mr Bellamy and he gave me his escort.'

Harriet sighed with exasperation. 'Go and change into something more suitable for a young lady at home and then come into my boudoir. We must talk some more.'

Molly obeyed and a few minutes later was seated watching her mother, who stood beside her bed contemplating what to wear for a visit to the theatre that evening. The choice was between a green taffeta, trimmed with pink silk roses, and a ruby-red velvet banded in black and white braid.

'Now tell me exactly what happened this morning,' she said.

'Nothing happened, Mama. We met while riding and Mr Bellamy offered to escort me, nothing more.'

'Who else saw you?'

'There were a great many people about, but they did not take any notice of me. Why should they? They do not know me.'

'Thank goodness for that. But you will not do it again, do you hear me? Until I decide what is to be done, you will confine yourself to the house and garden...'

'But, Mama...'

'I blame Tony Stacey. When he does decide to put in an appearance—which give me leave to doubt, for he is assuredly more concerned with his own pleasures than the ruined hopes of a young lady— I shall ring a peal over him for leading you astray.'

'Mama, that is unfair! He has not ruined my hopes and he did not lead me astray. He was always very proper and kind and generous. I told you that. If it had not been for him I would have had no clothes...'

'Rags!' her mother said, referring to Molly's purchases and not the velvet gown she had just picked up and was eyeing critically. 'I could wear my rubies with this. But I am not sure they suit my colouring. What do you think?'

Molly was fairly sure her mother did not own any rubies and the necklace which lay on her dressing table was almost certainly fake. 'I think they would look very fine.'

'But the green shows off my figure better, does it not?' She stood up and held the taffeta gown against her ample bosom, then clad in amber sarcenet. 'And the emeralds have more sparkle. The same colour as my eyes.'

'Whichever you like, Mama. They are both beautiful.'

'Of course they are! I am known for my elegance and would not be seen in such dowdy things as those Tony Stacey bought for you.'

'Oh, I know they are not of the first stare,' Molly admitted, 'for I have been looking at the pictures in your *Lady's Magazine* and *La Belle Assembly*, but they suit me very well.'

'Oh, they are quite good enough for someone living in the seclusion of the country, which is where you belong. I cannot think why he did not take you straight back to Stacey Manor when he first found you.'

'I think he had arranged to meet Sergeant Upjohn and there was no time. They had business together.'

'I am beginning to wonder if he is this Dark Knight you spoke of, after all. It is the sort of rig he would get up to. I collect he was always falling into scrapes when he was a boy. I would not be surprised if he weren't playing some deep game of his own.'

Molly was inclined to agree but did not say so. 'He cannot be that bad for Aunt Margaret is very fond of him.'

'That don't mean he ain't up to something. Are you sure you have told me the whole?'

'Oh, yes, Mama.'

Harriet looked closely at her daughter, wondering if she was as innocent as she sounded. 'You have not set your cap at him, have you? You will come home by weeping cross if you have. I believe he is still repining for Beth Gooderson and has forsworn marriage.'

'You mentioned the name of Beth before,' Molly said. 'And he did admit there was someone who disappointed him, which was excessively unkind of her.'

'She thought he was dead, killed at the Battle of Vittoria or some such, so how was it unkind of her?'

'She married someone else?'

'She married his brother.'

'Oh, poor Duncan! His brother took his title and his love! No wonder he is sometimes a little out of humour.'

'What I should like to know is what he is going to do about it. There will be a farrago over it, to be sure, and I wish we had not got mixed up in it.'

'I am not privy to his intentions,' Molly said, with a spirit intended to hide her misery. 'But I'll wager he will do nothing. I think he will go back to a life on the road. I doubt we shall see him again.'

The thought of never seeing him again made her feel very, very sad, as if something sweet and wonderful had slipped from her grasp before she had managed to catch it properly. And trying to convince herself there had never been anything between them and that he had kissed her when he was not feeling himself, and that her life from now on would be full of new experiences and new excitement, did not work at all.

Chapter Ten

Duncan took his mount back to Connaught House and then went shopping, taking in Weston's to have pantaloons and waistcoats made up and to Scott for a new frockcoat; they had made his uniform and he liked their military cut. He went to Hoby's for boots and Locks for hats and finally dropped in at Robinson and Cook in Mount Street on his way back to order a phaeton. None of it would be ready before the end of the week and by that time the money from the War Department would be safely in his bank to pay for it. Then he set out for Holles Street.

Molly was sitting with her mama in the small parlour when Betty announced his arrival.

'Oh, he has come,' she murmured, and found her heart lifting with pleasure.

'Show him into the withdrawing room,' Harriet instructed Betty, and then said to Molly, 'Stay here. I wish to speak to the Captain alone.'

'Oh, Mama, you are not going to roast him, are you?'

'Naturally I am. He need not think that I will allow him to play fast and loose with my daughter and do nothing about it.' And with that she swept out of the room.

The last thing Molly wanted was to be excluded from the conversation and she followed to listen outside the door.

'Your obedient,' Duncan said, sweeping Harriet a bow. 'I trust I find you well?'

'I would be better if you had not saddled me with that madcap of a daughter. She tells me you passed her off as your wife, and in a common tavern too.'

'She told you that?'

'Of course she did; she has no idea how to dissemble, as you must know by now. She is no more than an innocent child and has no idea how to go on in Society, but you should have known better. You have ruined her reputation and mine along with it.'

'Oh, I would not say that,' he said wryly. It was not that he was not sorry for what had happened, because no one regretted it more than he did, but he would be a sousecrown if he admitted that to Harriet, who had done more to ruin her daughter's hopes than anything he had done. 'No one will think anything of it if you take her out and about, which is all she wants. She has talked of nothing else since I met her.'

Molly, creeping to the door and putting her eye to the keyhole, saw her mother sitting on the sofa fanning her flushed cheeks and the Captain standing with his back to the hearth, looking down on her. He was still dressed in his uniform, which set off his broad shoulders and long, shapely legs.

'That will only make matters worse. If any of this is whispered over the teacups, we shall both be undone.'

'No reason why it should,' he said reasonably. 'I'm not about to noise it abroad and I'll wager you will not. As for Miss Martineau, all she wants is for someone to pay her a little attention.'

'Then I suggest you do it.'

'Perhaps I will,' he said, so softly that Molly, on the other side of the thick door, could not hear it.

'But not in town, not where we will be the laughing stock of the *haut monde*. Take her back to Stacey Manor.'

'Ma'am, you shock me. How could I do that? It would be highly improper and, besides, she would be so disappointed.'

'It is no more improper than the way you brought

her here. I think your disappointment over Beth Gooderson must have addled your brains. You cannot suddenly come to life again and think everything will go on as before. You should not be in town at all. I wonder at your audacity.'

'Oh, I have audacity and to spare, ma'am,' he said, smiling lazily. 'But there is no need for you to disturb yourself over it. I am a distant cousin of the Earl up from the country.'

'And you would do well to return there post haste before Beth comes to town. And take my daughter with you.'

'I cannot do that, ma'am; I have other engagements. Things to do, you know. Besides, she would not go.'

'She will do as she is bid.'

Duncan was not so sure. Molly had a mind of her own and if she decided she would not go, only tying her up and carrying her to a coach would make her budge. That was no way to treat her. She needed to be handled with affection and humour and persuasion— all attributes he had never pretended to have, though he was learning fast. 'Then you may look to someone else to take her back, ma'am, for I will not do it.'

Molly was near to tears. She crept away and climbed the stairs to her room and sat down on the bed to stare at the hideous green wallpaper. No one wanted her, not her mother, nor Captain Stacey, and she had been a ninny to think that she could turn up on the doorstep and all would be well.

Now she would never have the opportunity to wear that lovely ballgown the Captain had bought for her, nor would she go on picnics and to the theatre or to Almack's, which she understood was the height of acceptability. Her mother would go out tonight and she would be left behind, just as she had been at Stacey Manor.

She heard the front door shut behind the Captain and it was as if the door had been shut on her happiness. He would go back to his life on the road with Sergeant Upjohn, to have more adventures, while she would be sent back to Norfolk and her humdrum existence there until her mama remarried. If she remarried; it seemed that her unwelcome arrival might well have put that in jeopardy.

She heard her mother come up the stairs and looked up as she opened the door. 'There you are, child! I have told Tony Stacey straight what I think of his behaviour and given him his right about.'

'What did he say?'

'Very little to the point. Not even an apology.'

'He has nothing to apologise for. Mama, I wish you had not scolded him; you will give him an aversion to me, for he will think I wanted you to do it, and I do not at all wish him to think that. He was very brave and clever and saved my life…'

Harriet peered at her daughter. 'I was right. You *have* developed a *tendre* for him.'

'No, Mama, there is nothing but cousinly affection between us.' She was deceiving herself, she knew. The way she felt about him, the tingling sensation in her limbs when he touched her, the enchantment of his lips on hers which made her melt inside, was not a cousinly feeling at all.

'You noddicock! He will not marry you, even if I were to insist upon it, which I will not, for I would not saddle you with a rakeshame such as he is. You would do better to cultivate Andrew Bellamy.'

'Mr Bellamy!' Molly protested. 'Oh, Mama, no.'

'Now I am going to rest,' Harriet went on as if she had not spoken. 'I must be in looks when I go out tonight. Cook has instructions for your supper. Tomorrow we will sit down and talk about what is to be done.' She smiled suddenly. 'Do not look so Friday-faced; we will come about.' With that she was gone, leaving Molly to her tumbling thoughts.

Her mother's strange smile had disturbed her. Had Mama suddenly changed her mind about giving her a come-out? Molly's spirits lifted, but were as suddenly dampened. Two or three weeks before she would have been overjoyed at the prospect but now she was not at all sure she wanted it, if it meant she had to drop the handkerchief to Andrew Bellamy.

The dream of going into Society seemed hollow now, meaningless, a sham. She had grown up, just as Duncan had said she would. Duncan, Earl of Connaught, soldier, highwayman, rakeshame. She would rather be dashing about the countryside with him, taking risks, enduring discomfort, than be the finest, the most desirable young lady in town. But it was not to be. Her mother had sent him away and she would not see him again.

Duncan was puzzled when Molly did not appear at any of the innocuous entertainments he would have expected her mother to sanction, though Harriet was very much in evidence, parading the Marquis of Tadbury like a trophy. She had probably passed herself off as a widow with a fortune. If that were so, they were both in for a shock; the Dowager Lady Tadbury was a pinchpenny and kept her son on very short commons. She would make stringent enquiries before she opened the purse strings sufficiently to allow him to marry.

'Where is Miss Martineau?' Duncan asked Harriet when he met her at a rout given by Lady Driffield. It was a dreadful squeeze and he had spent the better part of the evening wandering from room to room and even into the conservatory and the library looking for her and her daughter among the guests.

'At home, in Holles Street; where else would she be, considering you would not take her back to Norfolk? I see now why not. You prefer to racket about town. I shall be interested to see what happens when someone recognises you.'

'I do not see why they should. I was a mere stripling when I left home and war has a way of ageing a man.'

'I cannot think what game you may be playing, unless you are planning to reclaim your inheritance.'

'And if I were?' he queried.

'It would be seen as an act of vengeance. Your brother took your title and your betrothed and you cannot forgive him, but I doubt it would make you popular.'

'If there was anything to forgive, I forgave him a long time ago,' he said, deciding to say nothing of the fact that he had received a letter from Carlton House only that morning telling him that he had been awarded a baronetcy for services to his country; he could now call himself Sir Duncan Stacey.

'And Beth?'

'Beth is my brother's wife. I wish them happy.'

'Do you mean that?'

'Indeed, I do. And if I hear that you have had a hand in spreading tattle to the contrary I shall fetch

Molly from the garret where you have imprisoned her and introduce her to the whole *ton*. You will have to acknowledge her.'

'I have not imprisoned her,' she said indignantly. 'Why, you know very well she has been out with Mr Bellamy.'

'Is he still dangling after her?'

'What a vulgar way of expressing it,' she said. 'But then I should not expect anything else from someone who has been out of Society so long— you have not the least idea how to behave like a gentleman.'

'Is he?' he persisted.

'He has called once or twice and taken her in the park in his phaeton. And do not look so shocked; she was chaperoned by Betty.'

'I am surprised at you allowing it, ma'am. His interest in Molly is not as a wife.'

'Oh, I think he can be brought up to the mark. Molly is not without breeding and she is a pretty little thing. I am persuaded she is already inclined favourably towards him. And anyone can see he is enamoured of her.'

Duncan was dismayed. 'You would not force her?'

'No, of course I would not force her. Do you take me for a monster?'

'Then you will give her a proper come-out?'

'There is not the least need for that; the whole thing can be managed very quietly.'

The interest in the evening's entertainment was gone and he took his leave, seething on Molly's behalf. How could Harriet use her daughter so? Not only was Molly not to have the Season she longed for, she was to be married off in a havey-cavey way which would break her heart. And his. He told himself he would not have minded seeing her at every Society function, beleaguered by eager beaux, if it meant she was happy. But to hide her away and only let her out with that rake, Andrew Bellamy, was an unkindness of the first water. He could not let it happen unless Molly herself told him she wanted it. If she did, he would withdraw, leave the country, die a second time.

Molly's disappointment was profound, but she did not blame anyone but herself. She should not have run away, nor inveigled the Captain into bringing her to London; her mother was right to be angry. Except for carefully orchestrated outings with Mr Bellamy, she was confined to the house and the overgrown garden and was expected to pass her time with no other company but the housekeeper and Betty, who accompanied her when she went for a walk in the park or to look at the shops or change her book at Hookham's library. How long would this punishment go on? Would she be sent back to Stacey Manor at the end of it? Would Lady Connaught even have her back?

It was at breakfast next morning that Harriet, enthusing to Molly about the rout which had, in the eyes of everyone there, been a great success, let slip that she had spoken to Duncan.

'The Captain is in town?' Molly's eyes lit up and then immediately clouded again. 'Why has he not called on us?'

'Why should he?'

'I hoped… Did he not even ask how I did?'

'No, but then I hardly said five words to him.' Harriet had no intention of telling her daughter the truth—that Captain Stacey had talked of nothing else; it would only unsettle her.

'How did he seem? Is he fully recovered?'

'I must admit he looked in fine fettle, flirting with every unmarried lady in the room, and even some that were not single.'

'Oh.'

Harriet looked closely at her daughter's dejected countenance. 'Molly, you must put him from your mind, you really must.'

Molly wished she could. Her obsession with the Captain quite spoiled her outings with Mr Bellamy when she found herself constantly comparing the two men. And though Mr Bellamy was the picture of elegance and his manners were excessively correct when they were in the presence of her mama she sensed a falseness about them.

He could turn a pretty compliment and brought her flowers and sweetmeats when he called, and she thanked him properly, but she did not think he was sincere. For one thing, she knew she was not the 'loveliest blossom in all of London', and it was a falsehood to say it. Mama said that was how things were done and she ought to learn to accept compliments in the spirit in which they were given. But what she could not fathom was exactly what was meant by that.

The Captain was different. He rarely praised, preferring to gammon her or even to scold, but when she thought about it carefully she decided she would rather that than Mr Bellamy's fulsomeness; it was more honest and easier to deal with.

'Will the Captain be at Lady Tadbury's masked ball, do you think?' she asked.

Harriet shrugged. 'I doubt it. He is, on his own admission, only a poor relation of Connaught's and only lately come to town, for all the silly articles swooning over him and calling him handsome and daring and mysterious. Her ladyship would have more sense than to include him.'

'Why?'

'Why? Because the ball is being given for her daughter Letitia, the Marquis's sister, and she has only just come out. Only the top one hundred will be invited and as far as the world is concerned Stacey is only a half-pay captain in the Hussars.'

'You will be there.'

'Naturally I will; the Marquis and I have an understanding.' She smiled suddenly. 'I shouldn't wonder if the announcement were made at the ball.'

Molly sighed. 'I wish I could go.'

'You know you cannot. It is not the thing for a young lady not yet out to attend a ball unless it be her own come-out ball.'

Molly concluded that her mother used the conventions when it pleased her and disregarded them when it did not, but she decided not to comment on that. 'I should so like to go to a ball before I return to Norfolk.'

'No, Molly. But do not look so glum. I promise you that if all goes as I hope it will I shall have a little supper party and introduce you to a few select people.'

It was not a supper party Molly wanted. She wanted to wear the lovely ballgown Duncan had bought her, to watch all the guests in their silks and satins, dancing under the chandeliers, to listen to the music and smell the flowers and, most of all, to dance herself.

It just wasn't fair that she should be left at home to dream while her mother, who had been to hundreds of balls and often pretended they were a boring duty, should go. It was to be a masked ball so how would anyone know she had not yet come out? No one of the *ton* knew her, except Mr Bellamy. Would he be there? Would Duncan? But her mother had said she was sure he would not be invited.

The more she thought of it, the more the imp of mischief which habitually sat on her shoulder when she was thwarted urged her to rebel. She would go. But how could she accomplish it? The problem occupied her mind to the exclusion of all else for the next three days.

On the evening of the ball, she sat on the bed in her mother's bedchamber and watched her dressing. She was going as Queen Elizabeth, in a brocade gown so impossibly tight over the bust, Molly wondered how she could breathe without popping out of it. She had fake diamonds in her great orange wig and a starched lace ruff about her throat which made turning her head difficult. Her skirt was four feet wide, looped and garlanded. The whole thing was finished off with a white satin mask, a chicken-skin fan and a quizzing glass dangling from a ribbon about her wrist.

'Lovely, Mama,' she said. 'Do you think anyone will recognise you?'

Her mother laughed. 'Not until we unmask at midnight. That is half the fun of it, keeping people guessing.'

'Does that always happen? I mean if someone knew you really well…'

'If they knew you well, naturally they would recognise you. Tadbury would almost certainly recognise me whatever I wore, but as I am going with him it is of no consequence. And I suppose if someone had a distinguishing mark, like a scar or a mole, or a figure you could not mistake, like the Prince Regent's…'

'But someone who was quite ordinary and had not been seen in Society before would remain anonymous?'

Harriet looked at her curiously. 'I suppose so. Why do you ask?'

'Oh, no reason. I was just dreaming…'

'That is half your trouble, Molly—you dream too much. Life is not like that. Now, I must go.'

She picked up her cloak and reticule as the front door knocker resounded through the house and Perrins came to tell her his lordship, the Marquis of Tadbury, was waiting for her downstairs. She pecked the air six inches from Molly's cheek, told her gaily not to expect her home before dawn and not to stay up reading too late, and disappeared.

As soon as she heard the front door shut, Molly

raced to her own room where Betty was waiting for her. 'They've gone,' she said, stripping off her day gown and slipping into the ballgown which she had persuaded the maid to clean and press. It looked as good as new; the blue-green crepe had lost none of its translucence and floated about her slim figure like a gossamer cloud.

She had removed the flowers which had trimmed it and replaced them with woodland greenery. Betty put her hair up in the Greek style, finishing it off with a coronet of ivy. Her mask of green velvet was tied on with a narrow green ribbon. The last thing she wanted was for it to fall off.

'There!' Betty said, standing back to admire her handiwork. 'You will be a sure hit.'

Molly took a deep breath, slipped on her Greek sandals and picked up her fan and reticule, in which she had put the last of her Newmarket winnings; her mother had not thought it necessary to provide her with pin money. 'I am ready. What time did you tell the cab to come?'

'Nine. Are you sure you want to go alone?'

'Oh, yes, for if Mama ever found out you had helped me she would turn you off.'

Betty realised the truth of this and was grateful. She led the way down to the hall just as Perrins opened the door to the cabman. Molly sailed out into the balmy evening air and climbed into the hackney with all the aplomb she could muster. How to get in to the ball without an invitation she was not at all sure, but her adventures with the Captain had taught her self-reliance and ingenuity and she would manage that when the time came.

She arrived within three hundred yards of the Tadbury mansion in Bedford Row in no time but then they came to a stop. Looking out of the cab, she could see a long line of carriages all waiting to pull up at the door. As soon as one had deposited its occupants, the empty carriage rolled away and the next drew up. It was going to take an eternity to reach the entrance and she realised, too, that each arrival was being carefully scrutinised by a footman and invitations checked. She could not go in that way.

'I'll walk from here,' she called up to the driver.

He was glad enough of that; time was money and he did not like wasting it sitting in a line going nowhere. He jumped down and opened the door for her. She gave him the fare he asked for and the cab rattled away, leaving her standing in the road, wondering how to go on.

She walked purposefully up to the house and then, with a quick look round to make sure she was not observed, skipped round the corner of the building and made her way stealthily to the rear of the house, guided by the tuneful music of a country dance. It was a warm night and the windows onto the terrace were open, their curtains wafting slightly in the breeze. She crept up and gazed inside.

The ballroom was brilliantly lit and crowded. Every historical figure she could imagine was represented: kings, queens, pirates, highwaymen, harlequins and columbines, milkmaids, court jesters, Roundheads and Cavaliers, Greek gods and goddesses whose costumes were so revealing she was shocked.

There were a few matrons and old men sitting on the sidelines watching the younger ones dance. Little huddles of young ladies stood and giggled, peering over their fans at groups of young men who pretended indifference. The music was setting her feet tapping and she longed to be in among them. The windows were deep and it was only a matter of stepping over a foot of wall and she would be in, behind one of the curtains.

'What are you doing there, miss?'

She turned to see a liveried footman advancing towards her. Her first impulse was flight, her second to stand her ground; he could not know every guest when they were all masked. 'It was so hot indoors, I came out for fresh air,' she said. 'Now I cannot find my way in again.'

'You will ruin your clothes going in by the window, miss,' he said. 'And there is a door not ten feet away.'

She did not tell him she had seen it and seen the footman who guarded it as well. 'Oh, what a ninny I am!' She moved towards it, wondering what she would do if the second footman stopped her.

'There you are, my dear,' said a familiar voice. 'I have been looking for you everywhere.'

She spun round to see a highwayman, complete with black three-cornered hat, cloak and black mask standing beside a garden seat not six feet away.

'Oh, Captain.' Although she tried to keep her voice light and unconcerned, she could not disguise the fact that she was unashamedly pleased to see him. 'I lost myself in the garden.'

He had accepted Tadbury's invitation in the hope of meeting her, but when Harriet had turned up without her he had been sorely disappointed, assuming she had been sent back to Norfolk after all. He'd been as sorry for Molly as he was for himself, and very angry with Harriet. Wandering out into the garden to calm himself, he had seen Molly contemplating climbing in a window. She had not changed; she was still the madcap Molly he loved.

'And now you are found. Come along in, my dear; I do believe they are playing a waltz.' And with that he took her arm and sauntered past the footman who had accosted her and the one who stood at the door and she found herself in the ballroom.

'I cannot waltz,' she hissed at him, blinking in the bright light.

'Of course you can. Listen to the rhythm of the music, follow my lead and don't you dare tread on my toes.'

He put one hand about her waist, took her hand with the other and whirled her into the middle of the floor. She had no choice but to do as he said and suddenly found she was enjoying it.

Everyone else faded into the background and it felt as if they were alone, moving in perfect rhythm to the music, at one with each other. Her temerity in coming, her nervousness, her fear of being caught all disappeared in a haze of joy. He did not speak and, for once, she was silent.

But it came to an end all too soon and he led her to a quiet corner, pushing two chairs close together so that they might talk uninterrupted.

'Now,' he said, admiring her composure; any other young miss would have been shaking with nerves. 'Tell me what you thought you were about. Climbing in at the window of a ballroom crowded with people is not the way to remain anonymous, you know. Or did you wish to embarrass your mama in front of half the *haut monde*?'

'How could I? No one knows me.'

'Not anyone?' he asked in surprise. 'Then who brought you?'

'No one. I came in a cab but as there was such a line at the door I sent it away and walked.'

'Why?'

'I told you, there was a long line and I would have had to pay for every minute we stood idle…'

'No, you goose, I meant why did you come?'

'I am to go back to Stacey Manor but I did not want to go without wearing this beautiful gown you bought me. I thought as everyone was masked…'

So, she thought the gown was beautiful. On her it was, though he realised most young ladies of her age would decry it as too plain. It had a simple elegance that enhanced her delightful figure. 'They will unmask at midnight.'

'Oh, I shall be gone by then.'

'Have you asked the cabman to come back for you?'

She looked nonplussed. 'No, I did not think of it…'

He smiled. 'I think I had better take charge of you.'

'Oh, no, that will not do.'

'Why not? Oh, I know you think I am an old goat…'

'I do not think anything of the sort, my lord.' That was perfectly true. She no longer thought of him as old, nor of herself as young; somehow or other she had grown up to meet him.

'My lord?' he repeated. 'I am not your lord or anyone else's.'

'Yes, you are; Mama told me. She said you were really the Earl of Connaught come back from the dead. And you were a rakeshame and always would be and Beth Gooderson has had a lucky escape…' The words tumbled out breathlessly.

'Undoubtedly she has. And so have I.'

'You cannot mean that. Mama thinks you are still suffering over it and that is why you have been riding about the countryside calling yourself the Dark Knight.'

'You were the one who clung to that notion— something to do with Don Quixote, or some such romantical nonsense, I collect. I never said it. Highway robbery is not romantic; it is a crime for which the punishment is hanging.'

'Do you wish to be hanged? Is that why you take such risks, because you are tired of life?'

He smiled. 'Molly, I am not tired of life. I am very glad to be alive, especially at this moment.'

She did not recognise the compliment for what it was and ignored it. She looked him up and down, noting that his costume was made of the very best materials, that the frills that fell from the cuffs of his shirt were of handmade lace and that a diamond pin in his skilfully tied cravat twinkled in the light from the chandelier above their heads. 'No, for I perceive the cards have fallen successfully for you again.'

He laughed. 'How well you know me, Molly.' He was suddenly serious. 'Or perhaps you do not know me at all. Perhaps I am Don Quixote, after all, rescuing a damsel in distress.'

'I am not in distress.'

'You will be when your mama finds you here. Why do you do these foolish things, Molly?'

'For the same reason you do the hare-brained things you do—for adventure. Life would be very dull without it.'

'True,' he said. 'But I am a man and you are…' He paused and finished softly, 'You are a dream.'

'You know, I dreamed of being a female high toby,' she said, disregarding the second compliment she had received from him in the space of a minute. 'A daring rider, known the length and breadth of the country for taking from those who did not deserve their wealth and giving it to the poor. That would be an especially commendable adventure, don't you think?'

He laughed. 'An impossible dream, my dear, and sooner or later we have to face reality.'

'Yes, I know. I must go back to Stacey Manor and you… What will you do?'

'Oh, I shall contrive.'

'By gambling and taking risks. I wish you would not. I should hate to see you hang.'

'How did we come to be talking about me, when it is clearly you who have the problem?'

'Please do not concern yourself on my account. I have worn my ballgown and had my dance...'

'And is that enough?'

'You told me I had to face reality.'

'So I did, but I think we can prolong the dream for an hour or two. Come, let us take a last turn about the floor before we go.'

And for a second time that evening she was on the dance floor being whirled round in a rapture of joy which was not lost on the chaperons who habitually sat on the sidelines making comments on everyone. 'It's the second time he has danced with her,' they said. 'Who are they?'

'I believe he is the Earl of Connaught's relative,' said another. 'But who the young chit is, I have no idea. Some barque of frailty, I shouldn't wonder; she don't seem to have a chaperon.'

Molly did not want it to end, but when it did she was surrounded by young men, all clamouring to mark her card, including Andrew Bellamy, dressed as a Cavalier. Duncan stood back and smiled stiffly as she was claimed and whisked away. It was what she wanted and who was he to deny her a little happiness?

'Miss Martineau, how lovely you look tonight,' Andrew said as they stepped hand in hand into the dance.

'You know me?' she said in dismay.

'Of course. Did you think a scrap of velvet would be disguise enough? I would know your figure anywhere—such grace of movement, such perfection. It would put Venus to shame. And those eyes! Ah, the eyes! What can I say to do justice to their colour, their brightness? And rosy lips made for kissing…'

'Mr Bellamy, I beg you, desist,' she said, laughing. 'You will make me puffed up with your flummery.'

The dance took them away from each other as they paraded down the outside of the line of dancers. At the top of the room, they came together again. 'There is to be a firework display at Vauxhall Gardens on Saturday evening,' he said as they promenaded in a circle round each other. 'It promises to be very fine and there will be musicians and tableaux. Will you allow me to escort you?'

She sighed. 'I think I shall have gone back to Norfolk by then.'

'Oh, you must not; you must not deprive Society of one of the brightest stars in its firmament.'

'It is not my choice.'

They moved hand in hand down the long line of dancers. 'I shall go at once and speak to your mama.'

'No, please don't. She does not know I am here…'

'Then who brought you? Could it be the highway-man? I fancy when we unmask we shall see the face of that rakeshame, Captain Stacey.'

'He did not bring me. I came alone.'

'Really?' He looked closely at her and smiled knowingly. 'Then if you do not want your mama to know I think you should repay me for my silence by allowing me to escort you home.'

'There is no need; the Captain has already offered and I have accepted.'

'Give him his right about.'

'Oh, no, I could not do that. I promised…'

'And promises count with you, do they?'

'Oh, yes. I should never break my word.'

'Then I must accept that, but you will come to Vauxhall Gardens with me on Saturday?'

The intricacies of the dance separated them before she could frame a reply and when they returned to each other the music came to an end. He bowed and she curtsied and put her fingers lightly on his arm to be escorted from the floor. 'I will wait for you in my carriage on the corner of Holles Street,' he murmured as he returned her to her seat. 'Eight o'clock. Please do not disappoint me or you will break my heart.'

'Then I am afraid your heart will have to break,'

she said crisply. 'I am not so lacking in sense as to agree to meet you in such a clandestine way.'

He did not answer because at that moment the Marquis of Tadbury bowed over her hand and requested the pleasure of dancing with her. She smiled at Andrew and allowed herself to be led away. The Marquis was hardly less fulsome in his compliments than Mr Bellamy, but he was certainly a much worse dancer for he trod on her toes several times, blaming her loveliness for his lack of attention. She was thankful that he had not realised who she was.

She could see her mother out of the corner of her eye dancing with an older man and coming perilously close. Surely she could not fail to recognise her? But her eyes were only for the Marquis. Could she be jealous? The idea would have amused Molly if she had not been so anxious to steer her partner away from her mother—a move which was not lost on Harriet and was entirely misinterpreted.

At the end of the dance, Harriet claimed the Marquis before he could conduct Molly to her seat. For a moment she stood alone in the middle of the floor, feeling lost, and then she saw Duncan leaning nonchalantly against a pillar, watching her from beneath his dark lashes, a smile playing about his lips.

She walked over to join him. 'Are you going to ask me to dance again?'

'Twice is considered enough for couples who are not engaged to be married, my dear. And you have had partners enough. You are the belle of the ball. I heard the tabbies whispering, "Who is she? Where has she come from?" They are all agog to see you unmasked.'

'Mr Bellamy knew me, but I made him promise not to tell Mama. He was vastly amused.'

'I'll wager he was,' he said laconically.

At that moment a drum rolled and a hush of expectancy descended on the company; it was time to unmask. Duncan grabbed her hand and marched her off the floor, out of the nearest door and into the garden. 'Home, before any damage is done,' he said, giving her no time to argue.

They walked quickly round the side of the house and along the alley to the mews where his horse and phaeton were being looked after until he was ready to leave. He helped her in, climbed in beside her and picked up the reins.

'I think the damage is already done,' she said, when they had safely negotiated the line of vehicles waiting to be called up, and turned into the street. 'I am sure Mama recognised me. She was certainly giving me some strange looks when I was dancing with the Marquis.'

'It would be an unnatural mother who did not know her own offspring,' he said, though secretly he thought the reason for the strange looks had another cause altogether. 'But you will know soon enough. If I hear you have been locked in your room, then I shall know the reason.'

'Mama would not be so cruel. After all, I have not spoiled her evening. She danced a great deal and I could see her fluttering her fan and enjoying the latest *on-dit* with other guests. Who was the older man she was dancing with just now? He seemed very attentive to her.'

'That was Lord Brancaster.'

'You mean Mr Bellamy's father?' she asked in surprise.

'Yes.'

'Then I think you were very rash to come tonight when you knew he could denounce you the moment you unmasked, if not before. I know Mr Bellamy knew you. You will be lucky if he has not pointed you out to his father.'

'What has he to denounce me for? I returned his lordship's coach and paid him for his inconvenience. And, like you, I have left before the unmasking.'

'Why *did* you come? I was sure you would be on the open road again with Sergeant Upjohn.'

'I think those days are numbered, Molly,' he said, his spirits suddenly lifting to know she had been thinking of him. 'A man must settle down some time.'

'Oh.' She was silent for a moment. Was that why he had been attending Society functions and, according to Mama, flirting with all the unmarried ladies in town? He was looking for a wife. Another Beth Gooderson.

'Nothing to say, Molly?'

'I wish you happy.' It was said in a whisper, for she had suddenly realised she could not bear to think of him married to anyone else.

'My happiness lies in your hands, Molly.' He pulled up outside the house in Holles Street, but made no move to get out and help her down.

'Mine?' She was looking at him with those wide blue eyes, and a puzzled frown on her brow which made his heart lurch. Gambler he was, but suddenly he could not risk declaring himself. It was too soon, much too soon. And she still had not been invited to any Society gatherings and he was determined to see her wish granted.

'Yes,' he said, thinking quickly. 'You will make me happy if you will consent to accompany me to Vauxhall Gardens on Saturday. I shall ask your mama's permission, of course. She may like to come too. We will make a party of it.'

She had been holding her breath, but now she let it out in a great sigh of disappointment. He did not think of her as a wife at all; to him she was a hoyden, a fribble without a sensible thought in her head. And how could she blame him for that? It was exactly what she was; she had proved it over and over again with her madcap behaviour.

She pulled herself together and forced herself to sound light-hearted. 'Oh, so many suitors, all clamouring to take me to Vauxhall, but you know you are too late, Captain. Mr Bellamy has already asked me. I am to meet him at the end of Holles Street on Saturday evening.'

'Molly, you cannot mean to go in that haveycavey fashion? It is unthinkable.'

His arrogant attitude annoyed her. Instead of telling him that she knew that perfectly well and had no intention of going, she demanded to know why she should not. 'He is very attentive. He says I am beautiful and though I know that is a hum it is nice to be told.'

'It is not a hum,' he said softly. 'You are very lovely.'

She turned in her seat to look at him in the light from the gas lamps that lit the London street, and was disconcerted to find him looking down at her with an expression in his dark eyes she could not fathom. Hurt? Disappointment? Tenderness? Amusement? But there was no laughter in his eyes. 'You do not mean that.'

'I am not in the habit of telling whiskers, Molly.

Nor will I allow you to make a cake of yourself over that scapegrace…'

She laughed. 'Listen to the pot calling the kettle black.'

He smiled ruefully. '*Touché*, my dear.'

He was ready to wager Bellamy had no intention of requesting Harriet's permission, and asking Molly to meet him away from the house boded ill for her. But if he protested too much he would almost certainly throw her into the man's arms, and once she had been compromised she would be at his mercy. 'If he asks your mama first and you are well chaperoned, I suppose there is no harm in it,' he said, pulling up outside the house in Holles Street. 'But you are not to meet him clandestinely.'

Again she was disappointed. She realised she had only told him about Mr Bellamy to judge his reaction and all he had done was give her orders as cool as you please! 'Who are you to say what I must and must not do?' she demanded, scrambling down. 'You are not my keeper.' Without looking back she marched to the door.

He strode after her and took her shoulders in his hands, turning her towards him, resisting with a huge effort of self-control the temptation to shake sense into her. 'Molly, don't you realise the peril you are in?'

'From Mr Bellamy?' she asked. 'Or you? I collect you are not averse to taking a lady by surprise…'

It was too much. He pulled her roughly to him and lowered his mouth to hers. It was a kiss that started in exasperation, even anger, and ended in sweetness and tenderness. He understood the reason for it, but did she?

She made no move to draw away, did not squirm in his arms or lift her hand against him. She settled herself against his chest, her head tilted upwards, and loved it. Loved him. Knew she loved him.

He broke away at last and stood looking breathlessly at her, wondering what to say and saying nothing. What good would words do? He had lost his patience and made a mull of it.

She was too confused to understand. She ran from him and pushed open the door, glad she had asked Betty to make sure it was left unlocked so she did not have to summon Perrins.

He watched her go inside and the door close on her and murmured, 'Goodnight, my love,' before reluctantly returning to his carriage. Harriet had been right; he had been so long out of Society, he no longer knew how to behave towards a young lady of tender susceptibility.

Chapter Eleven

Feeling nothing but contempt for himself, he returned to Connaught House. Birtwhistle admitted him, still fully dressed. 'Oh, sir, I am glad you have come. Lady Connaught has arrived.'

He was startled. The last person he wanted to face was Beth. 'Is the Earl with her?'

'No, sir, I meant the Dowager Lady Connaught, not the Countess.'

'Grandmama! Why, she hasn't left Norfolk in the last ten years.'

'She is here now, sir. Before she retired she left instructions that you were to present yourself in the library at nine in the morning.'

'Thank you, Birtwhistle. Do you think you could rouse me at eight?'

'Yes, sir.'

He went up to the room he had been occupying

for the last ten days and went to bed. He had a very good idea why his grandmother had come to town, but it was no good losing sleep over it.

At precisely nine o'clock the next morning, he strolled into the library to find Lady Connaught sitting behind the great oak desk from which her late husband had directed the affairs of his vast estates. Besides Connaught House, there was a parcel of streets in the metropolis, bringing in considerable rents, Foxtrees and several surrounding farms, a hunting box in Leicestershire and a grouse moor in Scotland, besides Stacey Manor and its surrounds in Norfolk, which had been left to his wife without encumbrance.

She looked up as Duncan entered, noting his brown single-breasted frockcoat buttoned to the waist, his nankeen trousers which were strapped under the foot, his biscuit-coloured waistcoat and perfectly tied muslin cravat. He had shaved himself and his hair had recently had the attention of a barber for it was arranged in the latest windswept fashion.

'Good morning, Grandmama,' he said, kissing the back of her bejewelled hand.

'Is it?' she queried. 'It is impossible to tell in this dreary city, what with the high buildings and the smoke and fog.'

Duncan had seen no fog, but he let that pass. 'What brings you here, if you find it so little to your taste?'

'You do. You seem to be in fine feather.'

'I am, thank you.'

'What have you done with that chit, Molly?'

'I have done nothing with her. I took her to her mother, as I said I would.'

'And what did Harriet say about that?'

'She was hardly in raptures. Molly is kept closely confined and Harriet will not even acknowledge her as her daughter. It is monstrous the way she treats her and I do not wonder that Molly rebels.'

'Harriet did not insist on you making an offer for her?'

'No. On the contrary, she told Molly she would not saddle her with a rakeshame such as I am. She has her mind set on pushing her onto Andrew Bellamy.'

'Bellamy. You mean Brancaster's only son?'

'Yes. We met him on the journey to London and since we arrived he has renewed the acquaintance-ship, dancing attendance on her and paying her fulsome compliments, but I am prepared to wager that all he has in mind is carte blanche. Molly is a sweet and innocent child, a little spirited perhaps, but none the worse for that; she can have no conception of what the phrase means…'

'I thought so,' she said, nodding her head sagely.

'A few weeks in her company and you have learned her true worth. I knew you would. Why have you not offered for her?'

'Grandmama, have you forgotten I relinquished my inheritance, every last penny? I am a gambler and a scapegrace, as you yourself pointed out, and…'

'It is not the least use you blustering.'

'I have nothing to offer a young lady like Molly; I have nothing to offer any young lady.'

'I have been thinking of that. I came to bring you this. It might help.' She picked up a sheaf of papers which lay on the desk and handed them to him. 'As you and your brother have exchanged roles and he has the Stacey inheritance, leaving you with nothing, you shall have what I intended to bequeath to him as the second son. And you need not wait for my death; those are the deeds of Manor Farm. You always said you'd like to breed horses and it is ideal for that. But you offer for Molly, do you understand? I want to see you settled before I hand in my accounts. I shall call on Harriet this afternoon…'

'I hope you do not mean to press my suit for me,' he said, and there was a warning in his voice she perfectly understood. He did not like being pushed even when it was in the direction he most wanted to go. If Molly ever got to hear of it, she would conclude he wanted to marry her for the sake of owning a farm and she would surely turn him down. She was too much of a romantic to consider wealth when choosing a husband, and she would expect the man she married to feel the same way.

'Do you take me for a noddicock, that I should do such a thing? I shall suggest taking Molly under my wing for the rest of the Season. She can live here with me and you can move into Fenton's Hotel; it would never do for you both to be under the same roof. Molly shall have her come-out; I know how much it means to her. What you do about it is entirely your affair. If you decide you would not suit, then find someone else.'

He smiled ruefully as she rose and swept from the room, her taffeta skirt rustling, leaving him to his thoughts. There was no one else; there never would be.

Molly spent what was left of the night in silent misery. She had been the worst kind of fool. Everyone at that ball had been talking about her; it was no wonder her mother pretended not to know her.

Duncan had rescued her, saved her from making a cake of herself, given her a little taste of what it was like to be the centre of attention, and for that she was grateful to him. More than that, she loved him. For one short minute, when he'd said his happiness was in her hands, she had thought he returned that love and was going to ask her to marry him, but he had not.

He had been no better than Andrew Bellamy, suggesting an outing which she did not think was at all proper. The fact that Duncan had said he would ask her mama and Mr Bellamy had suggested meeting him secretly she completely ignored.

Like Mr Bellamy, he had taken her for the kind of girl he could kiss with impunity. What was the phrase? A little bit of muslin? For all he pretended otherwise, he was a member of the aristocracy and he would not forget that when choosing a wife. She did not fit the bill.

She fell asleep as dawn lightened the sky and woke in the middle of the morning with a bad headache. She was not sure if it was caused by the unaccustomed champagne or the churning thoughts in her head, but whichever it was she could not lie abed.

As soon as she had drunk the hot chocolate Betty brought her, she rose and dressed in the plainest of her new gowns and went downstairs to eat a lonely breakfast. Then she went into the small parlour to finish reading her novel. But she could not concentrate and her mind kept straying to Duncan Stacey. Who would have thought that she would fall in love with a man who was not at all the lover of her dreams? Nor had she needed to come to London to meet him. But having met him, having melted under his kisses, having given him her heart, she had waited in vain to hear him speak of love.

All he wanted was an undemanding companion for whatever devious game he was playing, a ready accomplice. Once she would have been content with that, but not now. Now she wanted more. Don Quixote was not enough. She had grown up in the last few weeks and it was a painful business.

Going to that ball had been a mistake and now she would never have her longed-for Season. Not that it mattered any more. She would go back to Stacey Manor, which would please Mama, if no one else.

Harriet joined her at noon. Dressed in an undress gown of blue silk and with her hair loose about her shoulders, she sank onto a chaise longue in the small parlour with every appearance of exhaustion.

'Did you enjoy the ball, Mama?' Molly asked, affecting innocence. 'Were there many people there? Did you recognise anyone in their costume?'

'Oh, I knew most of them, they have been doing the rounds all Season, but there were one or two strangers who disappeared before the unmasking. Tony Stacey was there dressed as a high toby, though that was hardly a proper disguise; I knew him at once. I own I was surprised he should have chosen that costume considering what you told me about the Dark Knight. I am not at all convinced he wasn't bamming us all.'

'You said you doubted Lady Tadbury would invite him.'

'Oh, that was Tadbury's doing. He thinks we are related and as Tony is a Stacey…'

'Was the Captain alone?'

'No, he was not. He had a chit with him dressed as a wood nymph or somesuch and though I asked Lady Tadbury she could not put a name to her, for which I was vastly relieved.' She paused and looked closely at her daughter. 'Did you think I would not know you? I never felt so mortified in all my life.'

'Oh, you did recognise me.'

'Naturally, I did. It was a shock, I can tell you. It is a wonder I did not have a seizure. Whatever possessed you to do such a cork-brained thing?'

'I did so want to go and you would not take me.'

'No, and is it to be wondered at? You have no idea how to conduct yourself. Tony Stacey put you up to it, didn't he? It is the sort of rig he would indulge in. I think he finds pleasure in vexing me, though why he should I do not know. I have never done him any harm…'

'It had nothing to do with the Captain. I went alone.'

'Alone!' her mother shrieked. 'Oh, Molly, how could you? You do know you are the talk of the *ton*?'

Molly could not suppress a little smile. 'I do believe people were asking who I was. The Captain said I was the belle of the ball.'

'Thank goodness Stacey had sense enough to whisk you away before everyone unmasked. You must never do anything like that again. Never, do you hear? If the gabblegrinders find out it was you, we shall be undone. We might as well find a dark hole and live in it in penury.'

'Oh, Mama, why should they find out? No one knew me except Captain Stacey. And Mr Bellamy, but he promised not to say a word to anyone.'

'We must make sure he does not. If I could persuade him to offer for you...'

'No, Mama, no!' she cried. 'We should not suit; really we should not. I do hope you have said nothing to him.' Then, remembering her mother had been dancing with Lord Brancaster, she added, 'You did not speak of it to his father? Oh, do tell me you did not.'

'No, of course I did not. These things have to be done in the proper manner.'

'Then I beg you, do nothing. I will go back to Stacey Manor, I will never embarrass you again, but please do not make me accept an offer from someone I do not, cannot, love.'

'Love! What has love to do with it?' She stood up and shook herself determinedly. 'Now I am going to change. I expect Lord Brancaster to call.'

Molly was appalled. 'But you said you had not spoken to him.'

'Of you, no. You are not the only subject of conversation, you know. In fact, it is one I avoid if I can.'

'Then I think I shall go to the library, Mama. I have finished my book and need another.'

'You read far too much, and what you do read is a fribble. No wonder you have such romantic notions.'

'There is nothing else for me to do, Mama.' It was said with a heartfelt sigh.

When she returned, she was astonished to find Lady Connaught with her mother in the withdrawing room. Her ladyship was still dressed in her old-fashioned mourning clothes but they did not detract from her imposing presence. She sat bolt upright, sipping tea, determination on every feature of her face.

'Here she is,' Harriet said. Her face, Molly noticed, was as puce as the silk day gown she wore and she looked decidedly uncomfortable. 'Come and make your curtsey, Molly.'

Molly obeyed and went to kiss her godmother's cheek. 'Aunt Margaret, I am truly sorry that I worried you. I should not have run away as I did, but you knew I was safe with Captain Stacey, didn't you?'

'I did not doubt it.'

'Then why are you here? I thought you hated London.'

'So I do, but I could not stand idle, knowing he would be bound to make a mull of everything.'

'How? He has done nothing wrong…'

'Nothing right either.' She paused. 'Enough of that. Now you are here, tell me, have you been out and about with your mama, seen the sights, met some of the eligibles?'

'She has had one or two carriage rides in the park,' Harriet put in before Molly could reply.

'Incognito, I shouldn't wonder.'

'Not at all. But she is not yet out…'

'And when were you going to bring her out?'

'Soon. I have yet to settle my affairs.'

'And does this settling of affairs involve a certain marquis?'

'That is all over. I decided we should not suit. He is too young and I have discovered he is fickle.'

This was news to Molly, though she remained silent.

'So you have spent all your blunt to no good purpose.'

'There is some way to go to the end of the Season. And there is someone else…'

'Then you will be fully occupied, I do not doubt, and poor Molly will be left out in the cold, as usual.'

Molly was shocked to hear her godmother speak to her mother like that, and she could not let her mama take all the blame. 'Aunt, it is not Mama's fault,' she put in. 'I arrived inopportunely and spoiled it all for her. I will come back to Norfolk with you and not bother her again.'

'Fustian!' She paused to look at Molly. 'I ain't going back to Norfolk, not yet. And don't look so Friday-faced; you shall have your come-out.'

Molly looked from her godmother to her mother in surprise. Her ladyship was smiling but her mother continued to look uncomfortable. 'Lady Connaught has offered to sponsor you,' she said.

'Oh.' Her initial delight was tempered with doubt. The prospect of going out and about and meeting other young people was no longer the epitome of her ambition. In truth, she would not have minded in the least if Lady Connaught had insisted on taking her back to Stacey Manor. The Season had lost its magic. It had faded the minute she realised how much she loved Duncan Stacey and how hopeless it was. 'But I do not wish to embarrass Mama and...'

'Any embarrassment she endures has been brought on by her own silliness,' her ladyship said. 'I should never have agreed to it in the first place. Now, Harriet, you will give up this house. I wonder at you taking it on when it is so far above your touch. You will be dished up before the Season is out...'

'I could not allow the world to think I was a pauper...'

Her ladyship ignored that. 'You will both come and stay at Connaught House with me. We will do the thing properly.'

'Did Tony put you up to this?' Harriet demanded.

Her ladyship gave a chuckle. 'Duncan is a mopstraw, doesn't know what's good for him, but that don't mean he'd come rattling to me to set things straight for him. He knows I can't abide maunderers.'

Molly could not see what begging had to do with it, but it seemed her mother had lost control of the situation and it was now very firmly in the hands of Lady Connaught. She sat by helplessly as the arrangements were made and the following Saturday accompanied her mother and a mountain of luggage, very little of which belonged to her, to Connaught House. She wondered if Duncan might be there, but he was not. He had moved into a hotel at his grandmother's insistence.

It was not because of lack of space, she soon discovered, for the house was huge and several families could have lived in it without encountering one another; it was done, so she was told, for convention's sake and because the Earl and Countess were expected soon.

In the next few days Lady Connaught took her shopping for clothes, all of which were modish and expensive, but she preferred the simple garments Duncan had bought her, just because he liked her in them. Rags, her mother had called them, but to Molly they were the stuff of dreams.

As soon as the *ton* learned that Lady Connaught was in town and sponsoring her god-daughter, the invitations began to flood in, but it was all too late. Molly found herself at tea parties, picnics and routs and being introduced to other young people, but instead of enjoying their gossip she found it shallow and meaningless. The young ladies simpered and the men were so excessively polite, she wanted to scream at them.

She saw Duncan occasionally at these gatherings, and sometimes he asked her to dance, or sat beside her at supper and made light conversation. But he was as bad as the rest; he talked inconsequentially about nothing, affecting a style and mannerisms which she was sure were completely alien to him.

'I wonder you are still in town,' she whispered to him when they chanced to be sitting beside each other at a musical evening. She had been enjoying the music, but was all too aware of the immaculately clad figure beside her.

Not so long ago he had had pockets to let, but now he was wearing a double-breasted evening coat of black brocade, a shirt and cravat of such whiteness they dazzled the eyes, and shining black shoes. Was he still gambling and winning? Or was the Dark Knight still about his business? But he was not the Dark Knight she reminded herself, so that did not signify.

'How could I leave while you are still gracing the capital with your presence?'

'That is flummery,' she said as the music came to an end and the audience began to applaud. 'It does not suit you.'

He laughed. 'I thought that was what you wanted. A little attention, you said. And Mr Bellamy seems to succeed with it.'

'I was a ninny to think that was important. I have grown up in the last month.'

'Oh, I do hope not.' He was looking at her quizzically with his head on one side, his eyes deep pools she could not fathom.

'What do you mean?'

'I liked you best as you were. Madcap Molly, game for anything.'

'The Dark Knight would think that, but you must have moved on yourself. Are you not thinking of settling down?'

'Indeed I am. I am going to breed horses.'

'Horses?' she queried, with an attempt at a laugh. 'Not children?'

'To have children one must have a wife. At least, if one is not to cause the most outrageous scandal.'

'And is that why you have been seen about town? You are looking for a wife?'

'I do not need to look. I have found the one I want.'

'Oh. Then I wish you joy.'

'Do you?' he asked softly.

She forced herself to sit still, though she longed to flee. 'Yes, naturally I do. And I hope we can still be friends...'

His laughter was so uninhibited, everyone turned to look at him, but he was unaware of it. 'Oh, Molly, Molly, you little goose...' He looked up as a shadow loomed over them. 'Oh, it's you, Bellamy. What do you want?'

Andrew ignored him and spoke to Molly. 'Miss Martineau, would you take a turn about the room with me?'

She rose and laid her fingers on his arm, anxious to escape from a situation and emotions she could not control. She hated Duncan Stacey for making her feel the way she did. It was unfair in him to take all her cherished dreams and wreck them with casual words, strew them at her feet and reveal their emptiness. Now she had nothing, not even a sense of adventure, for without him even adventure seemed meaningless.

She walked sedately round the room, following other couples doing the same thing, only half listening to Andrew's complaints that she had not kept their tryst and he did not intend to give up. Molly then became aware that Duncan had left his seat and was taking leave of their hostess. The next minute he was gone and the crowded room seemed suddenly empty.

It was next day she learned from Lady Connaught that he had left town. 'He has gone to Manor Farm,' she said. 'There are alterations he wishes to make and he has gone to put them in hand.'

'He told me he was going to breed horses,' Molly said, wondering how she was going to bear having him living with his new wife not two miles distant from Stacey Manor. She was convinced that was where she was bound. Her Season had been a total failure.

'What else did he say?'

'Nothing, except that he had met the lady he wanted for his wife.'

'Did he, now?' She peered at Molly short-sightedly. 'And how do you feel about that?'

'I said I wished him joy.' She spoke flatly. She

could not put into words exactly how she felt. She wanted to berate him for his blindness, to shout at him in frustration, at the same time as she longed for him to put his arms about her and kiss her as he had done twice before. The memory of those two kisses would live with her for ever, though they could have meant very little to him.

'I did not ask what you said,' her godmother said. 'I asked how you felt.'

'I don't know. A little sad, I think. He is such a free spirit…'

'You mean a scapegrace.'

'No, I don't. He is chivalrous and caring and…' Her voice trailed off.

'I do believe you are wearing the willow for him.'

Molly sighed. 'Perhaps I am, but there is nothing I can do about it. I cannot make him love me and if there is someone else…'

'Fustian! He does not know his own mind. You must make a push.'

'Oh, no, I could not do that. It would not be fair.'

'All's fair in love and war,' her ladyship said bluntly. 'Men are all children at heart; they need to be told what is best for them.'

'My lady, I do hope you will not say anything like that to him. It will give him an aversion to me and I do so want to remain his friend.'

'Oh, give me patience!' her ladyship exclaimed. 'You should have your heads knocked together.'

Harriet came into the room then, bursting with energy. 'Lord Brancaster is arranging a party on Saturday to visit Vauxhall Gardens,' she said. 'We are all to go.' She stopped and looked at her daughter. 'Why the Friday face? It is ungrateful of you to look so solemn when everyone is doing their best to entertain you. Why, I do believe Mr Bellamy suggested the outing to his father in order to please you and you should be happy about it.'

Molly forced a smile. 'I am perfectly content, Mama.'

'Good.' Harriet took her at her word. 'Now we must decide what to wear. You must be in looks for Lord Brancaster will want to look you over.'

'Mama!' She was horrified.

But all her mother did was laugh gaily and take her off to the dressmaker to have a new gown made. It was an open gown of creamy muslin, decorated with pale lemon embroidery over a silk slip. There was a lemon caraco jacket and a chip bonnet trimmed with yellow flowers. 'The essence of spring,' her mother said, putting it on Lady Connaught's account, along with the ruby taffeta gown she had bought for herself. 'Unsullied youth—Lord Brancaster will like that.'

'What has it to do with him?'

'If you are to make a push to catch the son, you must impress the father, for he holds the purse strings. And besides, there are other reasons…'

'What other reasons?'

'His lordship is a widower and I've heard he is looking for a wife.'

'Oh. But I thought you were tired of old men.'

'He is not so very old and age has its compensations. It has a mellowing influence.'

Molly could not help smiling at this but decided not to comment. What concerned her more was her mother's conviction that Andrew Bellamy meant to offer for her. She did not want to marry him and must let him down as gently as possible; she hated hurting anyone's feelings.

The party, consisting of Lady Connaught, Harriet, Lord Brancaster and Andrew, Lord Tadbury and his sister, Letitia, Lord and Lady Bonchance and their daughter, Naomi, travelled in several coaches to have supper at Rules, before going on to Vauxhall Gardens to listen to the concert and stroll about the lantern-lit gardens before fireworks brought the evening to an end.

The musicians played with verve and several of the songs were tuneful enough for the audience to join in, but Molly's thoughts were far away with

Duncan in Norfolk and were only brought back to the present when the applause at the end of the concert impinged on her reverie.

'Miss Martineau,' Andrew said, jumping to his feet and holding out his hand to her. 'Tadbury and Miss Bonchance are going for a walk before the fireworks start; shall we join them?'

She looked at her mama, who was sitting beside her with Lord Brancaster on her other side. 'Go on, child,' she said, before turning her smile on his lordship again.

'What do you think of the Gardens?' Andrew asked as they walked slightly ahead of the Marquis of Tadbury who had soon got over his disappointment with Harriet and had fixed his attention on Naomi Bonchance. They were deep in conversation and not paying the least attention to Andrew and Molly.

'I find they are fascinating—so much going on at once and so crowded.'

'They are only crowded near the pavilion, and in the more common walkways. There is more to see than this.' He waved his arm around him to encompass the pavilion and mown grass, the little hedges and pergolas. 'Come, I will show you.'

The Marquis and Naomi had fallen so far behind, they did not notice Andrew take her arm and draw her into one of the less frequented walks where the light of the lanterns did not reach. 'This is better, don't you think? I dislike an audience when I have something serious to say.'

Her heart began to beat uncomfortably; she could see that the walkway was dotted with little arbours and in almost every one there was a couple in each other's arms and their antics dismayed her. 'Mr Bellamy, I beg you, let us return to the others. I am not at all sure we should be here.'

'Why not? You know I have lost my heart to you, don't you?'

'No, I do not.'

'How can you not? I have been most attentive; you cannot deny that.'

'Yes, but I thought... I did not think...'

'Come, let us sit on this seat, while I show you just how much you mean to me.' He took her hand and pulled her into one of the arbours. 'I adore you. I need you in my life. I cannot conceive of anything more pleasurable than loving you. The idea consumes me with passion.'

'Mr Bellamy...'

'Call me Andrew, please,' he murmured, burying his head in her neck and kissing her. 'If we are to deal well together, you must learn to be easy with me.'

'Mr Bellamy.' She tried again. 'I am very sensible of the honour you do me, but I cannot accept...'

He laughed suddenly but it was not a happy sound and she shivered with apprehension. 'What a pretty speech, learned by rote, I shouldn't wonder. And that before you have even heard my offer.'

'Then I have saved you the trouble of making one.'

He smiled and stroked the back of his finger down her cheek. She was so rigid with inner tension, she could do nothing to prevent it. 'You are not such a ninny as to believe I had marriage in mind, are you?'

'You haven't?' Her words were whispered.

'Of course not. You have nothing to commend you as a wife, no fortune and no breeding, but as a ladybird—that is a different matter. You have exactly the right attributes—beauty, the figure of a goddess, the necessity of making your way in the world, and you do not care what people think of you or you would not go racketing about the countryside with a half-pay soldier and riding in the park astride a horse where the whole *ton* can see you. Such aplomb! Only a high-class impure could carry it off.'

She was beginning to understand. That was why Duncan did not want her! Not as a wife, not as anything. No wonder her mother did not wish to own her! But that did not mean she would succumb to Andrew Bellamy's blandishments. 'Sir, you have quite mistaken the matter.'

'No, I do not think so and I will prove it to you.'

He took her face in both his hands and kissed her with more force than finesse.

She squirmed as his mouth opened and his tongue forced its way between her lips. It was horrible. She grunted and pushed at his shoulders, forcing him to lift his head. 'Mr Bellamy, please…'

'Oh, I do please. Very much. And so do you.'

'I certainly do not. Let me go at once.'

'Not until you've heard me out. You shall have everything a woman could desire, all the clothes and knick-knacks you need, a well-furnished apartment and a carriage. All you have to do is to be there for me when I need you and be agreeable to my friends.'

'If you think I would agree to such an arrangement you are a bigger sousecrown than I took you for,' she retorted, as angry with herself as she was with him. How could she have been such a fool? 'I am not at my last prayers yet, and even if I were I would not consent to that.'

'You are unlikely to get a better offer, certainly not from Duncan Stacey, and you would do well to consider it.'

She stared at him in the gloom. His eyes were pinpoints of light in a dark face; the rest was shadow. She began to be very afraid, but determined not to let him see it. 'I never will. Please take me back to my mama.'

'Mrs Benbright! She is a demi-rep herself; she

will thank me for taking you off her hands. I'll wager she told you to encourage me.'

She did not answer; her mother had said something like that, but she had surely not been thinking of anything less than marriage?

All she wanted to do was escape, but he held both her hands. She forced herself to relax because only that way would he loosen his grip. As soon as he did, she kicked his shins very hard and stamped on his toes. While he yelped with pain, she made good her escape. Down the dark paths she fled, making for the lights she could see in the distance.

She stopped when she realised she could not go back to the party in the state she was in, nor tell anyone what had happened. It would cause no end of a scandal, and though she was innocent no one would believe she had not enticed Mr Bellamy. Her mother might even be pleased and insist on him marrying her. The very idea was abhorrent.

She was standing, trying to compose herself, when a tall figure loomed in front of her and grabbed her. She opened her mouth to scream, but he forestalled her and put his hand over her mouth. 'Not so fast, my pretty,' he said.

She struggled in vain. And then she heard Andrew's voice behind her. 'Oh, you foolish wench, did you think you could escape from me?'

'She's yours?' the man queried.

'Indeed, she is. A little firebrand too. I thank you for stopping her, for there is no telling what she would do if left to herself.'

'She is certainly a handful,' the man went on, holding Molly at arm's length while trying to avoid her kicking feet. 'You should teach her manners.'

'So I shall. My carriage is on the road, will you help me to get her to it?'

'No! No!' Molly yelled, and was immediately cuffed about the ear. She spat in his face which was a bad mistake. He hit her so hard she lost consciousness.

When she came to her senses, she was riding in a closed carriage. Andrew was sitting beside her and the man who had captured her was sitting opposite her; beside him was another man. They were talking quietly together and she decided not to let them know she had regained her senses.

'It was a stroke of luck bumping into the little lady,' the first man said.

'Why?' Andrew asked warily. 'What is your interest in her?'

'Oh, we ain't interested in her,' the second man said. 'But she can lead us to the man we want. Been tracking him for weeks…'

'Who might that be?'

'The Dark Knight.'

'The Dark Knight,' Andrew repeated, while Molly held her breath. 'You mean the high toby who has been terrorising the countryside?'

'Yes. This little one is his accomplice. You would never think it to look at her, would you? Demure as a whore at a christening, she is.'

'That's ridiculous. No one knows who he is.'

'She does. An' so do we. She's goin' to fetch him to us.'

'What do you want with him?'

'He's got property that belongs to our master. Took it off him, he did. We've been sent to fetch it back.'

'Why don't you go to a magistrate and have him arrested?'

'That won't serve, not at all.'

Molly was beginning to realise that Andrew had lost control of the situation. She could tell by the tone of his voice he was afraid, and yet he was ready to bluff his way out of trouble. 'The lady is my mistress,' he said. 'I say where she goes and she goes with me to a little house I've got prepared for her…'

'A love nest. So be it. You keep her there. We will do the rest.'

Molly stirred a little and the first man leaned across and poked her ribs. She flinched. 'She's coming round,' he said.

'Where am I?' She struggled to sit up and stared at the two men. She could see little in the gloom of the carriage, except that they were both dark and wearing dark clothes. One had long hair and straggly moustache and the other was very thin. 'Who are you?'

'No need for you to know,' the long-haired one said, with a grin.

'What do you want? Where are you taking me?'

'Bless you, we ain't takin' you anywhere. Lover boy is the one who's doin' the takin'. We're just going along for the ride, so to speak.'

'Oh.' She turned to appeal to Andrew. 'Mr Bellamy, please take me home.'

'Home?' he repeated. 'Why, of course, my dear. I'll take you to the prettiest little home imaginable. Be patient.'

'I meant Connaught House.'

'I'm afraid that is out of the question.'

'But Mama and Lady Connaught will be searching for me. You cannot simply abduct me and think no one will look for me.'

'They will not find you until it is too late.'

'Too late?' she queried, wondering if he meant to murder her.

'Too late to save your reputation,' he said, then smiled. 'Once you have spent a night in my company, you will be ruined in the eyes of the *haut monde*, a fallen woman—not that you aren't already, for you spent a week on the road with Captain Stacey…'

'Nothing happened,' she protested.

'Then he is a bigger clunch than I took him for.'

'He is more a gentleman than you will ever be.'

'Such touching loyalty will not serve you when it comes to asserting your innocence, you know. Society can be very cruel. By the time the gabble-grinders have done with you, you will be pleased enough to accept my offer.'

'Never! I would rather die.'

She heard the dark man laugh and turned angrily on him. 'And you will be in worse trouble when you are caught. I have powerful friends.'

'Captain Duncan Stacey!' The man laughed. 'Yes, I do believe he will ride post haste to the rescue.'

'Stacey!' Andrew repeated, and burst into laughter. 'Is that the Dark Knight? A common high-wayman! Oh, what a rig!' He slapped his knees. 'Why, my friends, nothing would give me greater pleasure than to have him done for a scamp. Double vengeance, that would be.'

'Not before we've done with him,' the second man growled. 'Then you can do what you like.'

They left the lights of the town behind and Molly

could see nothing but hedgerows and realised she was being taken into the country. But where?

Fifteen minutes later they turned into a rutted drive and drew to a stop. Andrew jumped down and let down the step for her. 'Come,' he said, holding out his hand. 'It will not be so bad, I promise you.'

Neither of the other two men moved and she assumed they were going to take possession of the coach. Between the devil she knew and the unknown terror of the two ruffians, she preferred the devil, and, taking his hand, stepped down to stand beside him.

'Mind you keep her safe here,' the dark man said. 'We will be back.'

She watched the coach disappear into the darkness and then turned back. They were standing outside a small cottage.

'Where are we?'

'Home,' he said, taking her hand and leading her to the door. She tried to free herself but he whipped off his cravat and tied her wrist to his. 'I do like a little spirited resistance; it makes the conquest all the sweeter,' he said cheerfully as he unlocked the door and ushered her inside. 'You will be all smiles and womanly wiles tomorrow.'

She did not answer; her whole mind and body was centred on keeping her head and taking stock of her surroundings. The cottage was clean and neatly furnished and they were evidently expected, for the lamps were lit and a meal was set out on the table, with wine and glasses. But there was no sign of servants.

'This will do for a few days, until we are at ease with each other, then I will set you up in town.' He moved towards the table and because she was tied to him she had perforce to follow. 'Now we will eat and drink and after that…who knows?'

'It will be difficult,' she said, raising the hand that was bound to his.

He laughed. 'It will be a pleasure trying.'

'Please untie me.'

'So that you may run?'

'No, for I have no idea where to run to. I am per-suaded we are miles from civilisation.'

'You are right.' He went to the door, turned the key in the lock and put it in his pocket, before releasing her. She stood rubbing her wrist, wondering how she could escape before he compelled her to agree to his outrageous proposal. Not only that, but she must warn Duncan of the danger he was in. But how?

'Sit down, my dear,' Andrew said. 'Now we are alone, we may enjoy each other's company and get to know each other.'

She decided it would be expedient to obey. He

served her with food and though it was well-prepared and looked delicious her throat was so dry she could not swallow. He ate well and drank copiously.

'Come, try this wine,' he said, filling a glass for her. 'It really is very good.'

'I do not want it.'

'And I say you shall have it. It will make you more relaxed. You are as stiff as a starched cravat.' He stood up and came to stand beside her, holding the glass. 'Drink.'

'No.'

He held her nose so that she was obliged to open her mouth, and then poured the wine down her throat. She had to swallow or choke. 'That is better.' He made her take more until the glass was empty. It made her dizzy, through drinking it too quickly, but it did not make her feel any easier about what was about to happen.

'Now, come with me,' he said, picking her up and flinging her across his shoulder. She kicked in vain; he held her by her legs and marched from the room and up the stairs, where he took her into one of the rooms and flung her onto the bed.

She started to thrash about and scream. He stuffed a handkerchief into her mouth. When her flailing legs made contact with his shin, he swore. 'You are being a very silly chit,' he said. 'Tomorrow, when the world knows you for what you are, you will be happy to oblige.'

The door opened behind them with a crash. He looked up and swung round, allowing Molly a moment's respite. But if she hoped it would be someone come to deliver her she was disappointed. The figure in the doorway was not a rescuer, but the second of the two men who had helped Andrew abduct her. And he was grinning.

'Jeremy wants you,' he said, jerking his head backwards. 'Go on and be quick about it.'

Andrew hesitated, but one look at the man's murderous face decided him. He took Molly's hands and tied them to the bedpost. 'I fear I must leave you for a little while, sweetheart, but rest assured I shall be back.'

And then he was gone, followed by the other man, to her immense relief.

She struggled for several minutes, then lay back exhausted. The wine she had been forced to drink was taking its toll and though she tried to stay alert she was becoming more and more drowsy. How could two glasses of wine send her to sleep? Unless they had been drugged... Her head lolled on the pillow and her eyes closed...

Chapter Twelve

'Here's to you, sir.' The man raised his glass to Duncan. 'God bless you and grant you long life and prosperity.'

'Here! Here!' came a chorus of assent from the half dozen men in the taproom of the Lamb and Flag.

'If there's anything we can do for you, you have only to tip us the wink.' This from one of them who had identified himself as ex-Sergeant Ben Brightman.

'Thank you.' Duncan was in beneficent mood, having come from Manor Farm, where he had engaged a builder to make the alterations to the stables he needed and to refurbish the farmhouse. He had returned to London and gone straight to Tattersalls to look over some breeding mares. Coming upon the ex-soldiers on his way home, he had invited them to the inn to join him in a celebration and, realising he would need help on the farm and these were men accustomed to looking after horses, he had offered them work.

He left them singing 'Over the Hills and Far Away', with more enthusiasm than tunefulness. Now he could put the past behind him and make something of his life. Tomorrow he would tell Molly that he had only a few acres and his strong arm to offer her, and a heart full of love, and that if she consented to marry him he would cherish her for the rest of their lives.

Leaving Caesar at the mews behind Connaught House, he set off to walk to Fenton's. He would be glad when he need no longer spend his nights at the hotel; the beds were hard and he was sure there were bugs. Turning the corner, he paused outside Connaught House. He did not see why he should not sleep there; he had not been banned and everyone would be in bed and would not know he was there until the morning. And he would be near Molly. Near Molly, ready to speak to her.

He bounded up the steps to the front door, only to find it standing wide open. His grandmother was in the grand hall furiously directing the servants, sending them hither and thither; Harriet was weeping into her handkerchief, crying, 'My baby! My baby!' while Lord Brancaster stood over her, trying to calm her.

Andrew Bellamy, who had just that moment

arrived, was in the middle of explaining that he had seen Miss Martineau snatched by a band of ruffians who had knocked him to the ground when he tried to intervene and had then carried her off.

'Why? Why?' wailed Harriet.

Duncan pushed his way forward. 'What has happened?'

'Molly has been kidnapped,' Harriet cried, turning a tear-streaked face up to him. 'We were at Vauxhall. Why should anyone want to take Molly? She has no fortune, no prospects. Oh, my baby.'

'Hush, ma'am,' Lord Brancaster said. 'Calm yourself. No doubt we shall hear the kidnappers' demands in due time.'

'What is the good of them making demands?' Harriet went on. 'I have no means to pay a ransom.'

'Stacey has,' Andrew put in, looking at Duncan. 'I heard them mention his name.'

'Mine?' Duncan queried. He had made a good many enemies in his life, but he was dismayed to think that Molly should be made to suffer because of anything he had done.

'Well, not exactly.' Andrew, in spite of the seriousness of the situation, seemed to be grinning. 'It was the Dark Knight they wanted.'

'Good God!' The exclamation was wrung from Duncan, but it was no good flying into a panic. He forced himself to stay calm. 'Have you any idea where they might have taken her?'

'None. They took my carriage which is why I have been so long arriving.'

'Oh, pray they do not harm her,' Harriet went on. 'Or worse… Oh, the shame of it.' She resorted once again to her flimsy lace handkerchief. 'No one will offer for her if she has been despoiled. It is all your fault, Stacey, for encouraging her madcap ways. She said you were not the Dark Knight, but I always thought there was something smoky about the way you brought her to London.'

'There is no sense in blaming anyone,' Lady Connaught put in, losing patience with her. 'Duncan, have you any idea who these men might be?'

'No, unless they be connected with Sir John Partridge…'

'I have heard of him,' Lord Brancaster said. 'He has only today been arrested and thrown into the Tower. I believe he is to stand trial for treason. We heard of it in Parliament today.'

'Then you must use your influence to speak to him and ask him where the men have taken Molly,' Duncan said. 'In the meantime, I will make my own enquiries. And Bellamy, if you want to be useful, organise a search round Vauxhall Gardens; they might not have taken her far.'

'Where are you going?' Andrew demanded. 'There's no sense in both of us searching the same place.'

'To the Lamb and Flag in Covent Garden. There are some fellows there who will help.'

He did not wait for a reply, but hurried from the house, fetched Caesar from the mews where he had left him only a few minutes before, and set off for the inn where he had left the ex-soldiers. He dared not think of what might be happening to Molly, but if it was the Dark Knight the men wanted, then the Dark Knight they should have. And if the worst was to come about and he could not free Molly any other way he would barter her life for his and it would be a small price to pay. But he needed allies.

He had given the men enough money to keep them drinking the rest of the night and he hoped they would still be there. Some of them were and, though they were well disguised, they had enough wits about them to listen to what he had to say.

'We'll look for her, Captain,' Ben Brightman said, speaking for them all. 'We know all the kens hereabouts.'

In no time they had organised themselves with military precision and set off to scour the capital. Duncan was about to leave to resume his own search when he was approached by a dark man with a straggling moustache and long greasy hair who had just entered. He was wearing a suit of black clothes, shining with dirt. 'Heard you were looking for a certain ladybird,' he said.

'Yes, yes,' he said, ignoring the implied insult to Molly; it would not help him to find her to quarrel with a potential bearer of news. 'What do you know?'

'Small, hair the colour of ripe corn, eyes like blue-bells and a fierce temper, goes by the name of Molly.'

Duncan grabbed him by the coat collar and nearly lifted him off his feet. 'Where is she? If you have harmed a hair of her head, I'll…'

'Hold hard, old fellow,' the dark one said. 'It don't pay to shoot the messenger.'

Duncan released him. 'Who are you?'

'Box is the name. Jeremy Box.'

'Then, Mr Box, I suggest you tell me what you know. And then tell me where I can find Miss Martineau. Fast.'

The man looked at him, smiling. 'Now, as to that, it depends…'

'Very well. Name your price.'

'Money? No, money ain't the thing, but me and Danny wouldn't say no to a monkey apiece. But what's more important is them documents you took from a certain gentleman on the road to Cromer.'

He was about to say he no longer had the documents and Sir John had already been arrested on the strength of them when he realised that they were the only bargaining power he had. 'Oh, those. Bits of paper. No good as currency; can't exactly recall what I did with them.'

'Then you had better start remembering. No documents, no girl.'

'No girl, no documents,' he countered, hiding his impatience. 'Take me to her. It will have a wonderful effect on my memory to see her safe and sound.'

The man looked pensively at him and Duncan could almost see his mind working. 'You write home. Tell them to send someone with money and the papers.' He called the landlord and asked for pen, paper and ink, which was produced after a search which had Duncan hopping from foot to foot with impatience.

'Now write.'

Duncan sat, pen in hand, wondering how to word the note. There were no documents, except the mail he had left there when he'd first returned to London with Molly. None of it was of any importance. He dipped the quill in the ink and began to write, addressing the missive to his grandmother who seemed to be the calmest of the people at Connaught House. She also knew his connection with Sir John and might understand his predicament.

He wrote: 'My lady, I am unavoidably detained. Please give…' He stopped to look up at the man who stood reading over his shoulder. 'Who are they to be given to?'

'Mr Andrew Bellamy.'

'Bellamy!' he repeated in surprise. 'Why him?'

'The little lady trusts him and who are we to argue with her? Write.'

Duncan continued. 'Please give to Mr Bellamy the bundle of papers from the top drawer of the chest in my room and a thousand pounds which you will find in the same place.' He stopped writing again. A servant would not dare read the papers but Bellamy most assuredly would and he would know they were worthless as bargaining instruments. He dipped the quill again and added, 'Seal them carefully and tell him that he must deliver them with the seal unbroken…' Again he stopped. 'Where?'

'He will know.'

Duncan was puzzled. How had the man who stood over him now known where to find him, unless he had been told by someone who knew? Andrew Bellamy! Had he had a hand in Molly's disappearance? Frank had been right in saying he had made an enemy there. But to use Molly! There was no time to waste asking questions he knew would not be answered. He finished the letter and signed it.

The dark man snatched the paper as soon as he had dusted the ink and read through it. 'A sensible precaution, Captain; we don't want to give anyone any ideas, now, do we?' He called the innkeeper and gave him a handful of coppers. 'Send a servant to Connaught House with this. It is urgent.'

The innkeeper called to someone who was washing pots behind the counter. 'Hey, you, Abraham or whatever you call yourself, come here.'

A big black man joined them and was given the letter. 'Can you find Connaught House on the corner of Berkeley Square?' the innkeeper asked him, speaking very slowly as if the man did not understand English.

'Yes, sir.'

'Then off you go. And mind you come back. You ain't finished those pots.'

Duncan, glancing briefly at the man, was taken aback when he recognised the slave he and Frank had freed, not so much by his looks as the ill-fitting garments he wore, although now they were filthy and ragged. It was evident the man remembered him, for his eyes widened, but he did not speak. Duncan wished he could have given him a verbal message, but the kidnapper, if that was what he was, was too wary to allow that.

As soon as the messenger had gone, Duncan turned to him. 'Now you fulfil your part of the bargain, Mr Box.'

Molly woke feeling stiff and cramped and her wrists hurt. She realised why when she tried to move her hands. How long had she been asleep with her hands tied to the bed-rail? Where was Mr Bellamy? Was he downstairs drinking, or had he left the house? Could she free herself? She struggled but only succeeded in tightening her bonds. She twisted her head to look up at her hands. They were tied with Andrew's cravat and that was made of starched muslin. It would rip if she could only make the first tear.

Slowly she inched her way up the bed, thankful that her hands were tied in front of her and not behind her back. Craning her neck, she was able to get her teeth into the material. It was stronger than she expected and her jaw and neck began to ache. She gave herself a few moments' respite and began again, her senses alive to any sound from downstairs which would tell her Mr Bellamy had returned from wherever he had gone.

A tiny split appeared in the muslin. She strained her wrists apart with every sinew of her strength. And then it tore. She was free! But that was only the beginning; she had to escape from the house. She rubbed her wrists and padded across the floor to the window and looked out.

It was still dark, but the sky to the east was tinged with pink, and away to her right there were lights. They were the gas lamps that lit the West End of London and there were others that could only be the lanterns on moving carriages or those carried by linkboys. She was not so far from civilisation, after all. Below her a narrow lane, edged with bushes, led to the main road.

She re-crossed the room, picked up her shoes and carefully opened the door, freezing against the wall when it creaked loudly. No one came. Slowly and silently, one step at a time, she made her way down to the ground floor in her stockinged feet.

There was a sudden snort from the room where she had sat with Andrew and she nearly cried out, but managed to stifle it. There was someone in there. Creeping slowly forward, she peered round the door. A man was slumped in an armchair fast asleep, but it was not Andrew. It was the second of the two men who had helped Andrew abduct her. Beside him on the table was an empty wine bottle and a half-full glass.

She turned and made her way to the front door, hardly daring to breathe. Slowly she lifted the latch. The door opened and a blast of cool air hit her face.

She ran down the path, her relief so great, there were tears running down her face and she could hardly see where she was going. It did not matter. Anywhere would do. The gravel was hurting her feet but she dared not stop to put on her shoes until she was safe.

She heard horses on the road and just managed to hide behind one of the bushes when two riders turned up the lane. She recognised the first one, even in the dark, and ran from her hiding place, crying with relief. 'Duncan! Oh, Duncan!'

He turned at the sound of his name and flung himself off Caesar. She ran forward and into his arms. 'Molly. Thank God!' He took her head in his hands and lifted her face to his. 'Are you hurt? Did they hurt you?'

'No, but I was so afraid…'

'Afraid? Madcap Molly afraid? Who would have believed it?'

His slightly bantering tone was enough to restore her spirit. 'But I wanted to warn you.' She turned towards the other man, who was standing beside his horse, smiling cynically. 'About this man and another one who is in the house. They are…'

'I know who they are, Molly.' He spoke calmly, but his mind was racing. How could he get her to safety?

'And Mr Bellamy…'

'I know about him too.' His tone gave nothing away. 'It is over now. Try to forget it. You are safe.' On the ride to the cottage, the man had enjoyed relaying what Bellamy had said to Molly in the coach. 'She will be of no use to you, Captain,' he had told him, grinning. 'Soiled goods, that's what she is by now.' He had been seething with fury ever since and not only with fury but disgust. Had she succumbed? Would she have had any choice? Did he still feel the same about marrying her? They were not questions to be answered now.

'Very touching,' the man said, producing a pistol from his belt. 'Now back into the house with you.'

She looked up at Duncan. He smiled reassuringly. 'Don't be afraid. We have to wait for a messenger.'

'The messenger is here,' said a voice from the darkness of the bushes.

Startled, their captor turned towards the sound and his mouth fell open. Two big men emerged, carrying muskets. 'Put the gun down,' one of them ordered him, lifting the musket to his shoulder.

Molly heard Duncan chuckle as more men appeared—some from the ditch beside the road, others from behind the house, pushing the second kidnapper, securely tied, in front of them. And standing beside Duncan's horse, as if he had appeared there by magic, was the big negro, grinning in the darkness and showing even white teeth. Jeremy Box dropped his weapon with a clatter.

'What do you want done with them, Captain?' Ben asked, forcing the man's hands behind his back and tying them securely with a length of rope he had brought with him.

'Take them to the Westminster magistrate and tell him they are accomplices of Sir John Partridge. He will know what to do. And my thanks to you all.'

'It was Abraham what put us onto you,' Ben said. 'He don't speak much English, but he made us understand.'

Duncan left Molly's side to shake the black man by the hand. 'You have my undying gratitude. Go with these men. They will take you to Norfolk. I can find work for you. Paid work,' he added. 'You are a free man; if it is not to your liking, you are under no obligation to stay.'

The man nodded, showing he understood English even if he did not speak it well. 'I serve you good,' he said.

'How did you all get here?' Molly asked, looking from one to the other.

'Oh, we had a guide who knew exactly where you were,' Ben said.

'Mr Bellamy,' she murmured.

'Yes.' Then he said to Duncan, 'What do you want

done with him? He's sitting in his coach, awaiting your pleasure.'

'My pleasure would be to beat him to a pulp,' Duncan said.

'Oh, no, please don't,' Molly put in. 'I do not want anyone hurt. Send him away. I don't want to see him.'

'You heard Miss Martineau,' Duncan said. 'Turn him loose. Let him walk home.' He smiled suddenly. 'We will borrow his coach again.' Then he said to Molly, 'The sooner we get you home to your mama the better.'

Ten minutes later, Duncan and Molly were sitting side by side in the Brancaster coach, with the negro on the box. Ben and his companions were riding the horses and were slowly driving the two criminals in front of them with their hands tied behind them. The coach soon left them behind.

Molly was almost limp with relief that her ordeal was over, but she could not relax; she was taut with nervous tension. Any moment now Duncan would start to ask her about what had happened between her and Andrew Bellamy and how could she answer him? She did not know if anything had happened while she had been drugged. But perhaps he had guessed and that was why he was so silent. Was he condemning her, as Mr Bellamy had said everyone would?

'Captain,' she said, after they had been travelling in silence for several minutes. 'I am sorry to have been the cause of so much trouble, but it was not of my choosing. Please believe me.'

'Oh, I do,' he said, smiling at her. 'But it seems to me you are even more prone to fall into scrapes than I am—but I am persuaded that was one adventure you would rather not have had.'

'It was horrible. I never want to live through another night like it.'

'Are you going to tell me about it?'

'I…I can't.'

'I see.'

'No, you do not see,' she cried. 'You are blaming me, telling yourself that a well brought up young lady would never allow herself to fall into such a bumblebath…'

'How did you fall into it? Tell me from the beginning.'

'Mr Bellamy asked me to walk with him in Vauxhall Gardens while we were waiting for the fireworks to start. He said we would be accompanied by the Marquis of Tadbury and Miss Bonchance and I did not think it was wrong, especially as Mama agreed I could go.'

'Then what?'

'We became separated from the others. He…he tried to kiss me.'

'The scoundrel.'

'It is no more than you have done.'

'So I have.' He smiled, trying to lighten the feeling of gloom which pervaded the coach. 'And how did we compare?'

'I do not know how you can make a jest of it.' She turned on him. 'It is not the least amusing.'

'No, of course not. I apologise. What happened then?'

'I was angry and I left him. That big dark man suddenly appeared out of the bushes and grabbed me. Mr Bellamy came up and they put me in the coach and there was another man there. The other two men left when we arrived at the house. Mr Bellamy took me inside. He wanted me to have supper with him and afterwards…'

'Never mind,' he said. 'You do not have to tell me if it is painful for you. I understand.'

He *was* disgusted with her. She had never been more miserable, but she refused to be cowed. 'No, you do not. I did not want it. I never asked for it. I fought and was tied up for my pains.'

'Oh, my poor, poor Molly.'

'But he left me, said he wanted me to be willing and I would be, too, the next day…'

He looked at her and put his arm about her shoulders, squeezing her to his side. 'My poor, brave darling. How did you escape?'

'I bit through my bonds.'

He laughed. 'Bit them? Oh, you are priceless.'

'It is not in the least funny.'

'No, it would have been terrifying and my admiration is unbounded.'

Admiration, she noted, not love. 'Now you have heard my story, don't you think it is time you told me how you knew where to find me? How did you meet that dreadful man and who were all those other men and the big black man?'

He told her the whole truth, speaking gently to her to reassure her. His disgust was directed at Andrew Bellamy and not her. None of it was her fault. The blame lay with those around her, including and more especially himself. He should have spoken to her of his intentions before going back to Norfolk, should have asked her to marry him the moment he could see the way forward. His delay had cost her pain and misery.

'We are two scapegraces together,' he ended, smiling. 'I think there is only one way to cure us.'

'How?'

'To marry.'

'Yes, I collect you said you had found a wife,' she said solemnly. 'I wish you joy of her.'

'I meant each other,' he said.

She twisted in her seat to face him, wondering

whether he was bamming her, but his expression was perfectly serious. 'Marry you?'

'Do you still think I am too old?' he queried.

'No, I have decided age is not so important, after all, but Mr Bellamy said that after last night no one would marry me and I would have to be his ladybird. I do not know exactly what that means but I do not think it can be respectable. I think I would rather be an ape leader and live in seclusion for the rest of my days. I know you are always pulling me out of scrapes, and I am grateful, but this is one too many.'

'Scrapes. Do you think that is the only reason I spoke?'

'Only a moment ago, you said…'

'Then I am a clumsy oaf. I love you. I will always love you.'

She could hardly believe her ears, did not dare believe them. 'After all that has happened, I would expect you to have a disgust of me.'

'Oh, Molly, how can you say that?' It did not matter what had happened, if she loved him; he had been a cur even to think about it. 'All I need to know, all I want to know, is do you love me?'

'Of course I do. With all my heart. How can you doubt it?'

'And will you flinch and turn away if I kiss you?'

She laughed suddenly. 'Try it and see.'

So he did and it was as wonderful as it had been the first time and the second, and when he kissed her again it was still glorious. They would have gone on doing it, if the coach had not drawn up outside Connaught House.

They walked into the house together and were bombarded with questions by Harriet, weeping and full of contrition, and Lady Connaught who had a sparkle in her eye which could have been a tear. Lord Brancaster was there too, looking white and drawn. Molly felt sorry for him and made up her mind she would not distress him by telling them what really happened.

It was almost as if Duncan could read her mind, for he pretended Andrew had only been allowed to go free if he agreed to lure Duncan into a trap. 'He is on his way home and will be at Brancaster House very shortly,' Duncan ended. 'I am indebted to him for reuniting me with Molly.' He took her hand and smiled conspiratorially at her. 'You may offer felicitations.'

'Then I do, most heartily.'

And so did everyone else. After that, Lord Brancaster left and an exhausted Molly was packed off to bed with a tisane, leaving Duncan to fill in the details of what had happened for the benefit of his grandmother and Harriet, and then go back to his lodgings for a few hours' sleep before returning.

Her mother came to her as she was climbing into bed. 'Tony has just told me the whole and I am mortified,' she said. 'It was all my fault. I thought Bellamy could be trusted to look after you. I thought he would marry you. Can you ever forgive me?'

'It was not your fault, Mama. I should not have come to London and put you to the blush. I must have spoiled everything for you.'

'Oh, it has come out well in the end. Brancaster proposed during the fireworks. I was so pleased and longing to tell you, but you had disappeared. Thank heaven you were not harmed. And Tony Stacey has offered for you. Who would have thought it? 'Tis a pity about the earldom, but Aunt Margaret tells me he has been awarded a baronetcy, so you will not be without a title.'

'Mama, how can I marry Duncan? I know I did not spend the whole night alone with Mr Bellamy but surely it was enough to ruin me? He said it would be.'

'No, of course you are not ruined.'

'Duncan said it made no difference,' she said. 'But he does not mean that. I am disgusted with myself and I cannot go through with a marriage which will cause him distress. He will never be able to forget it and neither will I.'

'Fustian! He rescued you, did he not? And he said Andrew had been kidnapped too. Nothing will be said, you may be sure, certainly not by Andrew. He has too much to lose. Now go to sleep and forget all about it. Tomorrow we will discuss weddings. Though I think mine must come first, don't you think?'

'Of course, Mama.' Molly smiled as the tisane began to work and she drifted off to sleep; her mother would never change.

It was the middle of the afternoon when she woke and the whole ordeal came flooding back to her. But that was followed by a wonderful sense of well-being. She was loved. She had found the man of her dreams, her Don Quixote, and he loved her. It had not been the least necessary to have a Season; he had been there all the time. Sir Duncan Stacey, hero and highwayman, farmer and horse breeder, was to be her husband. She would be Lady Stacey. Her dreams had come true.

She could not lie abed when there was a glorious day to be lived, and not only one but many, a whole lifetime of them. She rose and dressed and went downstairs.

Duncan had returned and was sitting in the drawing room with her mother and Lady Connaught. There were also two others in the room she had never met before—a young man who was stationed in front of the hearth and a young lady who stood with her back to the room, gazing out on the garden.

Duncan jumped up when she entered the room and strode over to take her hand and kiss the back of it, his eyes dancing with something akin to mischief. Or was it simply happiness? 'Molly, how are you?'

'Quite recovered, thank you.' She knew she was blushing but could not stop herself.

'Good. Come and be presented.' He led her to the young man who stood by the hearth. He was very like Duncan in looks though not quite as tall and very much thinner. 'Hugh, this is Molly. Molly, my brother, the Earl of Connaught.'

Hugh smiled and took her hand, raising it to his lips. 'I am charmed to meet you, Miss Martineau.'

'If it please you, my lord, I am Molly.'

'Molly it shall be,' he said. 'And no more "my lord". It is inaccurate to say the least.'

'Hugh, I said we would speak of that no more,' Duncan put in, before turning to present Molly to his sister-in-law, who had turned from the window.

She was, Molly noted, tall and graceful and her elegant clothes set off a figure she envied. So this was the lady who had disappointed Duncan. She searched their faces for signs that the attachment still lived, but either they were skilled at hiding their true feelings or he had been telling the truth when he'd said it was all in the past.

Molly moved forward and curtsied. 'I am very pleased to meet you, my lady,' she said.

'And we you,' Beth said. 'Such tales we have heard…'

'Oh, I beg you, take no note of them. They are bound to have been exaggerated.'

'What? No abduction, no gallant rescue?' Hugh put in.

'Yes, but it is over now.'

'I must say you look remarkably calm about it all.'

Duncan laughed. 'It takes more than a kidnapping to unsettle Molly. She is the match of any ne'er-do-well, as I know to my cost. You may felicitate me.'

'Then I do. Heartily.'

'I wish you happy,' Beth said, moving forward to kiss Molly's cheek. 'It is time Tony settled down.'

'Oh, we plan to do that,' Duncan said. 'On Manor Farm, breeding horses.'

'No, that is not fair,' Hugh said. 'You must take up your rightful place as the Earl. I am an impostor and have no right to the title or the estate. I came to London to make a public announcement of the truth. Beth agrees with me, don't you, dear?'

'Of course.' She turned to Duncan. 'Since you came back from the war, Tony, we have been feeling so guilty. Hugh has been quite ill with it. I would rather have a healthy, happy husband than any title…'

'Then he should be happy. He is not depriving me of anything I want.' He reached out and took Molly's hand. 'I have my heart's desire.' He paused and turned to look at Molly, searching her face. 'What say you, my love? Do you wish to be a countess?'

'Seems to me she doesn't have any choice in the matter,' Lady Connaught put in. 'You cannot throw away the laws of progeniture to please yourselves. Duncan, you are the Earl of Connaught, whether you will it or not. And you will have children…'

Duncan smiled at Molly. 'I certainly hope so.'

'Whatever you do, you cannot deprive your son of his inheritance.'

'No, you are right, but I do not want to live at Foxtrees. Hugh, you will stay there and manage the estates on my behalf, until such time as my heir is ready to inherit. Molly and I will live at Manor Farm and I will be Sir Duncan Stacey. After all, it is a title I have earned for myself.' He smiled again at Molly. 'Does that suit, my love?'

'Yes, yes. As long as I am with you, that is all I care about.'

'Then that is the end of the matter,' Duncan said. 'Now, Molly and I are going to stroll round the garden. We have a lot to say to each other.'

But it was not words that passed between them once they were out of sight of the house and sitting in a little green bower at the end of the garden. It was smiles and kisses, and a great many of them.

* * * * *